Property Rites

A Deed of Enslavement

Han Li Thorn

velluminous

Published by Velluminous Press

www.velluminous.com

Copyright © Han Li Thorn, 2005

www.hanlithorn.com

The Author asserts the moral right to be
identified as the author of this work

ISBN-13: 978-1-905605-00-2
ISBN-10: 1-905605-00-5

Also by Han Li Thorn

Spike Trap
Rough Copy

1   birthday present

The day before Alasha's eighteenth birthday, her life changed forever.

The Matriarch was ill again. Judging by the doctor's grave face and half-disguised warnings, she was even worse than the last time.

After a while, Alasha came to understand that her mother was dying.

It was plain that Lord Jarvin and her brother knew it too, but they didn't speak about it, as if they thought her still too young for such things. When Alasha went to her mother's chamber in the south tower, the guard's words sounded kind enough, but that didn't stop him from turning her away.

"Your father's orders, young miss. I'm sorry."

It was one of the new men, otherwise she might have tried to wheedle her way around him. Otherwise, he'd have known her name.

It's not fair, she thought. *It's a daughter's right to bid her mother farewell. If anything, it's the husband and the stepson that should be waiting out here.*

Then the door opened and Jarvo was there. "It's all right, Hap. It's fitting that my sister should be present at the end."

"Very good, sir," said the guard, standing aside.

She went past him into the room and approached the big four-poster that had been part of her world for as long as she could remember: she'd been born in that bed, conceived in that bed.

Her father had died in that bed, twelve years before.

Alasha hardly recognized the old lady under the coverlet: her mother's skin was parchment-thin and pale as candle-wax, the wisps of hair so translucent that it would have been flattery to call them white. The Matriarch's eyes were closed under trembling lids, and each breath was a painful straining for air.

Alasha knelt at her mother's bedside, next to her stepfather's chair.

The doctor stood at the foot of the bed, his face grave.

There was an invalid's desk set across the covers, with a silver pen and an inkbottle, and a bundle of vellum that bore the Matriarch's unsteady but distinctive signature. Now, Lord Jarvin took the topmost leaf from the bundle and set it on the side table next to Alasha.

"You must countersign this, girl, in the presence of your mother."

"What is it?"

"It appoints me as your guardian until you are of an age to assume the Matriarchy. Until then, it will be my duty to protect you, to see to the running of the Malkenstorm estates, and to make sure that your holdings prosper."

Alasha studied the deed. Its purpose was unclear: it seemed to consist mainly of a bewildering number of schedules, appendices, and codicils. "I should like to read the rest of the document first."

"It contains nothing but tedious legalities, girl, and there is little time. Your mother is satisfied with it, and our family advocates assure me that it's been drawn up most carefully. If you fail to sign in the presence of the Matriarch, the choice of guardian reverts to the King. That is the law."

Alasha had learned nothing of this law in her studies, but then she'd never expected to be orphaned before her coming of age. The Matriarch was not yet out of her middle-years, and her illness and swift decline had seemed unthinkable when they began, less than twelve moons before.

The dying woman's lids flickered open for an instant, and Alasha saw her mother's dim eyes turn towards her. The Matriarch was look-ing at her, perhaps for the last time.

She's telling me to sign before it's too late, decided Alasha. *Anyway, better that Lord Jarvin should have the management of the estates, rather than some stranger.*

She picked up the silver pen and signed her name in the place indicated.

"Don't date it," said Lord Jarvin quickly. "That will be done in the lawyers' chambers."

Once more, Alasha was confused: surely, the signature should be dated when it was made? Reluctantly, she deferred to her stepfather:

this wasn't the place for argument, or the time to add to her mother's troubles.

Later, she came to realize how foolish that had been. Her mother's problems would soon be over forever, while her own were just beginning.

Alasha dreamed of the Matriarch that night, and when she woke she remembered her loss before the fact of her own birthday.

Her mother had always been distant; stern rather than loving and more concerned with Matriarchal duty than maternal affection. The young Alasha had grown up with nurses and tutors as her true parents, and now she felt a sense of bereavement, but not of inconsolable sorrow.

At eighteen, she stood at the threshold of life. She was still three years away from her majority and the assumption of her position among the Xendrian nobility, but from today she could own land and gold, and deposit money with the silversmiths (or borrow, if she had the mind, and be held responsible for her debts). She could even embark on business ventures of her own.

She considered what to wear. For her birthday, she would normally have chosen her favorite gown: tailored from deep blue silk that brought out the green of her eyes, with long rustling skirts and a flattering bodice, but today there was propriety to consider.

The mourning period must be observed, she thought. *I will wear black.*

Alasha couldn't find her slippers, so she crossed the icy stone floor of her dressing room barefoot and on tiptoe.

She opened her wardrobe and confronted emptiness.

Her gowns, her undergarments, her shoes, her riding clothes and boots – all were gone. Someone had been in her room and taken everything away.

All that was left was a light shift, suitable perhaps as an underbodice for a serving girl, but in no way appropriate for the future Matriarch.

There was a folded note lying on the shift. It was too dark to make out the spidery writing, so Alasha took the parchment into her bedchamber and drew the curtains back from the frost-rimed window. As the winter light streamed in, she saw that the trinkets, bottles and books from her dressing table were all gone as well.

She had to read the note through twice before her mind grasped its meaning, and then her hands started to tremble.

Stepdaughter,

You will understand that the previous contents of the wardrobe were unsuitable for your new station. You are to clothe yourself in the garment provided and attend me in my rooms.

Leave the nightgown in the bedchamber; neither gown nor bed belong to you any more.

It would be best for you to attend me directly you wake up.

Lord Jarvin

Alasha didn't even touch the shift. She threw the chamber door open and stormed off towards her stepfather's rooms in the south tower, the nightgown swishing around her ankles and the flag-stones cold against her bare feet.

"It's too late to back out, girl. I saw you sign the document myself, and since you're eighteen now, you are bound by its terms."

"So that's why you told me not to date it."

"I don't know what you're talking about. You can't possibly expect anyone to believe that a girl of your breeding would sign a legal document and then fail to date it."

"The witnesses know when it was signed."

"The doctor and my son both checked the time carefully, and they agree that it was after midnight. No one will believe your fantasies. You are mine now, to dispose of as I will. Signed and delivered by your own hand. Your mother's castle and lands are mine, too, and Jarvo's after me."

"My brother would never agree to this. You won't get away with it."

"We already have, girl, and it was Jarvo who came up with the idea. He knows that you're only his stepsister, even if you seem to have forgotten. Now. You were instructed to leave the nightgown and to put on the shift provided. You may disrobe now, and then return to the chamber for one last time to collect the proper garment."

Alasha simply shook her head and pulled the warm gown closer about her body. She would die before she went through the castle unclothed.

Or would I? she wondered. *Why is the idea of going naked through the torch-lit passages so enticing? Why have my loins become warm at the thought of it? Would I tremble and hurry, keeping to the shadows, or linger so that a passing guard or a servant might see me?*

She felt her nipples stiffening and loosened her grip on her garment, letting the tightly stretched fabric fall away before her reaction could betray her, but Lord Jarvin was already staring at her chest with a knowing smile.

"I didn't expect you to be sensible, girl. I didn't expect you to accept what you so obviously desire. Perhaps what you really want is to learn the hard way, eh?"

He rang a small silver bell, summoning two of the new guards into the room.

"My new slave girl seems to be in need of some help with her clothes," he said. "Would you be so kind as to assist her? After that, I'd be grateful if you would accept her as a guest in your quarters for an hour or so. Entertain her as you will, but leave her intact."

One of the guards stood in front of Alasha, while his comrade seized her arms and twisted them behind her. She struggled until he jerked her elbows upward with cruel force, making her gasp with pain. After that, she stood still, glaring at the guard who was drawing the lacings out of her nightdress, not quite able to believe that someone could be doing such a thing. The garment went slack, held up by no more than the faint friction of silk on skin, and then he reached forwards and brushed the fabric away from her shoulders so that it fell away, catching at her twisted elbows.

Alasha was half-naked now. The guard smiled and licked his lips, making no effort to hide his lust. She looked down at her bared breasts, hating the way her traitorous nipples basked so proudly in the rosy flush that spread around them. She felt her cheeks burning, too – from the outrage and shame at being stripped, but also because of her other responses, and her inability to disguise them.

The man in front of her wrapped his fingers about her throat, tilting her face upwards. He squeezed – gently enough so that he didn't quite hurt her, firmly enough to leave her in no doubt that he would if she showed any fight. She held herself quite still, and his comrade released her elbows for a moment so that her garment dropped away completely.

The guard let go of her neck, and his gaze followed the nightgown to the floor as it puddled around her ankles in a silken cascade. He let his eyes drift slowly back up over her exposed body, and grinned even more broadly. His teeth were stained, and riddled with crooked gaps.

Alasha had never been naked in front of a man before. Sometimes, alone with her dressing-room mirror, she'd wondered whether the body she saw reflected there would be pleasing to male eyes.

From the men's sharp intake of breath, she understood that it was.

The soldier grasped her left arm while his comrade maintained his grip on her right elbow. The whole thing seemed rehearsed, as regular as the new-fangled Marlish clockwork toy that had been in her room until last night.

These two have done this before, she thought.

Together they marched her out of her stepfather's apartment and down the stone steps towards the barracks.

Alasha struggled with three conflicting emotions.

The first was fear, of these men and of what they meant to do to her. She had led a privileged life, full of literature and astronomy to balance the archery and fencing lessons, but growing up in the Matriarch's northern fastness had offered little in the way of male society. Even so, the castle's library was well stocked. Alasha had no illusions about what would happen to a friendless girl who turned up naked in a barrack room.

The second emotion was embarrassment. She'd known some of the castle guards for as long as she could remember, and she was dismayed that they might see her like this.

The third was hope, because while the soldiers she knew might embarrass her, they surely wouldn't let anything really bad happen. They'd just laugh and enjoy the sight of her, as if she were a pretty serving girl. They'd probably still be joking about the time the Matriarch appeared bare-arsed in the barracks when they were old and toothless and wheezing over their beer in some dingy tavern, but that wasn't such a bad thing, either.

In fact, she found the thought almost gratifying, in a perverse sort of way.

Her captors dragged her down the final flight of steps. If her fantasy was to come true, there had to be some soldiers that she knew – some of the old guard who'd served the Matriarch for years – beyond the iron bound barrack doors.

There weren't.

There were only new faces, the ones recruited over the months by Lord Jarvin.

As Alasha's dreams of rescue crashed around her, she understood that these were the castle guards, now, and that her stepfather had sprung his trap only after every man whose loyalty was in doubt had been replaced.

Hope was gone, and in its absence, fear became irrelevant. All that was left to Alasha was the shame of being naked before these soldiers, because every man who cared to look could see every part of her body. The most humiliating thing of all was that they might see how hard her nipples were, or sense the warmth that she felt taking hold between her legs.

Even as Alasha squirmed with embarrassment, some more de-tached part of her was still observing, impressing the sights and smells of the barracks into her memory. She already knew that she would relive this scene in her imagination, once whatever this place held in store for her had been done.

The light was dim, filtered by mean, grimy windows, so that it was hard to make out details. The reek of tallow mingled with the fragrance of leather and aromatic smoke, and with the harsher scents of male sweat and harness oil. She took in the hard pallets on which the men slept, the cramped dirtiness of the room, and the packed earth of the floor.

"A birthday present from Lord Jarvin," said the man at her left. "Eighteen today! We've got her for an hour. Seeing as we're the ones that fetched her, we get first dibs. The rest of you can draw lots."

He brushed his knuckles over the hardness of her nipples, and then let his hand descend to her loins, where he pressed his fingers against her sex. Alasha tried to twist away from him, but his comrade held her still.

"Don't worry, lads. This one's warm and willing. Plenty to go round, eh?"

There was a chorus of deep guffaws. The guard brought his fingers to his nose and inhaled extravagantly, taking her most private scent deep into his lungs before licking it from his fingertips. "Sweet and fresh, too. Mind you lads, her cunny's untouched and Lord Jarvin wants it kept that way, understand? No one's to plant any seeds in her belly."

One of the soldiers searched through a iron-bound chest until he found a strap that might once have held a piece of armor in place, but now they made it serve as a slave collar. They tied her wrists behind her back with a length of rough cord that they secured to a harness ring looped onto the collar, so that her wrists were hoisted halfway to her shoulder blades.

"Put her on her knees," said the man at her left.

Soldiers surrounded her, jostling for a better view, and rough hands forced her to kneel. She resisted only for an instant: there were too many of them, and they were too strong. Collared and trussed as she was, Alasha knew she would have been helpless against any one of them.

The man stood in front of her and opened his breeches. The prim and flaccid diagrams in her anatomy books hadn't prepared her for this, and she couldn't help gasping at the sight of his engorged sex. He stood close to her and his man-scent filled her nostrils. She tried to squirm away.

Even as she struggled, she felt what had been warm and moist becoming hot and drenched, felt an unfamiliar itching between her thighs. *It can't be the stench of him,* she thought, but there was no denying it. The scent of the man before her, the constricting bonds at her neck and her wrists, and the rough sensation of callused hands against her soft, naked skin – all these were more exciting to her than she would have believed possible.

Which was wrong. *Everything about this is wrong.* She slid her knees closer together, trying to hide the tell-tale wetness between her legs, wishing her hands were free so she could cover her treacherous breasts.

Fingers twined in her hair, pulling her head backwards and tilting her face towards the male sex that stood proudly in front of her.

"No," she started to say, and he took advantage of her open mouth to push himself between her lips.

His taste and texture shocked her as much of the hard invasion of her mouth: the skin was velvet-smooth and flavored with salt that must come from his sweat, and with a yeasty sourness that she tried not to think about.

"Suck my cock, whore."

She tried to shake her head, denying what was happening as well as his command. *I should bite him,* she thought, but she knew she wouldn't do that. Not while she was so helpless, not while there were so many of them standing ready to take revenge.

Her mouth was full, yet less than half of him was inside.

"You can either suck my cock, or I can fuck you, like this."

He pushed himself deeper, all the way to the back of her throat. The hands in her hair held her immobile as the soldier rammed his sex into her mouth and filled her nostrils with his overpowering scent.

Alasha gagged on him, tasting the bile rising in her gorge, but the man pushed past that, pushed until her face was buried in the wiry hair that covered his belly. She had no choice but to swallow his sex.

He held that position for much longer than she could bear. She heard mewling noises, and was vaguely aware that she was making them herself. Her breath whistled desperately through her nostrils, overlaying the drumming of her ankles and calves against the hard-packed earth of the floor.

Then he was out of her throat and back in her mouth. "Suck me, whore," he said again.

This time, she obeyed, using her lips and her tongue – tentatively at first, because she didn't know what he wanted, and had to learn by listening to his responses and sensing the way he moved.

He was getting more excited, so she seemed to be pleasing him.

Against her will, that thought pleased her, too.

The speed of his strokes increased along with his arousal. It was becoming harder to keep her tongue dancing on the spot that seemed to please him so, to stop her teeth from snagging his velvet skin – and any hurt she did him would surely be viciously repaid. Her jaw began to ache from being forced open for so long, from the unaccustomed effort of accepting such a thing so deep into her throat.

Please let it be over soon, she prayed, though she had no idea of how much time a man might require to spend in a girl's mouth. The soldier showed no sign of wanting to slow down, or stop. On the contrary, the rhythm he adopted seemed to outpace her racing heart, and his cock plumbed her more deeply with each stroke, until it seemed to challenge even the depth of her humiliation at being used like this.

Just when Alasha knew she couldn't bear it any longer, her abuser gasped and went still for a long moment, before giving a final thrust that was even deeper than before. She sensed the pleasure-spasm of his climax, and tasted the hot seed that he pumped past the root of her tongue.

And then he was finished with her, turning away as if she was of no further interest. A rough hand seized her jaw, holding her mouth shut, and a finger and thumb clamped her nostrils closed. The hands in her hair tipped her head back until she was looking up at the circle of lustful faces that surrounded her.

I will remember these men, she thought, *and I will have vengeance.*

The seed ran deeper into her throat, and there was no choice but to gulp it down. When it was gone, they let go of her head.

Please let it be over now, but she knew that it wasn't; her stepfather had sentenced her to an hour of this. The man who had held her arms as she was undressed looped his fingers through her collar and led her to the end of one of the rough pallets.

He guided her to her knees and bent her over the end of the straw-packed mattress. Alasha co-operated, hating herself even as she did so, but knowing that resistance would only make things worse.

There was another reason to co-operate, too, one that she tried to push away but that remained lurking in a dark corner of her mind. She had tasted something that would have been inconceivable an hour ago, and despite herself, she wanted more. Now there was a yearning between her legs where she needed a man to plunge his sex, and a burning in her breasts that she knew could only be quenched by a man's rough fingers, or his sharp teeth.

It should be a man of my choosing, though.

She stiffened and moaned as the soldier behind her forced his hand between her thighs and ran a finger along the line of her sex. There seemed to be no choice but to open her legs for him. He chuckled softly, and his watching comrades sniggered. Now his fingers were inside her secret lips, compelling her to rock back and forward to the rhythm they dictated.

Oh, please don't. Stop. Oh, please don't stop. Please keep doing that for a few more heartbeats, for a few more minutes, please keep doing that until I'm ready for you to stop.

But his fingers weren't there any more, they were at the tops of her thighs, trailing through the slickness there. Alasha whimpered and tried to push her sex towards his hand again, but he was gone, he was moving upwards. His palm caressed her breasts for a moment and then he was smearing her own taste and secret fragrance over her nose and around her lips.

"Lick me clean."

The thought of tonguing the soldier's dirt-stained fingers disgusted her even more than the idea of tasting her own juices, and she kept her mouth firmly closed. Someone grabbed her wrists and twisted them brutally between her shoulder blades, until she whimpered and started to lick the proffered hand.

As soon as he had finished with her mouth, he pushed her face down into the rough mattress, so that her female scent mingled with the mustiness of old straw and the sharp reek of unwashed male. Alasha started to weep – perhaps because of what was happening, perhaps because of what she was discovering.

His fingers were back between her legs again, coaxing more wetness from her and carrying it back to his loins, carrying some of it to her most private place where she felt it returning to her in a shameful anointing, circling the tight entrance behind her sex.

As soon as Alasha realized what he meant to do, she went rigid and started to buck against the pallet. *No. Not there. Don't touch me there.* She tried to twist aside, but a strong hand pressed down between her shoulders, forcing her back down against the soldier's cot.

She heard the man behind her spit, and felt his hard fingers rubbing more saliva between her buttocks.

"No," she said.

His hand dipped to her sex again, and she shuddered with a mixture of revulsion and desire.

"Shut up, you randy little slut. Don't try to pretend you're not gagging for this."

She felt his cock pressing against the tight opening that should have been hers alone, and tensed herself, ready to deny him with all her strength.

He increased the pressure steadily, together with the pain. Alasha tried to keep herself clenched against his invasion but it was no use; his cock was breaching her defenses, sliding through the lubrication he had applied, too slippery and too strong and too hard for her to resist. He reached around and touched her sex again, and her body went rigid even as the orifice he was using finally yielded to him fully. After that, she lay defeated under his strength, unable to do anything other than weep as he transfixed her again and again, filling her with a defiling fire that grew more intolerable with every thrust.

It took far too long for the man to empty himself. When he was done, she remained kneeling at the foot of the bed, too stunned even to raise her head, feeling nothing except for the searing pain he'd left between her buttocks and his cooling seed trickling down her thighs.

Vaguely, as if from a great distance and through someone else's eyes, Alasha was aware of him wiping himself off with a rag and buttoning up his breeches.

"Right lads," he said. "Who's next?"

2

slave ring

At the end of the hour, Alasha felt light-headed from sex, and pain, and perhaps from relief that her ordeal was over.

The two grizzled soldiers who escorted her back up the stairs had been unlucky with the casting of lots: her allotted time in the barracks had passed before they could take a turn with her.

Perhaps that was why they handled her so roughly as they pulled her into an alcove just off the main stairway.

"Don't worry, pretty one. The youngsters won the lot-drawing today, but there might still be time for you to have a real man, eh?"

Alasha hoped with all her heart that there wouldn't be.

The taller of the men hurried up the stairs and returned a few moments later. "It's all right. Lord Jarvin's busy with the notary, recording this one's title. There's plenty of time." He turned to Alasha. "We're not brutes like the others, girl. We let our women decide what they want. So, what's it to be? Arse or mouth?"

Her heart sank and she felt tears springing to her eyes again, but she looked at him numbly and shook her head. *I won't give him the satisfaction*, she thought.

"I'll choose, then. Your arse. Don't upset yourself, it's not that you haven't got a pretty mouth, but your sweet little wriggling peaches are something else."

They laid her across a stone bench and the soldier plunged his sex into her. She was still slick from the others, and the ring of muscle that might have guarded her was exhausted, so he entered easily. Almost before he'd finished, his comrade was pulling him off, desperate to take his own turn.

As the second man moaned and bounced up and down behind her, Alasha heard footsteps on the stairs. A servant came into view and froze for a moment as he took in the tableau of the slave girl and the two guards.

It was Fryc. The man had served her at table almost every day since before she could remember, and had teased her as a little girl when she explored the kitchens where he worked. Alasha went rigid, her horror that he should see her in this condition even stronger than the pain of what was being done to her.

There wasn't so much as a spark of recognition in his eyes: all she saw there was resignation, and perhaps a hint of fear. The old servant looked away and hurried on up the stairs, as if this sort of thing had become commonplace in the castle.

Perhaps Alasha wasn't the first girl he'd seen being used by Lord Jarvin's new men.

Fryc carried on up the stairs. Alasha watched him go, trying to pretend that the thing going on behind her and inside her was happening to someone else, that she was just an observer. The servant glanced back before the staircase took him out of sight, then paused to watch from the shadows until the guard finished his business and let her rise stiffly to her feet.

"Come on, girl," he said. "You'd better clean yourself up before you appear before Lord Jarvin."

They led her up the stairs, following Fryc for a while, and into a small chamber where there was a stone cistern, a bucket, and a cloth. Both men watched as she started to clean herself.

"Ever had a noblewoman before?" asked the tall one.

"Never," said his companion.

"Well, you still ain't. She's just another slave girl, now. Is it a pleasant change, slave girl? You'd never have tasted cocks like ours if you was still a noble."

Alasha said nothing as she rinsed the cloth as best she could in the bucket, and used it to wipe away the man-seed that had dried around her mouth and on her breasts, and the mess that they'd left smeared between her buttocks.

She waited until they were gossiping again, and not looking at her, before she cleaned her own stickiness from between her legs.

Lord Jarvin left Alasha to cool her heels for some considerable time.

For some reason, waiting outside his rooms made her feel even more naked than being displayed for the pleasure of the guards in the barracks. It was certainly colder here. She thought longingly of her woolen gowns, and then of the nightdress that had been stripped from her. Even the thin shift that she'd rejected so casually earlier would have been better than nothing.

It might be icy, standing here unclothed among the great stones of the south tower, but at least there was a temporary safety: she was unlikely to be molested in the Lord's own vestibule. Alasha shivered as she considered how it would have been if she'd been condemned to wait in the barracks; the two men who'd brought her here were not the only ones who'd been left unsated.

The door opened and a well-dressed man emerged, carrying a ledger. *He must be the notary, and that book contains the record of my enslavement*, thought Alasha. *Now I am in the property registry. There can be no escape.*

That was the first moment that she truly comprehended what had been done to her. Everything else – being forcibly stripped, even being taken by the soldiers in the barracks and the alcove – could have happened to anyone who fell into the wrong hands.

Now, she was different. Only slaves had the title numbers of their deeds inscribed in the registry. Only the owner could have the record struck off.

The notary glanced at her as he left. His eyes were devoid of human recognition, as if he saw her only as something to be cataloged and recorded in his books. She wasn't used to that: ever since she had grown into a woman, she had seen male interest – ranging from the polite to the openly smitten – mingling with the respect that men always showed. To be displayed so brazenly without being desired was galling to some feminine part of her.

It's his profession: he must see slave girls naked like this all the time, she thought. *Or perhaps he prefers boys.*

"Your Master is waiting for you," said the notary. "You may go inside now."

Alasha pushed the heavy door open and entered her stepfather's study for the second time that day.

"I trust you enjoyed the society of my soldiers?"

Alasha chose to say nothing.

"Why so quiet? You're usually such a talkative girl … has something happened that I should know about?"

"You know very well what happened."

"Indeed I do. I've had a full report from the sergeant. I understand that you enjoyed the experience rather more than I anticipated. A shame: that wasn't part of my plan. Still, I shouldn't complain if you seek to make the most of your new station."

"My station is to be future Matriarch of this castle." Even as she spoke, Alasha knew that her words were hollow.

"Alas, no. The indenture that you and your mother signed has just been notarized. I imagine you saw the gentleman on the way out. Perhaps not, though: it's hardly your place to watch the comings and goings of people of quality, is it?"

"My place is as your liege-lady, as my mother was."

"I should have you whipped for that. In fact, I think I will. You have an appointment at the smithy, girl. If you're there within five minutes, I'll reconsider."

Prudence struggled against pride: *he'll have me taken there no matter what I do; at least if I go myself, he might not have me whipped…*

Pride won. She wouldn't give the usurper the satisfaction of submitting so easily. "You have no right of command over me, stepfather."

"We shall see," he said, as he rang his hateful bell.

The smithy was warm and dim, both heated and lit by the great forge. The forge boy working the bellows couldn't tear his eyes away from Alasha's body. *He doesn't know me either,* she thought. *He only knew the fine clothes and the deference I was owed.*

Casa the smith recognized her straight away. Alasha almost wished she hadn't, because anonymity was her final refuge, but it was comforting to see a friendly face.

"Wait outside," Casa told the guards. "I will call you when I am done."

"Lord Jarvin's orders are that we wait with the slave."

"And wait you shall, but outside. This is delicate work, and I need room to breathe."

The guards muttered about being given orders by a woman, but the smith made it obvious she wouldn't start until her smithy was clear, and in the end, they left.

"I am truly sorry that it's come to this, Lady," said Casa.

"Don't take any risks for me, Casa. I have been stupid, and now I must pay."

"There is not much I can do anyway, except refuse to tag you."

"No. They'd just throw you out, and find a new smith. In any case, I'd prefer it done by someone I know."

"Then I do it with a heavy heart, Lady."

Casa took a length of cord and measured around the innermost joint of Alasha's ring finger, the finger that she'd carelessly assumed would bear a wedding band some day. Then the smith selected two matched halves of a bright iron ring from a wooden box, and placed them in the fire.

"It has been many years since such a thing has been done here. Long before my time," she said grimly. "An evil fate brought me to this place, I think."

The smith set some tiny pieces of metal type in an ancient-looking press, and when the ring was hot enough, she took one half up with a pair of tongs and set it between the clamp's jaws before pulling the long handle down with all of her heavy-set strength.

"It is numbered," she said, shortly, as she set the work back in the fire. "Now we must do our best to protect your finger from the heat."

"I don't understand. Surely the ring is not to be set on me straight from the forge?"

"Not red-hot. But the two halves must be joined. The pegs will not fuse into the sockets if they are cold."

She placed a filigree tube over Alasha's finger. "This will help to keep the ring from burning you as I put it on. After that, you must thrust your hand into the quenching trough straight away."

"But that will seal the ring in place forever."

"That is so. But remember that the wires will not shield you from the heat for long. We have no choice in this, Lady."

Alasha nodded, and the smith took one half of the ring from the fire and set it in an iron form that rested on the anvil. Then she lifted the other half in her tongs, and glanced at Alasha.

"Wet your hand first, Lady. Best close your eyes as soon as your finger is in place. Let me do my job and then let me plunge your hand in the water. If you flinch, I may hurt you with the hammer."

Alasha dipped her hand in the quenching trough, and looked at her unadorned finger for one last time before putting it into the form. She heard the hiss of steam and felt her finger burning even before she had time to close her eyes, but she gritted her teeth and held her hand steady.

She heard the chink of the top half of the ring dropping into place, followed by the clear ringing of the smith's hammer, and then her hand was deep in the icy water, the tube was gone, and the unfamiliar heaviness of the slave ring was tight around her finger.

She opened her eyes and looked at the homely face of the smith. "Thank you, Casa."

"I fear there is more, Lady." The smith went to a shelf, and took down an iron harness of some kind. "You might be glad in some way to wear this, though I do not like its design."

"What is it?"

"It is a chastity belt, made to preserve the virtue of a lady's womb," she said. "Alas, it is intended to offer no more protection than that." Casa shook her head sorrowfully, fingering the large ring that opened towards the rear of the device.

"You're to lock this thing on me?"

"I fear so, Lady. I am truly sorry."

"It's as I said, Casa: better that this should be done by a friend."

The smith took the belt, and locked it around Alasha's waist and between her legs. "I am to hold the key for Lord Jarvin," she said.

"What's the purpose of this belt, Casa? I know that my stepfather's soldiers will obey him in this matter…"

"I am sorry, Lady. I have heard that you are being sent away."

"Where? Why?"

"I do not know where. As to why, I would guess that Lord Jarvin sees you as a threat. He seeks to pull your fangs while staying within the law."

"My fangs are not to be pulled by a ring and a belt. I will return. I hope we'll meet again then."

"I hope so too, Lady, though I do not know how long I will be able to stay here."

There was a banging at the door. "You've had long enough," called the guard. "Send her out, or we'll find another smith. One who works faster."

"Goodbye, Casa."

"Goodbye, Lady."

As Alasha left, the last thing she saw was the astonished O of the forge boy's mouth, as if he only now realized that it was the Lady of the castle who had been in his smithy, and whom he had just seen enslaved.

Alasha stood in the courtyard, shivering in the thin winter sun as her stepfather talked with the caravan master. Lord Jarvin didn't attempt to move away, or even to lower his voice. *He must want me to hear how much he's selling me for.*

There were three mule-drawn wagons standing in the snow, with their drivers lounging lazily in their seats. A dozen or so mounted soldiers – mercenaries, going by their varied weapons and armor – provided the escort. The trade goods of the caravan were chained behind one of the wagons: a long coffle of slaves, the males at the front, the females following.

In the days of the Matriarch, traders such as these hadn't been welcome in the surrounding lands: Alasha knew of such things only from books. There were slaves working on the farms and in the castle, of course, but they were treated more like indentured servants and certainly weren't traded like cattle. That sort of thing still happened elsewhere in Xendria, but not here in the north, not since people like her mother had come to power.

Things were to be different from now on, it seemed.

The caravan master turned to her, and walked around her slowly before putting his hand under her chin and tilting her head up towards him. "Open your mouth."

Alasha considered the ugly whip that was coiled at his belt and obeyed, allowing the man to inspect her teeth.

"Good enough." He turned back to Lord Jarvin. "Eighty silver pieces."

"Eighty? My friend, this girl was once a noblewoman. She has been educated by the best tutors, taught all the finer points of etiquette. And as you see from the belt, her maidenhead is intact."

"All of which would help your case, if only my buyers were in the market for a wife and not a whore. But since there's no denying she's exceptional, and since you're opening up your lands to me … I'll go to ninety."

"You know very well you'll sell her for ten times that, perhaps more."

"Only if she survives the journey. Which she certainly won't, if she travels in that condition. She's not even shod, man!"

"I'll be damned if she takes anything from here. My final offer: you provide what she needs for the road, and give me a good price on what I want to buy. In return, I'll look on your future operations with favor, and let her go for a hundred. You know she's worth it, my friend."

The trader hawked up a mouthful of phlegm, spat it on the ground, and looked at Alasha again. "Deal," he said.

"Excellent," said Lord Jarvin. "I promised the girl a whipping earlier, but I haven't had time to deliver it. May I pass that duty to you, my friend?"

The trader spat again. "Anything for a good customer such as yourself."

"How perceptive of you."

"Perceptive?"

"Indeed. I am a good customer. I'd like to buy the rest of your females."

"What, all of them?"

"All of them. For the wellbeing of my men, you understand? And I believe this one might have a more interesting journey if she's the only girl. Shall we say fifty silver pieces a head?"

The trader gave a thin smile. "I could let you have one or two at that price, for friendship's sake. But all of them? That would be my profit for the trip gone. Anyway, we can't travel with only one. She'd lose too much condition, perhaps she wouldn't even survive … and the men need their comfort."

"Then what do you suggest?"

The trader thought for a while, sucking his teeth. "I could let you have six girls of my choosing, the ones who might be too weak to survive the journey. That doesn't mean they're no good, just a little less strong than the others. Give them some gruel and a pile of warm straw to sleep on for a few nights, and they'll be fine. They're pretty enough, too, like all my girls. Sixty each."

"Agreed, if you throw in two boys on the same terms; I believe that some of my men have eclectic tastes. And not one of them is to be at death's door, understand?"

"Of course not," said the slave trader. "I'd be the last person to risk offending you, my Lord."

One of the slavers gave her a rough woolen tunic, clogs that were too big for her, and a handful of long rags to wrap around her feet and legs.

"You can pay me back later," he said, before he shackled her at the end of the chain by her left wrist.

The caravan moved out of the courtyard and through the deep shadow of the gateway. As they emerged into the sun again, Alasha looked back, up at the great south tower and its smaller northern neighbor, at the high battlements of Malkenstorm that had always been home. After a moment, she turned away to the town in the valley below.

I won't look back again. The next time I see those towers will be when I return to claim them.

Curious yokels lined the hedgerows, watching the unfamiliar procession. Alasha hung her head, staring at the shuffling feet of the woman in front of her. She was sure that her people would suffer horribly under Lord Jarvin's new regime.

She wondered if the farmers would all be bonded serfs by the time she returned: if she had fallen so low, so quickly, what hope could there be for them?

I have failed them. It was my place to protect them, and I have failed.

The caravan moved slowly with a creaking of wheels and a tinkle of chains, punctuated by the occasional *crack!* of a whip whenever a slave slipped and fell in the snow.

The other captives looked weak and starved. Alasha pitied them at first, but by the end of the day, she was stumbling along as blindly as they were. She lost her balance twice, and only avoided the whip by scrambling to her feet quickly enough to keep from holding up the caravan.

When they stopped to make camp, she collapsed in the freezing mud, huddling with the other women on the chain.

The slavers released three of the male slaves, hobbled them, and sent them to gather firewood. Then one of the guards turned to Alasha.

"Can you cook?"

"I've studied it, but–"

"You can cook. Go and prepare food." He unlocked her, and then released two of the other women.

"Come," said the first. "This place has been used as a campsite before: we must find the fire pit. What is your name?"

"Alasha."

"I am Mica."

Alasha looked at the second girl for a moment, waiting for her name, but she simply looked at the ground and said nothing.

"She does not speak," said Mica. "She is young, and it has been difficult for her. Her name is Zini."

The girl looked up at the sound of her name.

"Zini, come."

Mica led the way to the fire pit, and Alasha started to dig out the snow while the others fetched the ember box and dry wood from one of the wagons.

"Can you light the fire?" asked Mica.

"Yes."

"Then we will fetch the grate and the pots."

Alasha graded the wood and arranged kindling in the pit, then blew on the embers from the box in order to light the fire. When it had caught, she added a layer of larger pieces.

Thank the gods I have a task that keeps me warm, and thanks to those who taught me enough woodcraft that I know how to build a fire.

They prepared two meals: a watery porridge for the prisoners, and a richer stew of salt meat, vegetables and castle-baked bread for the soldiers.

Alasha spooned gruel into wooden bowls for the clinking line of slaves. The aroma wafting from the soldiers' pot made her stomach growl. She glanced over, trying to gauge its level, wondering if there'd be any left.

Mica was looking at the stew, too. "We get some, sometimes, if we submit to them willingly. They will take what they want anyway, so it is best to pretend to enjoy it."

"I won't sell myself for food," said Alasha.

"There will be more for me, then," said Mica, without smiling.

The gruel was bland and unwholesome, but even so, Alasha wished there was more of it. By the time she'd finished, the others had already scooped the last traces out of the cooking pot. She sighed and tried to clench her stomach muscles to stop the rumbling in her belly. At this rate, it wouldn't be long before she was as emaciated as the rest.

Later, the soldiers chained the workers back into the coffle and started to pitch their camp. The slaves huddled under the wagons for shelter, with a strip of canvas hung and weighted to keep out the worst of the wind. The stronger ones pushed deeper into the mass of bodies, seeking warmth, or perhaps safety from the slavers. Alasha had no stomach for such competitions, and simply curled up against one of the wheels.

It wasn't long before one of the mercenaries was pulling her out, unlocking her bracelet, and leading her into his tent. "This is no night to be sleeping under the wagon," he said. "Come and warm my blankets instead."

At least the tent was out of the wind and close to the remains of the fire, and at least there were only two of them.

"Undress for us, love," said the soldier.

Alasha removed her clogs and undid her leg-wrappings. The man whistled appreciatively, and his comrade chuckled.

"Nothing quite like a shapely pair of legs, is there?" he said. "Unless it's a firm pair of tits and a warm cunny. Let's see yours, girl."

Alasha pulled her tunic over her head, revealing the chastity belt.

"Now that's a crying shame," said the first soldier.

"Reckon we can make the best of it," said the other, eyeing her behind.

"Take her up the arse if you like, you dirty little bugger. I'll stick with her mouth. Pity, though; I'll wager she's got a real sweet pussy."

His partner pushed a finger inside the iron belt, as if to make sure, and traced a line through the moisture he found there. "You're right. This one's wet for us." He looked at Alasha. "Sorry, love, but if you will go around dressed like that, there's not much we can do for you, is there?"

Alasha shook her head silently, waiting to see which of them wanted her first.

"Ain't got no rings or nothing, either. Reckon the boss will want to put that right."

What does he mean? Surely he can see the slave ring?

The first soldier pulled his breeches off and lay back on his bedroll. "Come on, then."

His cock is hard already, she thought, shocked at herself for even acknowledging that such an unladylike word existed. *But then, I'm not a Lady, not any more. Cock. Pizzle. Pecker. Tool. Manpiece. Prickle.*

Alasha straddled his legs and bent forward, kissing his cock's velvety end gently before taking it into her mouth.

She sensed the other man moving behind her, heard the sound of buckles being loosened and clothes falling to the ground. Callused hands stroked her behind and spread her cheeks, exposing what was hidden between.

Despite herself, Alasha moaned around the cock in her mouth, mortified at being opened in this way, but also wishing he would touch her between her legs again, inside the iron bands that both protected and frustrated her.

Instead, he put a finger on her most shameful entrance, and she flinched away, still sore from her ill-treatment in the barracks.

"Faster, harder," said the man beneath her.

She did her best to comply, but now the things that were happening behind her were becoming exceedingly uncomfortable. Was that a wet finger against her entrance, or a hard cock? Whatever it was, it slid inside her, making her snort with surprised pain. A finger: no cock could be that mobile.

She started to buck her hips uncontrollably, urged up and down by man kneeling behind her.

The new motion sent the cock between her lips over the edge and it spurted into her mouth, its owner raising himself onto his elbows as if he wanted to watch her face while he spent himself.

She swallowed as much as she could, but some of it ran out of her mouth and back down his shaft.

I have to appease him. Do I need to? Or do I want to? Is there any difference? She chased the oozing rivulets with her tongue and recovered what she'd lost.

"That's the spirit," said the man she was serving.

The soldier behind her reached around to her face. "Give me some spittle, lass."

She spat into his palm once, then again, and looked down past her hanging breasts and the frame of her thighs, watching him use her saliva to lubricate his tool.

Then he was pushing against her.

Alasha's time in the barracks had taught her a hard lesson, and she did her best not to fight him. Perhaps that would have helped, if she hadn't been so sore, or if she'd truly been able to let go. As it was, she couldn't help straining against his invading cock, and she couldn't avoid clenching herself after each withdrawal, as he pressed himself against her quivering entrance, poised to plunge inside her again.

From the sounds he made, her lack of co-operation seemed to arouse him even more.

Soon, she was hoping he would empty himself so that it could be over, but when at last he finished, she knew that she needed more.

No matter how much they hurt me, it will always be over too quickly, there. That's not where I need to be fucked.

The soldier disengaged himself and rolled over onto his sleeping mat. "What do you reckon? I don't fancy all that cold ironmongery next to me. Shall we kick her out in the snow?"

"You're a hard man, you are. After what she's done for us, and would do again, eh love? Don't worry, you can share my blanket. You'd best get dressed first, though, and I'll have to shackle your ankles."

Alasha pulled her jerkin back on, and held her feet together while the soldier locked irons around them.

"Not that you'd want to run away from a warm tent on a night like this, eh? But I'd end up just like you, if I let you escape, and you wouldn't wish that on me, would you?"

He returned her to the coffle at dawn, and she spent the day trudging through the snow, hunched against the cold and dreaming about finding somewhere warm to lie down.

At nightfall, Alasha helped prepare the evening meal again and then collapsed under the wagon. When the mercenaries came to choose their sleeping companions, one or two glanced at her, but they all selected other girls from the chain.

She was already shivering, wishing she were free to sleep near the remains of the fire, wondering if she'd be snug and warm in one of the tents if it wasn't for the hateful belt.

It was a long night under the wagon, and the iron bands locked around her loins were as cold as the ground.

3   unfree market

The slavers' camp was a crude stockade that nestled in a hollow near the top of a tall hill. Alasha and the rest of the cargo were un-chained and deposited in two holding pens, men in one, women in the other.

Nearby were rows of wooden cages, made of stout saplings bound together with rawhide.

"What will happen to us now?" she said aloud.

"The ones who can tell us that are out there," said Mica, nodding to the open area outside. A work-party brought leather buckets of water, splashing it into stone troughs set in the corners of the pens.

"Don't drink it too quickly," said one.

Alasha looked at the murky water and hoped she'd be out of the pen before she had to drink any of it at all. It was food and warmth that she and the other slaves needed, more than water.

The memory of those who had died of hunger and cold under the wagons still haunted her. *Please let us be taken to southern lands, where it is warm. They can't leave us here for long, not if they don't want more of us to die.*

It was an hour before the caravan master appeared with a slave girl at his heel, and ordered that the females' pen should be unlocked.

"Follow this slave, and do as she says," he said.

The women filed after the girl, who led them into a building made of stout timber posts and planks.

"This is the bath house" she said. "It is to clean you and rid you of vermin. You must take off your clothes and then go through the pas-sage."

Alasha was glad to be rid of the jerkin and strips of cloth: they were indeed infested with creatures that crawled and jumped and bit. She stripped the rags off and went through the passage further into the building.

There was a trough sunk into the ground, filled with dark liquid that steamed and reeked of tar. Steps led down, but Alasha hesitated.

Something pushed her from behind, and she stumbled forward and fell into the tank. It was deep, and unpleasantly hot after the chill outside, and she scrambled to her feet, spluttering as her head cleared the surface. She just had time to take a lungful of air before a forked pole came down from somewhere overhead, catching her behind the neck and forcing her under the surface again.

It held her down until she was on the verge of panic, her lungs bursting, and then it released her. She managed to straighten up again, taking in air with great sucking gasps. There was a yelp and a splash from behind her, but she ignored them and made her way to the far side of the tank where she clambered out.

In the next room, two slaves sluiced her down with pitchers of water, washing her clean of the oily liquid from the bath, and after that, she came into the presence of the valuer.

There was an iron grille suspended against one wall, and a weighing platform with a measuring rod mounted beside it. The valuer sat behind a rough table, with his writing box in front of him and a stack of larger chests at his side. A youth, who was evidently the valuer's apprentice, waited near the door.

"Number?"

The apprentice took Alasha's hand and read the figures inscribed on her ring. "Number 1478923, sir."

The valuer consulted his notes. "Ah, yes. Alasha, former noblewoman. Hardly a fitting name, any more, but doubtless her new owners will change that if they wish. Your report, boy?"

The apprentice took Alasha's elbow and steered her onto a weighing platform, where he noted the reading and then measured her height. "One hundred pounds, sir. A shade under sixteen hands. Hair dark blonde. Eyes green. Rings none, brands, none. Teeth fine. No evidence of infestation; health appears good."

"What have you forgotten, boy?"

"Er, yes. The chastity belt, sir. Then … we can assume she's untouched?"

"Assume nothing. Always check. Here."

He tossed a key to the apprentice, who used it to unlock the belt before leading Alasha to a mat. "Lie down," he said.

As soon as she was on the floor, he opened her legs and then her more intimate parts, before examining, prodding and probing her. "You can get up now, girl. She's intact, sir."

"Good. Your recommendations?"

"Um, a collar and some rings, sir? And a light branding?"

"No branding, not matter how much you'd enjoy it. Try to be professional about this. Why devalue prime flesh with a generic mark? We leave that to the buyer. You are right about the rings, though. They'll set her off nicely on the auction block."

Alasha was so relieved that she wasn't to be branded that she hardly registered what he said about the rings. It was only when the apprentice fetched a long box of polished wood, and opened it to display the gleaming instrument inside, that she understood.

"No," she breathed, looking at the valuer beseechingly.

He just smiled. "She doesn't seem to like the idea, boy. Make sure you restrain her well. You don't want to tear her."

The apprentice led her to the grille and strapped her ankles and wrists to it, spread-eagling her across the unyielding surface. Then he secured her waist with a longer strap, cinching it tight until she felt the metal bars cutting into her back.

"Don't forget the collar," said the valuer.

The youth circled his fingers about Alasha's neck with efficient detachment, as if judging her size. Then he opened one of the larger chests and selected a collar, which he locked around her throat and chained to the grating.

Now, she could do no more than breath, and watch.

The apprentice took a bottle of clear liquid and poured some into a dish that stood on the table. Next, he scooped up some rings from the long box. Two were made of gold; the rest were of some glittering metal that looked like Marlish steel. He dropped all of them into the dish before swabbing Alasha's ear lobes with the same fluid.

Earrings: the adornments of slaves, whores, and gypsies. It doesn't matter. I'm already marked as a slave and a whore. It will be no disgrace to be taken for a gypsy.

The youth picked up the instrument that Alasha had glimpsed in the long box. It was a pair of long-handled tongs, with an intricate mechanism into which he fitted one of the golden rings from the dish.

She shut her eyes as he approached, and heard a clicking sound as he prepared the machine and then a cold pressure as he clamped it to her left ear lobe. There was a sharp crack and a sudden pain, and she felt the weight of her new jewelry hanging against her jaw.

He treated her right ear in the same way, and she opened her eyes, basking in a wave of relief that it was over; the piercing had hurt, but the pain and the sense of violation hadn't been nearly as bad as she'd feared.

The apprentice stood back to admire his handiwork, and then he retrieved his cloth, dipped it in the fluid again, and started to swab her left nipple.

O please no, not that, but her treacherous nipples had already grown hard under his touch. The boy looked at her face and then glanced at his master. The man was reading his notes. The apprentice grinned at Alasha, and rolled her flesh between his thumb and forefinger, pressing hard enough so that she would have flinched away from him if she'd been free. He stuck his tongue out at her.

The valuer rustled his papers and cleared his throat, and the boy finished swabbing her and picked up his piercing tongs once more.

This time, Alasha fought against her restraints, finding some mad reserve of strength that rattled the chains and swung the grating away from the wall. It was useless, though: flesh and bone could not master the unyielding iron that secured her. Soon, she was hanging in her bonds again, panting and staring fearfully at the awful tongs.

She watched the cold jaws closing over her puckered flesh, and felt the nipple hardening as if it welcomed the machine's cruel caress.

Alasha looked from her breast up to the boy's face, hoping to find a hint of pity or sympathy there, praying that he would smile and tell her this was nothing but a jest. All she saw was rapt concentration as he positioned the tongs and tightened their jaws further.

The crack of the machine surprised her almost as much as the sound of her own lament. This was far worse than before. A stabbing jolt of pain ricocheted around her breast before dissipating into a hot mist that obscured her vision with tears.

The apprentice waited until her howls had subsided into sobs before he started to swab her other nipple.

This time, she didn't struggle and she didn't cry out. She simply clung to the grille and listened to the sound of her own whimpering as she watched him fit the tongs again, and waited for the agony to return.

Crack!

The pain shot through her breast again, and Alasha looked down through her tears and saw the two silver rings that would mark her as a slave for the rest of her life.

Now that the torment was over, she found the sight both repulsive and fascinating. "You've done what you wanted. Please let me down now."

The apprentice simply looked at his master, who nodded back to him. "They will balance the others, and allow us to dispense with the belt."

And then it became even worse: he was swabbing the lips that guarded her sex, and his grinning face left her in no doubt that he could sense how aroused – and how repelled – she was by his touch.

This time, the ring he selected was less delicate than before. The steel of the piercing tool seemed to freeze against her labia, and the pressure as he tightened its jaws was exquisitely painful, so that she couldn't help wailing and challenging her chains again.

The pain she felt as the ring punctured her most delicate parts was worse than she could have imagined. So was the knowledge that it would happen at least once more, and that she was already thrice ringed, now and forever.

Alasha decided to salvage what dignity she could. As the instrument returned, she closed her eyes tightly against the tears that welled up, and clenched her teeth against the scream she knew would come. She couldn't help jerking against the chains as the final ring bit home, but she didn't weep, and she didn't scream, and when it was done, she felt as if she had reclaimed a tiny piece of her old pride.

The boy swabbed the blood away, and the valuer rose from his chair and came over to inspect the piercings. "Tidy work, boy. You'll be a journeyman yet, if you keep at it."

"Thank you, sir."

The older man indicated the rings that transfixed Alasha's sex. "Lock those two together and then send her to the premium auction."

"Premium it is, sir," the lad replied, and fastened an ivory marker to Alasha's collar.

When the apprentice released her from the grille, she found that her limbs were shaking so much that she couldn't stand. The boy caught her and held her until she calmed down.

"Don't worry. There's many that don't bear up as well as you." He glanced down at her loins and then grinned at her. "Reckon you'll start appreciating them soon enough."

Then he chose a light padlock and clipped it through her labia rings, fastening them together. She winced as he disturbed the piercings, and as the new weight settled on them.

"Be grateful you're rid of the belt, girl," said the valuer. "I can see where it's been chafing you … injuries like that don't look good on the block, you know."

The apprentice nodded his agreement. "Careful when you piss, now, and be sure to keep the lock clean and dry, or it'll rust and then where'll you be? Take extra care to keep the rings clean too, for the first few days."

Alasha looked down at herself, wishing there was a mirror. Her body had been transformed, almost as if in confirmation that it no longer belonged to her: gleaming ornaments at each ear and each breast, and a heavier weight that glinted like a jewel between her legs.

What sort of man will want me now, marked like this? The sort of man who buys what he wants, or just takes it. No man that I would choose for myself will desire me now.

"Off you go, then." The apprentice handed her a roughly woven blanket.

"Thank you," she said.

Alasha fingered the heavy ivory marker he'd fastened to her collar, and left the room.

At least the soup they were given seemed more nourishing than the trail rations, though the meat looked gray and of dubious provenance.

Alasha ate her bread and vegetables, and drank the broth. A skinny girl sitting nearby started to wolf her portion down.

"Take your time," advised Alasha. "You'll make yourself sick, otherwise. Here, I'm not going to eat all of mine; you can have some more when you've finished, if you'll just slow down."

The girl ate more slowly after that, chewing each mouthful and eyeing Alasha's bowl disbelievingly.

After they'd been fed and watered, they were herded into cages built onto wagon-beds, and the caravan set off again. Just before nightfall, they arrived at a large town. There was a delay while the lead driver negotiated with the gate guards, and Alasha saw two girls and a boy being taken from one of the wagons and hustled into the guard post.

A short while later, the three slaves were loaded into their wagon again, and the caravan passed through the gates and plodded through the town. Alasha wondered if the traders had a compound within the walls, or if the caravan would just stop close to wherever the market was to be and remain there all night.

The wagon lurched to a halt. Alasha, who was sitting cross-legged next to the bars, leaned forward trying to see through the darkness; there seemed to be some kind of disturbance at the crossroads ahead of them. An accident, perhaps, or a broken-down cart.

Two youthful voices – one Xendrian like Alasha herself, and one pleasingly foreign – were raised in friendly disputation as their owners caught up with the wagon. Alasha watched as the young men paced alongside and came into the circle of light cast by the driving lamps. They had a flask of wine, which they were passing back and forward between them like a debating baton, except that the one who drank was the listener and not the speaker.

The Xendrian was tall and raw-boned, with blond hair and an arrogantly hooked nose. The foreigner – Marlish, by his accent – was darker and smaller but still well made, and he moved with a lithe grace that his companion lacked. He had curly dark hair that hung to his shoulders, and a short beard trimmed in a manner that may well have been the height of fashion among the Marlish, but which seemed delightfully eccentric to Alasha's Xendrian eyes.

Her tall countryman was speaking as they drew alongside the wagon.

"...considering you hardly attended a single Philosophy lecture. That's not what he said, and it was someone else who said it, anyway."

"Then I pray you enlighten me, O learned one." The foreigner had a pleasing smile, and used it to disarm the mocking glance he gave his comrade.

"It was our own playwright Simeron, as you well know," said the Xendrian. "I'll not entertain the tired claim that one of your Marlish dilettantes could have penned the tale of Lysia and Landor."

"I'll grant you that Simeron made a passable translation, if you can live without all the nuances that can only be expressed in the original Marlish."

"Don't be so ridiculous. You Marlish may be great tinkerers and inventors, but to suggest that such great poetry originated in your smoky land ... the very idea is preposterous, my mercantile friend."

"Gods, give me strength. Is there not one person in this caste-ridden country that doesn't claim that every piece of art and literature across the entire globe originated here?"

Alasha wrapped her blanket around herself more tightly, and spoke up. "Indeed, sir, I'm forced to concede that much depth of meaning is lost in the translation." She switched to Marlish, doing her best to imitate the rounded tones of her language tutor. "Who but a Marlish poet could have glorified a land where liberty runs so deep that a slave is freed, simply by setting foot on its soil?"

Both the men halted and gaped at her, as well they might: a beauti-ful caged slave girl, collared and tagged for the market and dressed only in a blanket, holding forth on Marlish poetry. Alasha imagined how she must look to them, and felt suddenly foolish, like a serving wench interrupting a philosophical debate at table, or a child showing off to visiting dignitaries.

It didn't matter. Her embarrassment was nothing compared to the mortification she had suffered already, and she was glad of the fleeting chance to think and talk as she had in the old days. It would be over soon enough, and she would be back in her world of cold and hunger, and of constant scheming and bargaining to avoid them.

Both men were looking at her seriously, now.

"And what have we here?" said the Xendrian. " A whelp that has been penned too close to her Master's library, perhaps?"

"Hush, Rafe. She didn't learn such well-spoken Marlish in a cage." The smaller man gave a slight bow. "May I present Rafe Strongbourne, my helper and sometime friend in your country? And I myself am Aric Albigenses, a merchant-adventurer from the island of Marl."

He paused and glanced around, as if waiting for someone to present Alasha. The protocol of these things was so strongly ingrained that she hesitated too, before forcing herself to say her own name.

"Alasha, a slave girl of Xendria, as you see."

"I didn't realize that Xendria was so open handed with its education," said Aric.

"Come on, Albigenses. She's of no interest. She'll be on the auction block tomorrow; why waste your time?"

"On the contrary, my friend. When a girl speaks of the poetry of my land in perfect – if delightfully accented – Marlish, it brings forth a certain homesickness. The fact that she's in a cage and has a price tag around her neck is a matter of supreme indifference to me, though doubtless it will be the source of further philosophical debate between us."

Rafe leaned close to his friend, and made to whisper in his ear. Perhaps he would have spoken more quietly, but for the wine. "There's no point, Aric. You can't afford her. Anyway, you've sworn never to own a fellow human being."

Aric's quick glance told Alasha that he knew she had heard. He bowed again, his face flushing. "Permit us to take our leave, Lady Alasha, and I venture to hope that we may meet again. Come, Rafe. I grow weary. It's time to return home."

Alasha watched and listened as the two men walked away.

"What did you mean by globe, anyway?" said the Xendrian. "You can't possibly subscribe to those wild theories about the world being round … the wine fumes must have addled your brain again."

Aric just laughed, softly. Alasha wondered what he'd really

thought of her. It didn't really matter; she knew that she'd probably never see him again.

Alasha had never seen such crowds.

The marketplace was filled to bursting with people who had come to sightsee and to buy. Around the edges of the enclosure were rows of stalls selling many different things: trinkets, brightly woven cloth, metalwork and pottery. Here and there, a food stall attracted a crowd of hungry marketgoers; the air was rich with the fragrance of hot bread and searing meat, making Alasha's mouth water and her belly rumble.

The morning had been devoted to the selling of males. Among the customers for that sale had been many that wore the boots and smocks of farmers, looking to replenish their labor supply ready for the new season's tilling and planting. Alasha had also seen plump eunuchs and bejeweled priests among the crowd, bidding on the youngest and most innocent looking of the boys.

All morning, buyers had strolled up and down the line of wagons, inspecting the lots that were to be offered later. Alasha had lost count of the number of times she was ordered to stand, to drop her blanket, and to turn in place so that another man could see her body and watch the way she moved; there was always a whip-wielding slaver nearby to ensure co-operation. She soon learnt to tell the serious buyers: they were the prosperous-looking ones who ordered her to kneel at the front of the cage while they noted her tag number and examined her teeth.

Now it was afternoon, and the turn of the women. The younger girls were being sold first. It almost made Alasha weep to witness them being pushed onto the block, and to see the rows of bidders at the front, with the old men who had not come to bid but only to gawk sitting further back. There, dirty hands disappeared beneath stained robes as each one watched the girls being presented and disrobed on the block, and gently massaged himself.

One of the slavers approached Alasha's cage. "Your lot is next," he said as he unlocked the iron door. "Leave the blankets. Put on a tunic from the pile and then wait by the block until you're called for."

Alasha and the others climbed down from the wagon. Alasha

looked around. There were no walls and no chains here: just the fact of being in a slave market, surrounded by people who wanted to buy – or to watch. It was enough to deny any prospect of escape. She walked over to the pile of clothes and chose one of the tunics: thin to the point of translucency and cut scandalously short, with no other purpose than to arouse lust.

She put the garment on and waited for her turn. All too soon, the slave handler beckoned her to the block. Alasha climbed the wooden steps and stood in the pale sunlight, looking down at the crowd.

The auctioneer was rattling off some information that the crowd seemed to understand, but his words ran together and Alasha could make neither head nor tail of what he said.

The slave handler was hissing something at her. She stopped listening to the auction babble in order to concentrate on her orders.

"Turn around!"

She turned, slowly.

The handler stepped forward and took a handful of Alasha's shift, just beneath its low neckline. He pulled hard, and the seams gave way with a loud ripping noise, so that the entire garment ended up fluttering in his hand.

"Turn again!"

She obeyed, displaying herself to the marketgoers.

The crowd fell silent and gazed at her, as if she seemed extraordinary to them even after the parade of delectable flesh that had already passed across the block. The only sound was the high-pitched jabbering of the auctioneer.

Then the bidding began.

One by one, the bidders dropped out: richly-dressed eunuchs; hard-nosed traders, even one or two silk-clad beauties, signaling their bids from inside their slave-borne palanquins with the wave of a painted fan.

Great Ladies, diverting themselves with a day at the market, thought Alasha. *Who knows? I might have become one such myself, if things had been different.*

At last, there were only two bidders left. One was a corpulent eunuch, swathed in colorful silk that was incongruously belted with a well-oiled whip. He was standing close to the block, flicking his gaze between Alasha and the auctioneer with the same calculated acquisitiveness that she remembered from his earlier inspection visit.

The other stood further away, leaning on his staff at the edge of the crowd. The staff, the dark-curled beard, and the black-trimmed hood and cloak that he wore, marked him to Alasha's eyes as an Arbian trader from across the Southern Desert. She found herself hoping that the eunuch would win the contest: better to enter a harem now than to trek across the endless sands to another market and another auction block.

The auctioneer uttered another string of syllables, which Alasha judged to be an invitation to the Arbian to increase his bid. The man shook his head under the hood, and turned away. The eunuch watched him go and then turned back to the block.

The auctioneer's hammer fell, and he uttered the first words that Alasha found intelligible. "Sold to Lord Fiasco, represented by his agent Emon, for eleven hundred silver pieces. Next!"

The eunuch's eyes glittered as he looked up at Alasha, and smiled.

Emon gave her a new tunic, cut much like the one she'd worn briefly on the block, but made of finer material. It was still thin enough and short enough to reveal as much as it concealed.

He didn't provide her with sandals, but he linked a chain to her collar and led her barefoot across the market place to where his carriage was waiting.

"What is your name, girl?" he asked, as he opened the door.

"Alasha," she replied.

"Hmmm. I doubt that will suit. Lord Fiasco prefers his female chattels to have brief and lowly names, as befits their station. I will think on a new one, for which you will naturally be grateful."

"Of course, sir," said Alasha, carefully concealing any hint of irony.

"I know that you're clever, girl. That's one reason why your new Master will be interested in you. But I advise you not to be too clever.

You haven't tasted much of the whip recently, judging by that deliciously unblemished hide. That is something that could change quickly, unless you show the proper respect."

He looked at her, his lips twisting into a cold smile that didn't reach his eyes. "In fact, I think I can promise you that it will change, and sooner than you'd like."

Alasha thought of the few cuts of the crop that she'd earned from the slavers, when she hadn't understood an order or simply hadn't moved quickly enough. That had been more than she could bear, yet she knew that it had been no more than a warning, compared to what might lie ahead.

The eunuch eased his bulk into the carriage and settled himself into the broad seat before tugging at her collar chain. Alasha followed him inside and made to sit opposite him.

"Do not presume to occupy a place meant for your betters," he said. "It will be four days before we reach your Master's estate. I must be able to stretch my legs. You may kneel there, in the far corner. If you keep out of my way, I might take it into consideration when I decide what food and lodging you are to receive at the post inns."

Alasha knelt, and did her best to keep her balance when the carriage lurched into motion. She remained silent and kept her eyes downcast.

As the carriage moved away, she could see Emon's plump fingers playing with the whip that served as his belt.

4   slave mistress

"This is Liri," said Emon, indicating the curtseying girl. "She held the post you will be filling, until recently. It would be wise for you discuss the work with her: it might help you to avoid the mistakes she made. Liri, this is Ala. You will show her to your old quarters, and explain her tasks and how she is to comport herself. Provide her with any assistance she requires."

"Yes, sir," said Liri.

Alasha curtseyed too, wondering if her failure to do so before would cause problems, and what other etiquette she needed to learn when dealing with her new superiors. She held the curtsey until Liri rose, which wasn't until Emon had left the room.

Liri seemed to sense that Alasha had waited for her cues. "We always curtsey for the eunuchs, and we kneel for the Master or his guests," she said. "Come. I will take you to your chamber."

She led Alasha to a small staircase at the back of the house, and they started to climb.

"I have a bedchamber of my own?" asked Alasha. "That is unexpected. I thought we would sleep in shared cells, or worse."

"Our … your station in the household is special. You are to act as governess to the Master's boys. Your chamber was mine, until yesterday. Now I have nowhere."

"Then you must share with me," said Alasha quickly. "What a strange man, to entrust the education of his sons to a slave girl."

"I said boys, not sons. It is not in the Master's nature to have sons or daughters."

Alasha climbed in silence for a moment as she absorbed this information. "Then why does he keep girls?"

"The Master prefers boys for pleasure. He prefers girls for pain."

"You mean he likes us to whip him, or something?"

"No," said Liri. "I wish it were so, but that is not his way. He likes to torment girls, or at least to watch his boys torment us on his behalf."

They arrived at a narrow landing at the top of the house.

"This is your chamber," said Liri, pushing the door open and standing aside.

Alasha didn't need to enter to see the entire place. A thin pallet took up the whole length – and more than half the width – of the room. There were some roughly woven blankets and a chamber pot. A tiny window, too high and too small to offer any hope of escape, was nevertheless furnished with iron bars.

"Our chamber," said Alasha. "We're sharing, remember?"

"You are very kind, but it is forbidden. Girls may not share unless ordered to do so." Liri paused. "For their entertainment, you understand."

"Then where will you sleep?"

"I shall find somewhere. Now, I am to instruct you in your status and your duties. You are to be governess to the Master's two favorites. He changes his preferences from time to time, and then you will have new students. Some are easier than others; the current pair are challenging."

"What am I to teach them?"

"How to comport themselves. The Master takes one or other of his boys to many of the formal engagements he attends. He expects his companion to know which cutlery to use, how to greet a knight or a duke, and how to make polite conversation. Your task is to inform them about such things."

"Does he also expect them to attend him on less formal occasions?"

"Seldom. When he goes among other men, to drink or to play cards, he usually takes a girl. One who reflects well on him. I expect he will require you to accompany him, now that I am disgraced."

"You said that his current pair are difficult."

"Yes. Vermillio and Quinn are their names. They are bolder than our Master's previous companions, and more difficult to control."

"In what way?"

"Understand that every male in this household stands above every female in the hierarchy. If a gate guard or a kitchen boy wants you, you must do whatever he desires. I would advise you not to risk their displeasure. You will find that out for yourself, soon enough."

"So I must teach two boys who are set in authority over me."

"Yes, and I have no doubt that they will lust for you as soon as they see you. Now that they know enough not to drink from the finger bowls, their only interest is to see how quickly they can have their teacher stripped and bent over a writing desk."

"Does Lord Fiasco not require them to pay attention during lessons?"

"They are his lovers, Ala. When they tell him that their teacher is stupid and lazy, he believes them."

"Which is why you are no longer governess, and why I have been brought here."

"Yes."

"Then what is to become of you?"

"I think the Master will keep me for a while. If you can teach his boys to use the right spoon for their soup, and to listen to a discussion of politics or history without belching or scratching their behinds, then I will be sold … and there are even worse places than this."

"And if I cannot?"

"Then perhaps I'll be re-instated as the boys' teacher, or more likely I'll be punished for not assisting you properly." Liri shrugged her thin shoulders. "There is no certainty in this house, not for the likes of us."

Alasha fixed her two students with a gaze that she hoped radiated confidence and authority.

"To begin, perhaps you could tell me what you have already learned?"

The one called Vermillio eased his rangy body back in his chair. "We learned what a girl looks like when she's naked." He smirked and tossed his oiled curls, wafting perfume into the air.

"I think I forgot," said Quinn. "I think I need that lesson again."

"Quite right," said Vermillio. "There are probably differences between girls that we need to know about, anyway."

"You're right. The other one had bigger tits."

"Take it off, teacher."

Alasha regarded them for a long moment. "Our Master is giving you an opportunity to learn things that will be useful long after he has tired of you. Please work with me, for all our sakes."

"Too right, teacher. Our next position might be with a Lady, right? There must be all sorts of things we need to know."

"Indeed; Ladies desire companions who understand the social graces. We shall start with the order of precedence on entering a banqueting hall."

"No. We'll start with the order of precedence on entering a sluttish slave girl," said Vermillio. "Me first. Take it off, teacher, and get on the table."

"Take it off," echoed Quinn.

"Or do you need some help?"

"We'd be glad to oblige."

"Just like with the other one. Liri, or whatever she was called."

"I am not Liri," said Alasha firmly.

"Of course you're not," said Vermillio. "If you were Liri, we wouldn't be nearly as interested. We've already seen Liri without her clothes. We've had Liri."

"I think I'll have her again, when we're finished with you."

These were boys, not men: perhaps a year or two younger than Alasha herself. She knew that they were dangerous, but she also remembered a time when they would have been terrified of her. If only she could recapture some of that presence…

"As I mentioned, I am not Liri." She looked at Quinn, whom she judged to be the more compliant of the two. "Consider that you are at a banquet with our Master, and he is speaking to the Lady sitting opposite him. Her goblet is empty, but the table slaves haven't noticed. What does protocol demand that you should do?"

"Er…"

"Protocol be damned. You're the only thing we're going to do," said Vermillio.

"And when it happens at the next banquet? Or any of the other thousand things you will be required to know?"

"We'll blame it on you, just like we did with Liri."

Alasha kept looking at Quinn. "Do you imagine your Master to be a fool? How many times do you think you can tell the same story, and have it believed?"

Quinn turned to his friend. "Maybe she's right."

Vermillio lounged in his chair and sneered at her. "We could have you whipped, you know. One word is all it would take. We could have you brought to Fiasco's chambers tonight, and thrash you ourselves, until you bleed. Your Master would enjoy watching."

"Then no doubt *our* Master will order it done himself, whenever he wishes. In the meantime, he desires that you be educated."

Alasha could see that Quinn was defeated, and that left to his own devices, he would have co-operated. Both she and he would have profited by that.

Vermillio was not Quinn, however.

"We'll make a bargain," he said at last. "For the first hour, we study. At the end of the hour, you take that delightful shift off, and we'll decide whether to continue our lesson with you, or in the tavern. If you're as clever as you seem to think, you'll have no problems teaching us what we need to know in an hour each day."

Quinn perked up when he heard this proposal. "And if she's really nice, we might not whip her later, right Vermillio?"

"Agreed," said Vermillio.

Both of the boys smiled expectantly and looked at Alasha. She knew she had made the best of an impossible situation: they had started with the right to do what they pleased, and she had pushed that boundary back a little. To have them undertake to study for an hour each day represented a small victory.

She hoped it would be enough to stop her from ending up like Liri.

Alasha heard the sound of tapping and turned away from the blackboard. Vermillio was flicking the side of the hourglass, where the last few grains of sand were slipping away.

"Time's up, teacher. I hardly noticed it at all; you must be good at your job."

"I hope I am." Alasha put down the chalk and stepped away from the list of honorific titles she'd been writing.

"I hope you're as good at keeping your bargains," said Vermillio.

"What shall we do with her?" asked Quinn.

"First, I want to see her naked." Vermillio nodded at Alasha, and she pulled her shift over her head, revealing herself for them.

Both boys fell silent for a moment, gazing at her and licking their lips.

"Are we going to fuck her?" asked Quinn.

"No. I want to touch her, first. I want to feel every part of that soft skin while it's still perfect and smooth, and find out what she smells like close up. Then I want to try her mouth, and see how it compares to the other one. There'll be plenty of time to fuck her later. Come here, teacher."

Alasha approached him, and stood with her eyes downcast.

"What's this padlock?"

She hesitated, fearful that they would rip it away from her. The chastity belt had been heavy and chafing, but it hadn't left her feeling fragile and vulnerable like these captured rings.

"It is to preserve my maidenhead," she said at last. "I believe that owners value such things."

"Fiasco cares bugger all for such things. Where's the key?"

"I think the eunuch must have received it, along with my deeds of indenture."

Alasha half-hoped that they would obtain the key and use it to gain full access to her. She knew that they would find other ways to use her, if needs be, and she had no doubt that her virginity would be short-lived in this house, padlock or no. At least they might free her of the restraint, and the risk of it being torn from her in a moment of careless lust. At least it would be easier to relieve herself, and to keep herself clean.

"You're very free and easy with that information, teacher. It almost makes me wonder if you're panting to have my cock inside you, and my seed planted in your belly."

"I want to be rid of the padlock," said Alasha carefully. "I'll keep my promise and give you what you want freely, if you can get the key. But I have no wish for a child."

"And we have no wish to father one on you, eh Quinn?"

"Um, no. Such a thing would not please Lord Fiasco."

"Though his displeasure would fall on her more than on us, since
he could hardly be certain who was responsible. Still, best to tread
carefully, eh? I understand there are ways to avoid such things? Herbs
you can take, or certain days when it's best to entertain ourselves in
other ways?"

"I have read of such things," said Alasha, "though I have no way of
obtaining the herbs."

"Then you'll tell us which days are safe for you, once I have the key.
We'll arrange it so that those days are less unpleasant for you in other
ways, and then there'll be no reason for you to cheat us. For now, just
stand there and turn around. Show yourself to me."

Alasha complied, fighting down her embarrassment at displaying
herself for these youths that had so recently been her pupils.

Vermillio was silent for a while before he spoke again. "You're
truly beautiful, did you know? Wasted on an old bugger like Fiasco,
wouldn't you agree, Quinn?"

"Yes, but we can make up for that. I'm glad you got rid of the other
one, Liri or whatever her name was."

"Come here, teacher. I think that Quinn wants to see your arse close
up. Don't you, Quinn?"

"Oh, yes."

Vermillio took her by the elbow, and positioned her between them.
She felt Quinn's fingers at the small of her back, slowly tracing downwards over her bottom cheeks and then between them. At the same
time, Vermillio lifted one of her nipple rings, and let it fall again. Her
body stiffened, as did her nipples, at the boys' touch.

"This one's hot for it, Quinn. We'd better get hold of that key soon,
or she might burn up completely. What do you say, teacher?"

Alasha found herself caught between conflicting emotions, and it
was a few moments before she was able to reply.

Her logical mind wanted no part of these boys, yet their inexorable
caresses aroused something in her, something that was beyond logic. It
had been the same with Lord Jarvin's guards, and with the slavers who
had taken her, and with the valuer and his boy when they had ringed
her. Part of her railed against the men who used and controlled her, but

a deeper part relished the experience of being used and controlled. The revulsion she felt at their unchosen touch only fanned the treacherous flames.

At last, she gasped a reply. "It … would be good … to get the key."

"Consider it done. In the meantime, perhaps you'd care to get on the desk?"

To her dismay, Alasha found herself scrambling to obey. "Like this?"

"That's it, on your back. Arch that beautiful body and bend those shapely legs a little; I want to see daylight between you and the desk. Rest on your shoulders and your arse and your heels. Point your toes. Doesn't she have dainty ankles and pretty feet, Quinn? Doesn't her body make a pleasing set of curves?"

"I suppose so. I'm a tit man, myself."

"Well, there they are, naked and awaiting your pleasure, and very shapely too. Perfect, if you're not too greedy."

"You know, she looks exactly like that girl in the book from Fiasco's library…"

"That why I arranged her like this, you idiot."

"Oh."

Alasha's neck was beginning to ache from the strain of holding her head clear of the desk. Shoulders, arse, and heels, he'd said. She'd probably be whipped if she didn't obey. She felt herself beginning to tremble from the effort.

"It's all right, teacher. You can put your head down. In fact…"

His hands were on her, urging her gently backward until her neck was level with the edge of the desk.

"Now, just relax and let yourself hang back, while we consider the convenient position your mouth happens to be in, and what we might do about it. This one's eager to please, isn't she? I think she'll work out very well. I'm glad we've decided to keep her for a while."

"Me too," said Quinn. "When are you going to have her mouth?"

"Everything in good time; we've got hours yet. Don't worry, you'll get your turn."

She felt one of Vermillio's fingers slipping between the padlocked rings and running gently up and down, just inside the moist lips of her sex. The sensations stole the strength from her body, and she almost straightened out against the desk.

"Look at her tremble, Quinn. I've made her go all sloppy, can you smell her scent? Keep her back arched, would you?"

Quinn seized her waist and pulled her back into position, as Vermillio's finger probed deeper and explored her hymen. "Ah, I've found the problem, doctor. There's not enough clearance here, not for big lads like us. Don't worry; we'll cure that in no time at all."

"Cure what?" asked Quinn.

"Her maidenhead," replied Vermillio, continuing to move his finger along her sex, sending shivers through her that whispered he was near a place that, if he could but find it, would take her to a different world.

Alasha heard herself moaning and became aware that she was straining forwards with her hips, and making circling motions as if she could guide his finger to the right spot. She fought for control, but there was no helping it: the frustrated arousal of Vermillio's finger, and the eroticism of her situation, were too powerful to resist.

"Let her go."

Quinn relaxed his grip around Alasha's waist, and she let her loins sink to back down. Her own panting was loud in her ears.

Vermillio was at the end of the desk. He opened his jerkin and his breeches so that his erect member sprang out, bobbing against her face. "You know what to do, teacher."

Alasha strained backwards, awkwardly capturing the very tip of his cock, then clamping her lips and tongue against it so as to draw it deeper and prevent its escape. Vermillio responded with a deep groan of pleasure. Then he twisted his fingers into her cascading hair so that she could not withdraw from him, and began thrusting himself into her mouth. Alasha heard herself whimpering under this careless cruelty, but that didn't stop her from sending her tongue scurrying around his shaft, encouraging him towards his climax.

Vermillio froze, inserted so deeply that she could feel him in the back of her throat, could see his male jewels dangling before her inverted eyes. Some instinct of self-preservation took over, and she held herself perfectly still.

"Don't try to rush me, you randy little slut. We have plenty of time. Quinn doesn't mind waiting, do you, Quinn?"

"Of course not. Take as long as you like."

Vermillio withdrew far enough so that Alasha's head emerged from between his legs. He looked down at her. "I can tell you haven't done this often, or if you have it was with men who didn't expect much, so I'm going to be patient. Turn onto your side, and then lick and suck me here, as fast as you can."

He eased himself out of her mouth, and indicated the point just beneath the head of his cock.

Alasha twisted herself sideways and placed her lips where he desired. The soldiers and slavers had all been happy simply to be sucked and stroked until they climaxed, and this was new for her; she wasn't quite sure what to do. She decided to experiment; no doubt Vermillio would let her know of any shortcomings.

She sucked gently, and was rewarded with a deep sigh of approval. Then she pushed her tongue between her lips and onto his scented skin, and started to stroke him in time with her suckling.

"Much better. Don't forget to use your hands."

Alasha reached up and encircled him with the fingers of one hand. He was slick with her saliva, and she started to pump her hand back and forward along his shaft.

"That's it. Use your imagination."

She explored between his legs with her other hand, and cupped his scrotum, squeezing it lightly.

Vermillio gasped and splashed his seed onto her face. Alasha took him into her mouth as quickly as she could, and extracted all that was left in him. He caressed her cheek almost tenderly, collecting what he had deposited there and then pressing his palm over her mouth until she had lapped up every single drop.

"Plenty more where that came from," he said, and let his hand drift over her breast and down her exposed flank, tracing a slow tingling path towards her sex.

Again, Alasha fought to stop herself from straining towards a man's defiling touch, and again she cursed the moist heat in her loins that overmastered her.

"Your turn, Quinn," said Vermillio. "What do you want to do with her?"

Quinn was already pulling his breeches off. "Between her tits, with her lying on the desk."

"You heard the man."

Alasha rolled onto her back again, and arranged herself in the way that they seemed to find so pleasing. Quinn climbed onto the desk and straddled her, with his cock laid stiffly against her breastbone.

"Push your tits together," he said.

She raised her hands and pressed her cleavage firmly around him. He thrust himself into the orifice so formed, rubbing his cock between her breasts. "It's not slippery enough. It wasn't like this in the book. What should I do?"

Vermillio just chuckled. Quinn looked down at Alasha. "Please?"

"It's too dry," she said quietly. "Men use spittle, sometimes."

"I'd have thought that scented oils would be more your style, teacher," said Vermillio.

The thought had never occurred to her; her tutors would never have considered such knowledge appropriate for a Lady, and while her books had held plenty of practical information, there had been little more than veiled references to the sensual details. She twisted her head to look at him. "Do you have any?"

"No." He laughed again. "Spittle it is, Quinn. I hope you're not too parched. I'll contribute some of mine, if you like."

"I have enough," said Quinn shortly, and spat directly between Alasha's breasts.

"Use your hand, man," said Vermillio. "Are you some kind of barbarian? Allow me to apologize for this brute, teacher. Perhaps he needs your etiquette lessons more than we thought."

"Sorry," said Quinn, and spat for a second time, into his hand.

"That's better."

His need was far more urgent that Vermillio's had been, and it wasn't long before she felt the hot splash of his seed against her throat, and his fingers trailing through the glistening liquid and smearing it between her breasts.

Alasha did her best to clean herself up, uncomfortably aware that

Vermillio was still watching her. "Same time tomorrow," he said. "I never realized I'd look forward to lessons so much. Hurry up with those breeches, Quinn. I can hear the tavern calling to me."

When they had gone, she put her garment back on and hurried back upstairs.

Liri was waiting for Alasha on the landing outside her room. "How did the lesson go?" she asked.

"Better than I expected," said Alasha. "At least they listened for an hour."

"Then you did well. They never paid any heed to me at all."

"They only listened to me because I bought their co-operation. I hope that my payment continues to be acceptable to them. Is there somewhere I can wash?"

"Yes, in the cistern room across the landing. We must keep it filled from the well in the rear courtyard; it is best to go early in the morning, before anyone else is around."

"You mean before there are any men around?"

"Yes. If we are late because they delay us, or if we fail in our duties because they have not allowed us to sleep, the fault is ours."

"And we are the ones who are punished?"

Liri nodded. "That is why it is best to go early. Keep to the shadows and hope no one notices you. I filled the cistern this morning, so you may wash if you please. You should perfume yourself too, ready for tonight."

"Tonight?"

"Lord Fiasco will certainly be curious to see you. You will probably be summoned to his chambers."

"I thought he only liked boys?"

"Oh, Vermillio and Quinn will be there too. The Master won't touch you, but he may wish to watch his companions have their way with you."

Alasha hesitated, and decided this was no place for coyness. "They already have. Both of them, straight after the lesson."

The other girl shook her head, and Alasha glimpsed something between sorrow and pity in her eyes.

"That's not what I meant," said Liri.

5 teaching post

Alasha had eaten nothing since her frugal breakfast, and she felt light-headed as she entered Lord Fiasco's bedchamber. She approached his couch sedately, keeping her eyes modestly downcast. The room was warmed by an open fire and dimly lit by silver lamps, and the carpet was thick and luxurious under her bare feet. The air was heavy with incense, and rich with a sharp herbal fragrance that she couldn't place.

Her studies had taught her nothing of the etiquette of slavery, but she knew how a commoner should approach a King, and she had learned something of appearing submissive. The eunuch had ordered her to disrobe before leaving her outside the door, and now she was naked except for the constricting collar and the cold, heavy rings.

The fire provided enough warmth for the comfort of the men, who were well fed and fully clothed. To Alasha, there was still a winter chill in the air, and she was aware of goosebumps rising on her exposed flesh. She was trembling a little, too.

Vermillio and Quinn were waiting in the room, dressed in fine silks and sitting on either side of the man who could only be their Master.

Lord Fiasco was middle aged and grossly overweight. Looking at him, Alasha imagined some insane sculptor using a mountain of flesh to fashion a crude parody of a man, and for a moment she felt sorry for Vermillio and Quinn, imagining the stifling treatment they must endure in his bedchamber.

She stopped in front of Lord Fiasco and made the same formal obeisance with which the former Lady Alasha would have greeted royalty, except that she continued the curtsey past its deepest point and so ended up on her knees. She kept her eyes downcast and placed her hands on her thighs.

"Very prettily done," said Lord Fiasco. His voice was a sonorous rumble, as if his vocal chords could do no more than to set up vibrations deep inside his grotesque frame. "I presume that you hope to save yourself, by behaving with such exquisite submissiveness."

Alasha's mind raced as she tried to guess how this leviathan would expect to be addressed. "I am yours to order as you will, Master. There is no question of seeking to save myself."

"Oh yes there is. You continue to try, even now. Unless you mean to contradict me?"

Alasha began to understand what manner of man she faced, and how hopeless her position was, and her heart sank. "Oh no, Master. I do not mean to do that."

"Good. Then it is clear: you were trying to save yourself." He paused, leaving Alasha in no doubt that she had to reply.

"Yes, Master."

"As you have no doubt concluded, I am not a particularly active man." He waited. "Well, answer me, girl."

"No, Master."

"I'm not sure I understand. 'No, Master' can mean so many things: that I am not an active man, or that you disagree with me, or that you refuse to answer me. Which is it?"

A prickling sensation started at the back of Alasha's neck, and despite the chill of the room, sweat pooled under her armpits and trickled coldly down her flanks. Her trembling was becoming more violent now; try as she might, she couldn't master it.

"You do not look like an active man, Master."

"How remarkably brave of you to tell me so to my face. Fortunately, I have little need to exert myself personally. I have a number of willing hands that do whatever I wish."

Alasha saw no obvious sign, but Vermillio lifted a piece of fruit to his Master's lips, as if to confirm the man's words. Quinn remained perfectly still, his gaze fixed on Alasha's naked breasts.

Lord Fiasco chewed the morsel carefully and spat several pips into Vermillio's outstretched hand. Quinn wiped the man's glistening lips with a spotless napkin.

"I am informed that you were once a Lady," said Lord Fiasco.

"Yes, Master."

"How fascinating it must be to see so many different sides of life.

I've only ever been on top, you see, but I've often wondered how it must feel to be at the bottom. Perhaps you could enlighten me, some time."

"It would be an honor, Master."

"Good. Though you have some way to go yet, before you reach that point. What has happened to you so far? You've satisfied the appetites of a few soldiers? Suffered a few scrapes? Any tavern wench could say the same."

Alasha fought the desire to contradict him: to tell him of the barracks, and the nights under the wagons and in the slavers' tents, and of being weighed, pierced, and sold at auction. She kept her face impassive. She was certain that he planned to do something terrible to her before the night was through, but he might do even worse if she provoked him.

Lord Fiasco shifted his bulk slightly, but did not take his eyes from Alasha. "How do you think we should entertain our guest, Vermillio?"

"I am at my Lord's command in this, as in all things."

"Hmmm. Any ideas, Quinn?"

"I await your Lordship's instructions most eagerly."

"Of course you do. Stand her up, then. I want to see her properly, before I decide."

Vermillio and Quinn sprang to their feet and came to Alasha's side, where they seized her by the arms and raised her up from her knees. She wondered if they'd been able to see how much she was shaking, before they touched her. She wondered if Lord Fiasco knew.

"What is that?" asked Lord Fiasco, pointing to her loins.

"It is a lock, my Lord," said Vermillio. "To preserve her maidenhead, I believe."

"By the gods, she's a virgin. And an uncommonly pleasing one, too. Perhaps I shall deflower her myself, one of these days. Indeed I shall; I swear it. Have Emon keep the key safe against that day."

Alasha felt the men holding her freeze for an instant, before relaxing again.

"You seem to be puzzled by that, my boys. But after all, why shouldn't an old leopard like me change his spots from time to time, eh?"

"No reason at all, my Lord."

"And if the cubs know that the leopard still has an appetite, they won't eat his meal up, will they?"

"Indeed not, my Lord."

"Then we understand each other. She may be tasted and tested, but not consumed. That pleasure is reserved for me. Vermillio, you will pass the word to Emon."

"Very good, my Lord."

"As for you, slave girl, you should be flattered. It's many years since I've devoured one of your kind. I had believed that particular appetite gone from me forever."

Alasha hoped that he wasn't speaking literally, or that she'd misheard. Even if he only meant to sleep with her, she was horrified by the idea of sharing his bed, and terrified she wouldn't survive such a night without being crushed and suffocated under his bulk. Lord Fiasco disgusted her, and this time her revulsion was unadulterated with lust.

She did her best to hide her feelings. "Thank you, Master."

"I can see that you are less than pleased with the idea. You tremble at the very thought. But perhaps I can persuade you to appreciate me. Vermillio, Quinn: show her, and explain."

They kept a tight grip on her elbows and steered her through a door opposite the one where she had come in. Alasha was dimly aware of Lord Fiasco lifting his body from the creaking crouch and making his ponderous way after them, into what was clearly a torture chamber.

"This is the whipping post, to which you will be chained tonight and on future visits," said Vermillio, indicating a pillar of dark wood that ran from floorboards to beamed ceiling. "As you can see, there are a variety of iron rings set into the post, to facilitate the restraint of the girls who are engaged here."

Alasha studied the pillar without really taking it in. At its base, the timber seemed pale and untreated. Around the level of her knees, it gradually darkened to a well-aged smoothness that faded again towards the ceiling. Alasha tried not to think about how such an effect might have been achieved, or about how many naked girls had been engaged in the polishing of it. Her mouth was dry and her tongue felt as if it was made of leather. Her nostrils were full of the scent of her own terror; she had no doubt that Vermillio and Quinn could smell it, too."

"Show her the whips," said Lord Fiasco.

Vermillio opened a cabinet, displaying the row of whips and riding crops that hung inside. "These are the lighter whips, such as we will be using tonight," he said. "Judging by the responses of previous girls, they cause significant pain, but they do little lasting damage. They are useful for entertaining slaves who are sufficiently submissive and obedient; with careful use, the girl will recover after a while, and the marks on her flesh will fade."

He opened the next cabinet. The whips inside looked harsher and heavier. "These are for when a girl is so disobedient that his Lordship condemns her to be blemished forever. They cut deeply." He indicated the dark stains on the floor around the whipping post, with a delicately slippered foot. "The girls bleed. Normally it's a few months before they progress to this stage. The treatments are planned so that the intensity increases over time, in the hope of correcting their behavior."

Lord Fiasco broke in. "It must be comforting to know that each whipping represents a new starting point, which will never be re-visited. Rather like those newfangled Marlish ratchets, you know. Ever-increasing sensation, with no need to worry about returning. Truly a fascinating subject; I almost envy you."

Vermillio waited politely before continuing. "This is the last cabi-net. The whips in here are only used when a girl is no longer required. Note the barbed strands on this cat, and the chain links on that one. And this one is made of wires, to be heated in a brazier so that the wounds are cauterized as soon as they are made."

"I do not permit those to be used here," said Lord Fiasco. "Only downstairs, where the cells can be sluiced down properly."

Alasha felt the last remnants of her strength leaking away, drained by hunger and by the horror of what they were showing and telling her. She knew that she was about to faint.

Her vision closed in and became dark, and she sensed her legs folding beneath her. She wasn't aware of hitting the floor.

Alasha struggled against consciousness, knowing that oblivion was preferable to what awaited her. Several nagging sensations called her back, though: a harsh surface against her cheek, and a weight on her wrists, and an unaccustomed tension around her neck.

They had chained her to the whipping post. Her collar was fastened to one of the rings, forcing her face hard against the beam. Her hands were tethered above her head, her arms and shoulders protesting at the load they carried. She scrabbled for support and managed to find the floorboards with the balls of her feet.

Alasha twisted her head, trying to see the men. Vermillio stood to her left, gripping the handle of a long leather whip. There was no sign of the others, but from directly behind her came the creaking of furniture protesting at an unnatural weight.

"I'm so glad that you're awake," rumbled the deep voice of Lord Fiasco. "Sleeping in my presence is not permitted. We will start with a few light strokes to make sure you understand that. Introduce her to the whip, Vermillio."

Vermillio nodded. He was looking pale and slightly sick, his white silk shirt less perfectly crisp than before. He had put on a pair of black leather gloves. Even as she noticed these details, Alasha was wondering why she cared about them, instead of worrying about her own plight.

Which was graver than she had imagined it could be: her new owner had turned out to be a sadistic madman who seemed to enjoy whipping his slaves half to death – or maybe all the way. She thought of the hooded Arbian trader who had been bidding for her, and longed for the warm desert sands.

Vermillio flicked the whip and sent its end over her shoulder with almost supernatural skill, so that the supple leather slipped gently over her bare skin. She had never felt so naked, or so vulnerable.

Or so aroused, she suddenly realized. If only this were a game. If only they would stop now and move on to other pleasures. Would it help to beg them not to continue, to offer herself to them? *No. This isn't a game. They aren't playing with pain in order to kindle pleasure; they truly mean to hurt me.*

The whip shifted again, and she looked down at her shoulder with unwilling fascination. The thing seemed alive, almost like a serpent: diamond indentations between delicately braided strands; oiled leather against pale skin, gleaming in the lamplight. Alasha's scalp tingled and her heart hammered against the whipping post. She wondered how bad it would be when the serpent struck.

Vermillio moved closer, until she could smell his perfume. He placed the handle of the whip just behind her shoulder so that its length dangled in front of her body with its tip barely brushing her foot. He held it there for a while and then pulled it away very slowly, snaking the lash back over her shoulder, along the path down which it had come.

"How is she?" asked Lord Fiasco. "Tell me what effect this is having."

Vermillio insinuated his gloved fingers between Alasha's body and the whipping post. Her naked flesh burned at his touch, and it was all she could do to keep herself from twisting towards him. He tested her left nipple, and then he slid his hand downwards, between her legs, before examining the fingertips of his glove.

"She appears to find it quite stimulating so far, my Lord."

"Excellent. Then we will start gently and chart her responses as we increase the intensity. How long before she shrivels up, Quinn?"

Quinn's voice was shaking as he answered. "Ten strokes, perhaps, my Lord?"

"Vermillio?"

"Less than that, my Lord. Six strokes, I'll hazard."

"Slave girl? Ala, isn't it? How many do you think, before you stop enjoying it?"

The question made no sense to her, but Alasha knew that no answer would cost her even more dearly than a wrong one, so she groped for something he might wish to hear. "One, Master."

"So few. What a shame it will be, if that proves to be the case. Still, at least you've admitted you're enjoying it so far, haven't you?"

"Yes, Master."

"Good. Do your best to hold yourself still. Quinn, observe her, and note when she stops enjoying it. Vermillio, you may begin. Six strokes to start with, at my count."

Vermillio swung the whip back, and held it ready.

"One."

There was a loud crack and a line of icy fire blossomed across Alasha's buttocks. She heard herself gasp as the air was driven from her lungs, and there was a rattling noise coming from somewhere: the chains at her wrists, she realized. She knew that sobbing and struggling might fan Lord Fiasco's flames higher, and fought to master herself, to stand still ready for the next blow.

"Two."

This time, she heard the whip cut through the air and tried to prepare herself for the blow. It didn't help: Alasha jumped against the post as Vermillio laid a new stroke across the first one. The chain that was fixed to her collar brought her up short, and she slid back down. There was a drawn out wail and a hollow sound as her bare feet hit the floorboards.

With two strokes, Vermillio had set her whole behind on fire. There were four more to go, and then who knew what? Alasha was certain that she could not endure this.

"Her nipples aren't hard any more," said Quinn.

"There. You lasted twice as long as you expected. Aren't you proud of yourself? Three."

The whip licked out again and set a new line of flame at the top of her thighs, just below the other burning welts. She tried to twist away again and yelped even more loudly.

"Four."

A new stroke bloomed, once more laid across the previous one, as if Vermillio was writing a message of fire on her skin. How could she stop this? There had to be some way. It was inconceivable that they should have the power to do this, and that she should be so utterly helpless to prevent them. Her mind raced through a maze of blind alleys, trying to escape the pain, seeking a key that didn't exist.

She could hear herself screaming at them, begging them to stop, to give her a few moments respite so that she could think what to do.

"Five."

The part of her that understood the futility of pleading was very small now. All it could do was to wrap her fingers around the chains that tethered her, to save her wrists from more hurt as she twisted against the bonds. It waited until she had done that, and then it fled.

"Six."

Peace descended. The whip had gone away, at least for a while.

Gradually, Alasha's mind returned from the places to where it had escaped, and she was back in the room, sobbing and chained to the post again. Her face was soaked with tears; her rump and the backs of her thighs were in agony, but it could be endured. Anything could be endured, apart from the return of the whip. She blinked hard, and did her best to dry her eyes by rubbing them against her chained arms.

"That must have been a most interesting experience for you," said Lord Fiasco. "Fine work, Vermillio. Such bold interlocking weals always make a pleasing start to these decorations. The riding crop for the finer details, wouldn't you say?"

"Indeed, my Lord. That will bring the pattern out very nicely."

"Would you care to take over, Quinn?"

"It would be my pleasure, if that is my Lord's wish."

"Good. Then let us sit together and study the merits of Vermillio's work for a while, before we decide how to proceed with the design. I'm sure that the girl will find our discussions most enlightening."

"Of course, my Lord."

That was when Alasha truly understood that the six strokes that Vermillio had placed on her so carefully were the basis of something far more intricate, and that her ordeal had only just begun.

She hated Lord Fiasco, and she dreaded what was to come. Even so, part of her was fascinated by what had happened: how her mind and body had reacted, and how it had felt to be so utterly controlled that she must simply stand and accept the impossibility of whatever punishment they chose for her.

All three of them stood behind her now, remarking on the pattern they had made on her body – and on how best to complete it. She trembled at that completion, yet paradoxically she needed it, too, if only so that this night might be over.

Hanging from her chains, reduced to an object for display and discussion by her betters, Alasha was acutely aware of the coolness of polished wood against her naked belly and breasts – and of how firmly her nipples and her loins pressed against the unyielding timber. At least that was some small distraction from her tormentors' calm debate of the artistic merits of what they had done, and how pleasingly their slave girl had responded to the whip.

When Alasha awoke in her room the next morning, her feelings about what had happened were even more confused. Her rump and the backs of her thighs were hot to the touch, still burning. She had slept lying on her stomach, unable to bear even the weight of a blanket below the waist.

She was certain that she never wanted to endure such a night again, but still … the helpless vulnerability she'd felt disturbed and com-pelled her in equal measure. She quailed at the thought that it would happen again, but some traitorous part of her was already eager for further punishment, curious to discover if it had truly been as bad as she remembered. That part, she knew, would welcome the next beating when it came.

Until the whip started falling again. She was certain that she'd be pleading for mercy then, just as she had the night before.

She slipped down to the courtyard well in the dawn twilight and filled two buckets to bring back to the cistern room. There, she bathed in the cool water, and used the crude mirror to examine what they had done.

There was a striking pattern of welts on her backside and thighs: Vermillio's six strokes had formed three interlocking X's: one on her rump, one at the tops of her legs, and one just above her knees. They had already turned into long bruises, outlined in purple.

The livid stripes that Quinn had left with the riding crop were more precisely grouped, carefully placed to embellish what Vermillio had done. Looking at the angry weals that crisscrossed her skin, Alasha shuddered at how close the whips had come to slicing into her flesh and drawing blood.

She pulled her shift on over her head, wincing as the material settled over her bruises, and inspected herself again. The marks showed plainly through the thin fabric. When she turned around, she saw that her nipples and pubis were clearly visible too.

Alasha sighed and left the cistern room. She hadn't eaten for twenty-four hours; her stomach was growling and she felt light-headed. She hurried downstairs, following the aroma of baking bread towards the kitchens.

Vermillio and Quinn seemed subdued during their lesson, and they let it continue for much longer than the promised hour; they didn't even set the hourglass.

"I'm sorry about last night," said Vermillio, at the end of the morning. "I won't deny that I'd enjoy a bit of rough stuff with you, but in truth, I have no stomach for such torments as Fiasco commands."

"He's never pushed us that far before, not with a new girl," said Quinn. "I don't think he likes you."

"Of course he likes her. Why else has he reserved her maidenhead for himself?"

"Oh, yes," said Quinn. "I'd forgotten about that."

"Anyway, Ala, it's plain that you need some time to rest. We won't call on your favors until you're feeling better, all right? He won't summon you again for a long while; he wants to keep you marked permanently, but it will be weeks before last night's weals fade. So there'll be plenty of time for us to renew our acquaintance."

Alasha looked at them. A rest would have been most welcome, but the burning welts of the beating had ignited a different sort of fire in her: a slow and smoldering one that she needed to quench regardless of the pain, or the difficulty she'd face if they wanted her on her back.

She simply smiled at them, and raised her hands to her shoulders. There, she pushed the straps of her shift aside, so that the garment fell, first to the crook of her elbows and then, when she straightened her arms, into an insubstantial heap around her ankles.

"Quinn, Vermillio," she said. "A promise is a promise, and I always keep mine. Now, how would you like me?"

6 hazard inn

Alasha couldn't help looking at herself in the hallway mirror.

She was properly dressed – in an elegant evening gown and pretty shoes – for the first time since the night her mother died. Lord Fiasco had ordered her to accompany him on an evening of drunkenness, gambling, and other debauchery. She had no doubt that the gown would come off later, but for now, she was enjoying wearing it.

She didn't have to wait long before Lord Fiasco came downstairs. He descended slowly, gripping the banister and breathing heavily, and she wondered for how much longer his heart would be able to keep pumping blood around his quivering bulk.

Alasha had returned to his inner torture chamber twice since that first night, many weeks ago now. Despite the intervals, the whip marks remained well defined: Vermillio was occasionally ordered to renew them with the riding crop that Lord Fiasco kept by his bed.

Those lesser beatings were more than she could really bear, but they were nothing compared to the nights in the torture chamber. Each time she was summoned to Lord Fiasco's rooms, Alasha feared another repetition of that, and she couldn't look at the inner door without trembling.

Lord Fiasco left her in no doubt that she would be passing through that door regularly, and that she would renew her acquaintance with the whipping post whenever Vermillio's restorative handiwork became unsatisfactory.

Today, her owner was full of concern, playing the part of the elderly gentleman accompanying his youthful ward on an evening's entertainment. He even held the door open for her and handed her into his carriage.

"Sit down, my dear," he said, before turning to Emon the eunuch, who was waiting anxiously to see his master off. "I'll be staying at the inn tonight. This seems like an ideal opportunity to unlock the girl and sample what she has to offer."

"I see. Then I pray you allow me to fetch the key, my Lord." Emon bustled away, to return a few minutes later with an ivory scroll tube. "The key is sealed in here, together with her letters of indenture. Should I remove it for you, my Lord?"

"No," said Lord Fiasco. "I am in haste; simply give me the tube. Perhaps I will even set her title deeds at stake on the gaming table, eh?"

"Very good, my Lord."

The carriage lurched on its springs as Lord Fiasco heaved himself up and sank into the seat opposite Alasha. He shook the ivory tube gently, and Alasha heard the rattling of the key inside.

"How delightful you look in that gown, my dear. I'm so looking forward to this evening. Aren't you?"

From the length of the journey, she decided that the inn must be near the border of Lord Fiasco's lands. It was dark by the time they clattered into the cobbled courtyard and saw the welcoming yellow lamplight at the windows.

"Here we are," said Lord Fiasco. "On occasions such as this, you are to refer to me as 'my Lord'".

"Yes, my Lord."

"Good." He opened the carriage door, stepped out, and then handed Alasha down into the courtyard. There was a soft rain falling, and the cobblestones were slippery. Lord Fiasco took her arm and leaned on her as they walked to the main door of the inn. Behind them, the coachman and footman struggled with Fiasco's luggage, which seemed excessive to Alasha: they were only due to stay here for a single night. She wondered what devilry the big chest might contain. *Perhaps I will find out later*, she thought.

They paused under the porch for a moment, waiting while the carriage trundled away towards the inn's coach house.

"Make me proud of you, girl," Lord Fiasco said, before he pushed the door open.

They entered the inn, and Alasha saw into the tap room, which seemed like a marvelous place to her, filled as it was with the warm glow of fire and companionship. Alas, that was not to be their destination: Lord Fiasco guided her along the passage, up a dark stairway that creaked alarmingly as he climbed, and finally ushered her into a private chamber.

The room was dominated by a circular gaming table. Sitting around it were a number of men, whom Alasha judged to be nobles and rich merchants by their dress, and by the beauty of the female companions that waited on several of them. Each girl stood behind her Master, ready to fetch whatever he might require from the sideboard, which was spread with wine bottles and silver trays of tidbits.

One of the men spied them entering and called out a greeting to Lord Fiasco as he made his way across the room. "So, what's this? Is that a new filly you have there, Fiasco?"

"A recent acquisition. I'm still breaking her in, but I thought it worth bringing her."

"I'll say it's worth it. Is she for sale?"

"Not tonight, my friend. I have plans of my own for her, which I have no intention of giving up, not even for you."

Most of the men laughed, as if there was some running joke between Lord Fiasco and his questioner, but Alasha had no idea what that could be.

She looked around the circle of faces at the table, seeing little in any of them except for scornful lust. Only one of the men returned her gaze in a more appraising way. He looked familiar, and after a few moments she saw that he was the bearded, long-curled Marlish merchant-adventurer who had lingered to speak with her the night before she was sold. She met his eyes briefly, and then dropped her own gaze, feeling her cheeks tingling and her heart beating faster. *What must he think of me, coming here in a fine gown and with a man like Lord Fiasco, when the last time he saw me I was half-naked and locked in a cage?*

Alasha knew the answer to that, and she hated it. She kept her gaze firmly averted as she poured wine for Lord Fiasco, and then she stood behind her Master, where she could see when his glass needed to be re-filled and keep his plate stocked with delicacies from the sideboard.

She studied Lord Fiasco's cards, trying to fathom the rules of the game. It only took a few hands before she had the hang of it: they were playing a collecting game, involving much bluffing and guessing and watching of the opponents' eyes.

She risked a look at the Marlish merchant. He glanced up from his cards at the same moment, and met her gaze. He'd been betting heavily against Lord Fiasco, and the pile of gold before him had dwindled sadly. Alasha glanced down at her Master's cards, and offered what she hoped was a faint but encouraging smile: Lord Fiasco's hand was a weak one.

There wasn't even a flicker of understanding in the merchant's eyes, but he pushed half his remaining stock of gold onto the table.

"As well to get it over with," he said with a sad smile.

Lord Fiasco laid his cards down. "I'll not back this hand any further."

"How gratifying. Perhaps my luck is changing at last," said the merchant.

Alasha made sure that it did. When Lord Fiasco had a strong hand, she adopted a sad expression. When his position was neither weak nor strong, she looked grave. And when he held dross, she let a hint of a smile play about her mouth. The merchant understood her cues immediately, though he took several small losses, and occasionally a big one, as if to allay any suspicions that he had a secret ally.

Even as she helped him, Alasha wondered why she was doing it. Lord Fiasco would surely take a terrible revenge on her, if he ever discovered her treachery. The only reason she could find was that her accomplice had stopped and spoken to her once, and treated her kindly, when she was waiting in a cage to be sold.

She decided that he had nice eyes, too. It had been too dark to tell when they met outside the slave market, but tonight she saw that they were between blue and green, and for a moment she was reminded of the color of the sea around his Marlish island.

"Dammit, sir, you have ruined me!" said Lord Fiasco, as the last of his gold disappeared into the merchant's growing hoard. "I intended to make an evening's entertainment of this, and now I have nothing left. Who will take my paper?"

"We play for gold here, Fiasco," said one of the others, to growls of agreement. "Paper leads to duels. You know that."

"Perhaps you might reconsider selling the filly," said the Marlish merchant, with a smile and a nod at Alasha.

"As I believe I mentioned, I have plans for her. The girl isn't for sale."

"Truly? I am almost embarrassed to be spoiling your evening by taking all this gold from you. Would it not be sporting to set her at hazard on the table, if you don't wish to sell her outright? The girl against all that I have won from you tonight?"

Alasha looked at the pile of coins, and her heart started to beat faster. The merchant's winnings were worth many times more than she was; she knew that from the bidding at the marketplace.

"Are you mad, sir? You have won over a thousand gold pieces from me. You'd stake that against a girl who only cost me that much in silver? Buy your own at the next slave market, man."

"I've taken a fancy to this girl. It's a cold night and I have no doubt that she would cheer my bed. You won't sell her, so perhaps I can win her. After all, the game's the thing, not the girls or the gold. Don't you agree?"

Lord Fiasco flushed and took the ivory scroll case from an inner pocket and laid it on the gaming table. "These are her deeds of indenture."

The merchant pushed most of his gold towards the scroll case. "My winnings from you."

"Then it seems I will be able to afford to stay at the table. More wine and food, girl, while I get my gold back from this fool."

Alasha turned towards the sideboard, cursing inwardly. Her ally would have to manage this round on his own, and going by his previous performance, she was doomed to remain with Lord Fiasco.

The fact that she hadn't the slightest idea of what the merchant planned to do with her seemed irrelevant: whatever his intentions, they could hardly be worse than Lord Fiasco's.

She loaded a plate with choice morsels of meat, pastries, and pickles, and selected one of the better bottles of wine. When she returned to the table, the game was over.

The ivory scroll case had joined the pile of coins in front of the merchant.

"You may finish serving your ex-master, if you will, girl. Then I must ask you to collect my winnings and accompany me to my quarters, for I am overcome with weariness and must be put straight to bed."

All the men laughed, except for Lord Fiasco. His face was flushed and his eyes were full of rage. "I may have lost you for the moment, you wretched girl, but I still own the gown and the shoes." He gestured at the table beside him. "If you please?"

All eyes were on Alasha as she reluctantly removed the dress and slippers and set them next to Lord Fiasco.

"Keep the shift. Your new owner's eyes are popping far enough out of his head as it is. Your name, Sir Merchant?"

"I am Aric Albigenses."

"And I am Lord Fiasco de Bacle, and you have made an enemy of me tonight."

"It was merely a game of chance, my Lord Fiasco."

"Was that all it was?" Lord Fiasco's jowls quivered as he shook his head. "I would almost have said there was more to it than that."

Another of the men broke in. "Come, Fiasco. There's no need for such talk. The man won fairly enough. Let us continue; I will advance you some gold on your word alone, so there will be no need for any paper between us."

Lord Fiasco's face was a rigid mask, apart from one eyebrow that fluttered uncontrollably. "Why didn't you offer me that before I lost the girl?"

Alasha didn't linger to hear the answer. She gathered the gold hastily and deposited it in her new owner's moneybags. Once filled, she could barely lift one of them, let alone all three.

"Let me," he said, and scooped the remaining pair up from the table with casual ease. "Come, girl. It's past my bed time."

There was only one bed.

"Where would you like me to sleep?" asked Alasha.

"That isn't a question we need to consider at the moment, since we can't stay here."

"What do you mean?"

"This room belongs to Aric the Marlish merchant, enemy to Fiasco, who happens to be the most powerful and ruthless of the local lords. Further along the corridor is room four, which was taken earlier by Alahim the Arbian slave trader. Alahim is traveling through this area on his way to deliver a girl to her new owner. He has no known enemies, so he's likely to be left alone. I don't know about you, but I'd prefer to sleep in his room."

"But what of this Alahim? Will he allow us to stay there?"

"I think so. He's a good friend of mine, and anyway he's away from the inn at the moment. I understand that his girl left, too. Come; let them think we departed by the window. Alahim and his companion made some suitable footprints in the mud outside, earlier on."

Aric began to knot the blankets and bed sheets together. After a moment, Alasha moved to help him. She tied the end of their makeshift rope to the bedstead, while he cast the other end out of the window.

Aric peered out into the darkness. "Good enough. At least it reaches the ground."

"The rain will ruin the bedclothes."

"Yes, remind me to reimburse them later, would you? Anything I leave in the room will probably be stolen when the place is searched."

"You're sure they'll come here?"

"I saw the man's eyes, and I heard what he said about having plans for you tonight. We're still inside his lands; he won't let us escape so easily. Come, I will check that no one is watching, and then we shall slip into my friend's suite. We should be safe there for one night, I think."

There were candles and a fire burning in Alahim's drawing room, and the window and shutters were closed against the rain. The room was small, hot, and stuffy.

"Shall we open the window, Lady Alasha?" asked Aric.

The form of address, and the fact that he remembered her name, threw her into confusion. "I beg your pardon?"

"The window. It's windy and wet outside, but it might be more pleasant if we opened it."

"Of course." She moved to the window and opened the casement and then the shutters.

"I'd have done that," said Aric, mildly.

"It's my place to do it."

"Nonsense. Now, I must change, and so must you, I'm afraid."

"I don't understand."

"I must become Alahim, and you must become his slave."

He went to a chest that stood in a corner of the room, and took a set of Arbish robes from it. Then he handed Alasha the sandals and gauzy garment of an Arbian slave girl, and one of the belled ankle bracelets that they wore.

"My apologies, but I must ask you not to wear the shift under these. Our disguises must be perfect."

Alasha made to pull her shift over her head.

"Um, would you like to change in the bedroom?" asked Aric. "Alahim ordered a bath to be prepared in there, too, if you feel the need."

"I'm sorry. It's been a long time since anyone cared about my modesty. I suppose I have become accustomed to being watched."

"It's never necessary to apologize for beauty," he said. "I just thought you might prefer to change your clothes in privacy."

"Thank you." Alasha went through into the bedroom. There were two beds set against opposite walls, and a copper tub full of steaming water stood behind a screen. She opened the door again, and poked her head through into the drawing room. "Won't your friend mind me using his bath, and his girl's clothes?"

"Not at all," said Aric. "He arranged everything especially for us."

"He must be a good friend."

"The best."

Alasha left the door ajar, in case her new Master wanted to speak to her. She slipped off her shift and stepped into the hot bath: another unaccustomed luxury. The water was perfumed with sandalwood. Alasha lay back and drifted away for a while.

"Are you hungry?" he called.

"Yes."

"As am I; the sweetmeats and pastries were not to my taste. I shall send for a proper supper as soon as I have bathed myself."

Alasha stood up so quickly that water cascaded down her body and slopped onto the floor. "Oh! I should have let you go first. Now the water is dirty, and less hot than it was … I'm sorry, Master."

"Truly, Alasha, it will be no hardship to bathe after you. Take your time."

She was already out of the bath and drying herself on a corner of the towel, leaving the rest for him. "Almost finished."

She fastened the Arbish chain about one ankle, and dressed herself in the translucent silks. The garment was little more than a set of veils lightly stitched together and fashioned to move against each other: never to conceal completely, and now and then to fall open for a tantalizing moment as its wearer moved. The carpet was deep and warm, so she carried the sandals back out into the drawing room rather than putting them on. Her anklet bells tinkled as she walked.

"There," she said. "I am your Arbian slave girl."

In truth, she wished that he would consider her so. Being owned and desired by a man like this was the best that she could hope for, now that she was a chattel; she knew in her heart that part of her would remain enslaved forever. Even if she won her freedom some day, and regained the Matriarchy, she would still need a strong man at her side, to make his mark on her and to bend her to his will.

A man like this, perhaps.

Alasha watched carefully to see if Aric would acknowledge what she had said, but he simply smiled as he looked her up and down, as if she had spoken in jest.

"Very becoming," he said, and then he disappeared into the bedroom, and she heard the soft sound of splashing water.

When he came out, he too had transformed himself into an Arbian. Even his beard seemed to be combed differently, so that it looked even more exotic than before.

"Now that I see you dressed like that," she said, "I believe I have seen this Alahim before."

"It's true. I was there on the day Lord Fiasco's eunuch bought you.

Unfortunately, he had more silver than me."

"Then Alahim doesn't exist?"

"Of course he does. He's as real as I am."

"I see," said Alasha with a smile.

Aric rang for a servant, and ordered a jug of wine and a platter of bread, meat, cheese and fruit. Alasha could hardly believe that she was to share such things: she hadn't tasted wine at all in her new life, and her rations had been meager and poor. Sure enough, when the tray arrived, Aric began setting two places at the small table.

"Let me do that, Master."

"Almost done. And my name is Aric."

"Still, I should do it. I wish you'd let me."

"Very well, if it will make you happy."

"Thank you, Aric." It was puzzling, the way her tongue hesitated over his name, as if it wanted to start along the older, more subservient path.

As soon as Alasha had finished setting the table, she drew out a chair for him.

"Shouldn't it be me holding the chair for you?" he asked as he sat down.

"Indeed no. After what you paid for me, you're entitled to waited on." Alasha sat opposite him and saw that it was too late: he'd already filled her wineglass.

"I didn't pay anything, if you recall. I won the trick, though I believe from the way you looked at me as you left the table that you didn't expect me to, without your help."

"Still, you wagered a huge sum. Far more than I'm worth."

"No amount of gold is worth more than a person," said Aric.

"I fear you are muddling my brain with your Marlish philosophy." Alasha was feeling remarkably bold, considering that this man had the power of life and death over her. It must be his manner, she decided. He hadn't frowned at her once, and he looked at her face instead of her body, most of the time. He almost made her feel like a Lady again. "I'm afraid you won't find a very sympathetic hearing for such ideas here in Xendria."

"Not even among the people who'd benefit from them?"

"Perhaps from them, unless they know how the workers in your smoky Marlish factories live."

Aric gave a rueful smile. "I see you know something of my home-land; it is less enlightened than many of our people would have you believe. Still, our workers are free. They may seek other employment at any time. They may not be beaten, or sold to a different master. They are at liberty to depart over the sea, if they wish."

"Perhaps. But our Xendrian system isn't all bad, you know."

"How has it treated you, Alasha?" he asked, gently.

She thought of all she had endured, and everything she had learned about herself. "It's had its moments," was all she said.

Heavy footsteps and jangling steel sounded along the passageway outside.

"They're about to enter my other chamber," said Aric. "They will conduct a room-to-room search, once they find we are gone. Best put on your veils."

She obeyed, pulling the wispy folds of fabric that hung from her neck over her head and face. She was acutely aware of how sheer the upper part of her garment had become, once she had done that. She glanced at herself in the mirror that hung over the mantel, and per-ceived the outline of her breasts through the gauzy fabric. The nipple rings, too, would surely be apparent to anyone who looked closely. *At least such piercings are common among slave girls; they will not recognize me from those.*

"How do I look?" asked Aric.

"Every inch the Arbian. How about me?"

He chuckled. "I prefer to be able to look into a woman's eyes, but what I see of you is perfectly delectable."

Alasha felt herself blushing under her veil, and hoped it wouldn't spread to anywhere he could see.

"You'd best go and kneel at the foot of my bed," he said. "As if you were waiting for me."

"I understand."

There was an impatient banging at the door, and Alasha hurried through to the inner room and took up her position.

"Ho! You inside! Open up; we're looking for a runaway slave."

Aric said something loudly and fluently in Arbian, before dropping back into Xendrian. His accent had changed completely, his soft Marlish pronunciation giving way to a more strident Arbish delivery.

Alasha heard the outer door opening.

"What do you want?"

"Open up. We are searching for a runaway."

"No runaways here."

"We will be the judge of that."

There was the sound of heavy footsteps entering the drawing room, and of Aric's protestations.

"Silence, you Arbish dog, or we'll fillet you. You're in Xendria now, and this is Lord Fiasco's domain. You'll abide by his laws or pay the consequences."

"Then do what you must quickly, and leave me in peace. I am about to retire for the night," said Aric in his Arbish-accented Xendrian.

Two soldiers came into the bedroom. One of them glanced at Alasha. "That's not her, is it?"

"No. This one's on the innkeeper's register; the Arbian's body slave. Lucky dog. Just make sure there's no one else hiding here."

They looked under the beds, in the closets, on top of the closets, and one of them even plunged his hand into the cooling bath water.

"All clear here."

"Good. Check this one off and let's move on."

With that, the soldiers left with much stamping of feet and clashing of armor, to disturb the occupants of the next room.

The rain had stopped. Outside the window, there were stars in the sky.

Alasha lay in her bed, close to the open shutters, pretending not to watch Aric prepare for sleep.

He combed the Arbish curls out of his beard and then turned his back as he pulled the robes off over his head. His body was tight, his muscles well defined. She glanced at the hard-looking dimples in his buttocks for a long moment before tearing her gaze away.

She was just in time: he turned towards her, slipped under his covers, and blew out the final candle. It would have been hateful to be caught studying him, when he had so gallantly permitted her to prepare for bed alone.

Such thoughts didn't help with her immediate problem, though.

"Aric?"

"Yes?"

"If Alahim and his slave girl were here, how would things be between them?"

"He would have commanded her into his bed, I expect."

"Would he have had to command her, I wonder?"

"Well, she was his slave girl, so she'd have had no choice anyway."

"Do I have a choice?"

"Of course."

Alasha slipped out from under the covers as quietly as she could, and padded silently through the darkness between their beds. "May I join you, then?"

There was no answer, except for the rustle of linen and the gleam of white sheets in the moonlight as he pulled back the covers and made room for her.

She lowered herself onto the pillows and into the crook of his arm, enjoying the fresh sandalwood scent of his skin. When she turned her face towards him, his breath was sweet too. Among the Xendrian men she had known, few bothered about such things. The Marlish were probably different, she decided.

She shivered as he caressed her hair very gently, and then his mouth was pressed hard against hers and she was returning his kiss with all the passion in her soul. Fireworks shot across her skin as his hand moved over her shoulder and down to her breast, and her whole body stiffened as he found the ring that pierced her there. He tugged it gently, launching a stream of tiny shooting stars that exploded inside her head, coaxed to life by Aric's twisting fingers.

"Do you like these?" he whispered.

She fought her way back through the pleasure haze, and tried to think. She'd hated them at first, but now they had come to symbolize what she was. Most men seemed to appreciate them, and there was a good chance that Aric did as well, even if he wouldn't admit it. From the feel of him against her thigh, she judged that he appreciated it deeply.

"Yes. Do you?"

"Very much."

"Then I'm glad I have them."

His hand lingered there for a while, and then he placed his mouth over her other nipple, where his lips and tongue played sweet encircling games that made her gasp with pleasure. At the same time, his hand moved down over her taut belly and brushed the curls at the top of her sex.

She needed to tell him something about that, but she couldn't think clearly, or control the sounds she was making. Nothing really mattered anyway: she was in his arms and she knew that everything was going to be all right.

Aric's fingers encountered the padlock that held the lips of her sex together. His mouth froze against her breast for a moment, and then he lifted his head away. "What's this?"

Again, she struggled to regain her senses. "I have been pierced and ringed there, too. There's a padlock, to preserve my maidenhead. I'm sorry, Aric. I should have spoken of it before. Now I've ruined everything."

"Nonsense. We can still enjoy each other. Don't worry, we'll get the rings removed, as soon as we're somewhere safe."

"There's no need for that. The key's in the scroll case; Lord Fiasco was going to unlock me tonight."

Aric struck one of his curious Marlish fire sticks and then went about the room lighting the candles. Now, Alasha gazed with open pleasure at the way that the shadows flickered on his body as he moved; her embarrassment at watching him had vanished.

He returned with the scroll case and sat next to her as he eased it open. He shook it over his hand; the rolled parchment stayed inside, but a fine chain holding two keys tinkled out into his open palm.

"One is for my collar, I think."

"Let's take that off too, then." He reached for the padlock that hung at her throat.

Somewhat to her surprise, Alasha realized that she wanted to keep the collar. She liked the way that having it locked about her neck made her feel, and she liked the idea that Aric – and no one else – had the key. In some way, it had come to define who and what she was.

"Please, Aric. I should keep it, if I'm to pass as an Arbian slave girl tomorrow."

"Very well. The other, then. Perhaps if you stood up?"

Alasha swung her legs out from under the covers, noting with satisfaction how Aric's eyes followed the motion of her ankles and calves, and stood before him. He knelt before her and peered at the padlock.

"This feels wrong," she said.

"What do you mean?"

"It should be me on my knees, in front of you."

"Nonsense." He fiddled with the lock, and little shivers ran up her belly and jumped right through her body before continuing their journey up her spine.

"No, really. It just feels wrong. After all, legally you're my owner and my Master."

He had the lock open, and eased it out from between the rings. *Thank goodness I bathed and took care to cleanse myself down there,* she thought.

"It feels right to me," he said, and planted a long, spine-tingling kiss on the shivery spot at the pit of her thigh, between the taut curve of her belly and the warm softness of her loins.

Alasha's consciousness extended through her entire body, pulsing in her fingers and her toes and most especially in her most feminine and pleasurable places. She closed her eyes. Nothing existed except for the sensation of being touched and the need for more. The strength went out of her knees, and she groped blindly behind her and clutched the bedpost.

Aric's beard didn't tickle at all.

He was working his way over to the other side of her pubis. She heard herself moaning, and risked removing one hand from the bedpost so that she could twine her fingers through his hair.

He ran his tongue up and down the lips of her sex, barely parting them. Alasha trembled, vaguely wondering how so much wetness could have been caused by one man's mouth.

His tongue was warm and soft, exploring the very top of her pussy and gently teasing the pearl that she had read of in books but had never truly understood.

And then she sensed that something delightfully unexpected was happening. Aric was guiding her to a hidden place where she had never been before, an undiscovered region that no one else had ever found. Alasha stood at the brink of a new world, a world whose existence she could scarcely have imagined, before tonight.

She opened her eyes and glanced down her lover. She was almost sorry for that, at first, because her movement distracted him from what he was doing, so that he paused in the midst of a most wonderfully intimate kiss and looked up at her.

Their eyes met, and she sensed the crackle and spark of the world's oldest language passing between them. The endless words she wanted to say to him, and everything she wanted to hear in return, all became unimportant, already reflected in the mirror of understanding she saw in his eyes.

He smiled at her tenderly, as if acknowledging that some deep and secret pact had been sealed, and pressed his mouth against her again.

An instant later, her world exploded into a long, shuddering climax.

When she returned, she was lying on the pillows next to him, cradled in his arms. She reached down and felt him. He was ready.

"My maidenhead is yours, if you desire it," she whispered. "As is anything else you require from me."

Aric straddled her, and then kissed her. He moved his hand to her loins again, and placed his open palm on her sex, making small circular motions. She abandoned herself to his strength, to the hardness of his hand pressed hard against her and wet with her juices.

For a moment, Alasha imagined that she was a flower, unfolding dew-damp petals at the start of a new day, and then she was simply a girl, opening herself at the touch of the man that she already loved.

"Fuck me," she said.

He pressed his cock against her pussy very gently, barely entering her. She wrapped her arms and legs around him, and pulled him into her in the same instant that he thrust, so that the act of pushing beyond her hymen was no more than a moment of discomfort, swiftly replaced by the smooth delight of feeling him moving inside her.

Alasha raised her hands above her head and gripped the iron bars of the bedstead, pretending that he had tethered her wrists with steel bracelets and restraining chains. She closed her eyes, letting her climax build, and sensed Aric spending himself inside her in the same instant that the wave broke over her.

Afterwards, they were both slick with sweat, and with each other. Aric's encircling arms told her that she was both cherished and adored, and his gentle caress seemed to promise that she would never be treated harshly again.

If only he knew, she thought.

"You are more beautiful than any woman I have ever known," he said, "and I loved you since the moment I saw you in that wagon."

"I love you, too."

"Will you bathe with me?"

He took her hand and led her to the cooling bathtub, where they knelt together in the water and sponged one another down.

"What's this design on your skin?" he asked, as he trickled cool water over her flanks and legs.

She didn't answer for a moment, ashamed of what had been done to her. "Lord Fiasco kept me marked with a whip. He likes to sign each of his girls with a specific pattern."

"Lord Fiasco does not deserve to live."

"He's a Xendrian Lord, Aric. It would be unwise to challenge such a man in his own domain."

He pulled her towards him and kissed her on the lips, gently and sweetly. "I challenged him today, my love, and won. That turned out to be a very wise thing to do. One day I may face him again, but not here; we are too close to the heart of his power. The hardest blow we can land now will be to escape."

7 arbish caravan

It seemed to Alasha that she had hardly fallen asleep before Aric was waking her again. She was still in his bed, and he was leaning over her with a candle, shaking her gently.

"We must get ready to leave," he said.

"What time is it? What's happening?" she asked, sleepily.

"It's an hour after midnight, and I've just been outside to say my nightly prayers. I overheard two stable lads who are still awake, celebrating their good fortune. They've been paid a few coppers to summon Fiasco's people as soon as anyone calls for a coach or riding horse. Each guest is to be questioned before leaving the inn."

She got out of bed and picked up her clothes. She had long lost any shame at being naked before a man, but this was the first time she had known the secret pleasure of carelessly displaying herself to one.

"Nightly prayers? At this time?" she asked, as she slipped into the slave veils.

"I take my Arbish duties very seriously, even though I was somewhat distracted earlier. Luckily for you, the Arbians hold that women and slaves have no souls worth saving, so you are under no such obligations."

"Then the lack of a soul is a great relief to me," Alasha said with a chuckle. A more serious thought struck her. "If we leave secretly, won't you lose your coach?"

"I don't have one, just a couple of riding horses and a pack mule. I don't mean to abandon the horses if I can help it, but the mule will be too slow."

"I'm sorry. I have cost you much."

"Nonsense. I can buy every beast in the district with the winnings from last night. We'll have to bury most of the gold somewhere; it will weigh us down too much even if we retrieve the horses, and it would make us too tempting a target for thieves."

"You instructed me to remind you to leave payment for the bedding we turned into a rope."

"Indeed I did."

Aric left a few silver coins on the table and then hurriedly packed the remains of the previous night's meal into a leather satchel. He removed Alasha's indenture from the scroll case, wadded it into a fat bundle, and stuffed it together with her collar key into a velvet purse that he kept hanging from his neck, under his jerkin.

"The scroll case is too cumbersome," he said. "We must travel fast and light."

Aric gave her the smallest of the moneybags, and she cradled it in her arms. He took the other two and tested their weight doubtfully. Alasha tried to hide the fact that she could barely hold her burden.

"This is no good," he said. "That's too heavy for you, and the extra burden will slow our horses. We'll just have to hide it in the room."

"On top of the wardrobes," she said. "There's a narrow gap. The soldiers looked up there last night, but no one would bother, not unless they were searching the room."

"Good idea." He took the moneybag from her and transferred most of its gold into the two larger sacks, before stuffing them into the gap and pushing them into the corners. "There. Now we have another reason to come back this way, sometime." He tied the remaining bag to his belt and picked up his staff before sweeping his gaze around the room. "I think we have everything."

"What about your clothes chest?"

"It's nothing I can't afford to lose; I half expected to have to leave it. Now, we must sneak downstairs and out to the coach yard without anyone noticing us. Fiasco's men made the mistake of giving the stable lads part of the fee in advance, and they have obtained a flask of wine."

"Someone might hear us on the way out. Could we not do as we did before, and make a rope of knotted sheets?"

"It's a long drop, if you lose your grip."

Alasha peered out of the window. "I see what you mean. Let's take the stairs."

Aric snuffed out all of the candles except for one, which he took for himself. "Go ahead of me, if you will, and carry this wineskin. If the stable boys are still awake, it might help you to distract them."

"I understand," she said, taking the wineskin and hoping that she would be able to play her part without letting him down.

Aric held the door open as Alasha passed into the corridor. She waited just beyond the threshold as he locked the room and slid the key under the door. Then she tiptoed along the passageway, following her own flickering shadow towards the stairs.

The inn was dark apart from Aric's candle, and silent apart from the slow rumble of snores that came from some of the rooms. Alasha eased her weight onto each step, waiting for one to squeak, but the staircase bore her with better grace than it had Lord Fiasco, and made no sound. Then she was back in the entrance hall, passing the tap room that had looked so snug but was now shuttered and dark. The front door was bolted.

Aric was close behind her. "There's no help for it: they must sleep with the door unbarred tonight," he whispered as he unlatched the door and pulled it gently open. His candle hissed between his fingertips as he extinguished it.

Alasha stepped out into the courtyard, which had turned into a far more forbidding place than she remembered from her arrival. The cheery, welcoming lamplight had given way to shuttered windows and gray walls. The moon was pale, lending an eerie quality to the yard, too dim to let Alasha's eyes pierce the shadows that lay between the buildings.

Her silks were warmer than she'd expected, but they provided little protection against the chill night breeze, and she felt goosebumps rising on her skin.

Something scampered along the base of a nearby wall – a cat, she hoped, or at least nothing worse than a rat – and a horse stamped and snorted somewhere in the darkness. That must be where the stables were. Alasha took one look back at the reassuring shape of Aric, and started across the courtyard, clutching her wineskin.

Someone was awake inside the stables; there were scraping sounds coming from within, and a glowing lantern stood on the windowsill. If Alasha hadn't been watching the open window, she might have noticed the figure outside before she was too close to avoid him.

She shrank towards the deeper shadows around the window, but it was too late. The stable lad turned away from the clump of weeds he'd been watering, buttoning his breeches. Both of them froze.

Alasha recovered first. She moved into the shaft of light that fell from the window. "I couldn't sleep. I was hoping to find some company."

The boy stepped forward and grinned. "What have we here, then?" His eyes flicked towards the stable. "Merv told me there was an Arbian slut at the inn, and we were just wondering what it would be like to have one. Don't worry lass, we'll keep you–"

The boy's speech was interrupted by a sharp rapping sound. He looked puzzled and vaguely hurt for a moment, and then Aric appeared out of the shadows and caught the lad as he crumpled to the ground.

Aric handed his staff to Alasha. "Let me get this one out of the way, then you fetch his friend out here."

She watched as he manhandled the boy's inert body into the dark corner between the stable wall and the gatepost. As soon as he was done, she returned the staff and slipped inside.

The other boy was reclining on a pile of hay, whittling at a stick with a well-honed knife.

"Excuse me, but if you're Merv then your friend wants you. He's not very well," she said.

The boy sprang up. "Where is he?"

"Outside, by the gate."

Shortly afterwards, there was a second hollow thud and some scuffling noises, and then Aric joined her in the stables. He took the lantern in among the pens, searching for his tack and his horses. She heard his gentling voice, and flinched at the racket of hooves on the stone floor as he brought one of the mounts out from its narrow stall.

"Will those lads be all right?" she asked.

"They'll wake up with sore heads, and a headache of another sort from Fiasco, but no more than that. Do you know how to saddle a horse?"

Alasha thought of the days she had spent riding through her mother's estates with a blade and a bow at her side, and smiled in the darkness. "Yes," she said.

"Good. This one is for you. There's a poncho in the saddlebag, if you need it."

They unbarred the main gates and led the horses out onto the road. There, they pushed the gates closed again before they mounted: Alasha onto the bay gelding he had given her, and Aric onto his big gray. They walked the animals until they were out of earshot of the inn, and then Aric urged his horse to a trot.

Alasha followed suit, and soon caught up with him. "How did you know I could ride?" she asked.

"You are obviously a lady of quality," he said. "I have no doubt you are skilled in all the noble pursuits."

"And where did you learn so much about the accomplishments of Xendrian ladies? You must have spent much time in their company, I think, before you ever met me."

"Um, no, very little, really." Aric sounded abashed, and Alasha's heart soared with the knowledge that he cared for her good opinion.

They rode through the moonlight under softly dripping trees. The air was cool, but she was warm under the poncho. After months spent doing the bidding of others, sitting in the saddle made her feel that she was in charge of her own destiny again. Now, she had no demands to meet, no commands to obey, and no plans to make. All she had to do was to sit in the saddle and follow Aric, wherever he might lead her.

It was the happiest night of her life.

Mid-morning found them riding under a hot sun. The poncho was back in the saddlebag, and Alasha was enjoying the cool breeze that blew through her silken garment.

Both of them were fearful of pursuit, and neither had spoken of resting: they were eager to push on and cross the border out of Lord Fiasco's lands. Alasha was tired after her sleepless night, almost nodding off in the warmth. Aric must have been tired, too.

She was startled awake by a string of harsh syllables. There were men blocking the way. She reined in her horse. Beside her, Aric did the same.

A group of Arbians had stopped for the night at the side of the road, and the drowsy fugitives had ridden right up to their camp. A black-cloaked soldier held a short bow fashioned from gleaming animal horn; his arrow was nocked but pointing to the ground for the moment. Another man held a drawn scimitar.

A third Arbian, taller than the others, strode out from the verge and into the road. Alasha blinked, wondering if she was dreaming in her saddle. The man was dressed in black-trimmed white robes, exactly as Aric was. He pointed at his own garb and then at Aric, and a stream of angry gibberish came from his mouth.

Aric replied in fluent Arbian, sounding conciliatory but not intimidated. He started to ease his mount around, screening Alasha from the archer, who now bent his bow and trained his arrow on Aric.

The tall man gestured at her, and said something to his men. The man with the sword moved towards Alasha's horse; she backed away, wishing that Aric would just make a break for it.

"Ride, Alasha," said Aric.

The black-feathered shaft struck him squarely in the center of his chest. A look of surprise came over his face and he toppled sideways.

Alasha had no knowledge of dismounting, or of running towards him. All she had afterwards was the memory of her cheeks being wet with tears, and of the soldiers who seized her before she could reach her Master's side.

The last that she saw of Aric was the red stain spreading across the white robe where the arrow pierced his chest. Then the tall man pushed her lover's body with his boot, and rolled it out of sight into the ditch at the side of the road.

"I don't speak Arbian," said Alasha through her tears. "Why won't you believe me?"

The tall man settled himself more comfortably on the cushions that were strewn over the floor of his tent, and shrugged.

"I believe you," he said, in Xendrian. "You were dressed as one of our slave girls, yet you are fair, and I see by your ring that you have been enslaved according the customs of Xendria. A shame: our troupe needs another Arbian dancing girl. No matter, though. We offer other entertainment too. Have no fear, Xendrian. I will find a way for you to earn your keep."

"I must go back to my Master. He was not Arbian either, so your law does not apply to him, or his property."

"He was Arbian. No foreigner has ever shown such mastery of our tongue. Anyway, he is a day's ride behind us; the wild dogs will have found him by now. Face it, girl: he trespassed on my rightful territory, and tried to steal my livelihood, and now he is gone. You belong to me now, along with his horses." His eyes were hungry. "I will inspect my new chattel: take off your clothes."

Alasha was too numb to resist, and she knew that the soldiers waiting outside the tent would be more than happy to enforce his command. She slipped her garment over her head, and stood naked while the man gazed at her.

"Stop crying, girl. Female slaves change hands all the time." He rose to his feet and examined the whip marks on her legs. "It is written plainly on your flesh that your old Master was not gentle with you; why do you mourn him so?"

The tears wouldn't stop, but at least she wasn't sobbing uncontrollably any more. "He was kind to me. I loved him."

"I see. Then you are one of those girls who enjoys a firm hand."

He twisted his fingers into her collar, and pulled her towards him. His other hand dropped between her legs.

"Dry as the desert sand," he said. "But I do not believe I have misjudged you. You are simply upset. I have something that will help with that."

He released her, and took a flask from among several others that nestled in a small case.

"Drink this," he said, unstopping the flask.

"What is it?"

"Fewer questions and more obedience, girl. Drink it."

She took the flask and sniffed it suspiciously. Its neck narrowed sharply at the end, almost as if it was meant to act as a funnel, and its contents smelled of honey and fire. Alasha shook her head; she had heard tales of Arbish potions before, and she had no intention of being poisoned or drugged.

The man moved so swiftly that she hardly saw what happened, and before she knew it he was behind her, squeezing her throat in the crook of his elbow and bending her backwards over his hip. She didn't have the flask any more, either; it was in his hand, its pointed neck already pushing between her teeth.

He twisted her head back and forced the flask in further, pinching her nose closed with his free hand. It was unbelievable, how strong he was and how quickly he'd moved. The bottle's pointed neck disgorged the first slug of fiery liquid deep into her throat, and she understood its odd shape: there was no way to spit it out, and no way to breathe until she'd swallowed it.

As soon as she'd done so, before she had time to draw another breath, another mouthful gurgled out of the flask. Alasha realized that he wasn't going to let her breathe until she'd swallowed every drop. At least it tasted sweet. She gulped the second mouthful down, hoping that was the last of it.

It wasn't. The flask held much more than she had expected, and she began to panic. She put her hands against his wrist and tried to push his hand away.

It was like trying to move an oak tree.

The Arbian forced another dose of the fiery liquid down her, and then it was over. He released her and she fell to her knees, coughing and retching.

"There. You feel better now, no?" said the Arbian.

It was true. The sweetness and warmth was spreading into her body and through her limbs, and she felt no need to weep any more; she still mourned Aric, but the loss seemed distant, as if it had happened to someone else.

Alasha wondered what was in the flasks, and how long the effect would last.

Then she started to wonder when she would be given more.

She rose to her feet, shakily. He was still behind her, and he put his arms around waist her as she stood up.

Alasha found no reason to resist; instead, she just leaned against him and tilted her head back against his shoulder.

"All my girls love the fire drink," said the man, with a chuckle. His voice was a honeyed caress, and Alasha felt herself going weak at the knees as she relaxed into his strength.

"What is your name?" she asked.

"You may call me Mussuf." His fingers strayed up to her breasts and tugged gently at her nipple rings. "Such a charming custom. I would not want to see an Arbian girl marred like that, of course, but you Xendrians are different, are you not?"

Alasha said nothing, lost in the sweet drink-haze. His placed his other hand on her hip and then allowed it to play across her bare stomach for a while, before working his way up to the space between her breasts. Alasha's skin tingled under his exploring fingers, and the sound of her own sighs was sweet in her ears.

His hand strayed downward, dropped to her loins again and finding the second pair of rings before testing the slick length of her sex. "The drink works quickly with you, girl. You're ready for me."

Mussuf spun her around so that she was facing him, and unbelted his robe. His monstrous cock bobbed out from between the folds of fabric, and Alasha gasped, wondering how any woman could accommodate such a thing.

Then his hands were on her hips, lifting her up with the same easy strength that had trapped her and forced her to drink his potion. A small, distant part of her watched in horror as she parted her legs helplessly and prepared herself to accept him.

He held her on the cusp of penetration for a long moment, and then drew her onto himself gently. Alasha felt herself filling very slowly, like a glass receiving a stream of carefully poured wine. She looked down and watched him disappearing into her, opening her and stretching her beyond what she would have believed possible. She started in sudden pain: the glass was very nearly full now, yet he was barely halfway inside her.

"Let yourself go, girl," he said. "Let the fire take you."

It was true: the drink was doing its work: honing the feelings of pleasure that came from his penetration, drowning any thought of loyalty or denial in a limitless ocean of lust. His cock pushed past her slackening resistance, and she sensed that undiscovered depths were opening up, deep inside her body.

Then he pushed her away again, slowly easing her off him until the moist lips of her sex were barely kissing the tip of his glistening cock.

Alasha felt a wave of relief that she had not burst open, that nothing inside her seemed to be broken, and then it was replaced by an urgent need to do it again, to test her limits for a second time.

To push a little further, this time. Harder and deeper.

She looked up at his face, and he met her eyes.

"Again, please," she said.

He lowered her back onto himself, less gently than before and with no pause to let her relax. Alasha winced in pain as he pushed past the point that had resisted him before, and then she was full to bursting again.

This time he didn't leave her immediately. Instead, he carried her, still transfixed, to the low cot that stood in a corner of his tent, and knelt so that he could lay her down without disengaging himself. Then he was on top of her. His weight seemed to double the pressure inside her, and she heard herself mewling – not in pain, exactly, but from the level of sensation she was experiencing – as his hands found her ankles and spread them even wider.

He raised himself away from her, and brought her legs around so that his shoulders were pressing against her calves and his head was framed between her bare feet. Now she was open completely, unable even to tense herself against him. He drew back a little, allowing her legs to rise and her body to close itself as he pulled away, and then he pressed forward again, re-opening the path as he thrust into her again.

Alasha felt a clot of honeyed fire building inside her. Mussuf seemed to sense it too, because he grinned down at her and started to move faster, which he mustn't do because she was going to burst. *O please don't let him push any harder, any deeper* she thought, just before her orgasm exploded through her body and into her brain.

She came back, a few heartbeats or a few hours later. Mussuf hadn't finished. He was still moving in and out of her mechanically, and with Alasha's arousal spent, it was beginning to hurt. She felt the warm pleasure leaving her body, to be replaced by the beginnings of dry pain.

Perhaps that was what pushed Mussuf over the edge: suddenly he was pumping gouts of hot liquid into her. From the pressure that she felt inside, he seemed to be as productive as he was well endowed, and for a moment Alasha wondered if his spurting would be the final straw that would burst her asunder.

Finished, he rolled off her and stood up. "Well, you have passed your test, girl. You will make a fine camp whore. Now get dressed and get out of here."

"Camp whore?" she repeated, still befuddled by the sex and the fire drink.

"Yes." He was wiping himself off, not giving her so much as a glance. "You cannot dance, as you are not Arbian. But the dancers are very alluring; many of the customers require personal attention after the performance. It will be one less job for the girls to do. They will be very happy that you have joined us."

Two of the dancing girls took her into their care. Neither of them spoke much Xendrian, something that disappointed Alasha because her brain was overflowing with questions – about Aric, about Mussuf, about the fire drink, about where the caravan was going … but at least it meant the girls couldn't give her orders.

It didn't make much difference in the end; they found other ways to communicate with her.

Xero held Alasha's arms while Zanya straddled her belly, pinched her nose, and forced a few mouthfuls of firewater down her throat. Mussuf had been right: the two dancers seemed very pleased that another girl had arrived to take over one of their less pleasant duties.

Once Alasha's will had surrendered to the drug again, they pulled her into a wagon that was hung with silks and lined with a deep covering of furs. There, they chained her to an iron ring set just behind the driver's seat. She watched numbly as they bound her wrists with short leather thongs and tethered them to her collar ring, so that she could reach no lower than the top of her breastbone, and so that she wouldn't be able to resist whatever was to be done.

Then Xero grasped Alasha's knees and forced them apart, while Zanya unstopped a small pottery flask and poured a slow stream of oil

into her palm. She applied the liquid to Alasha's opened body, smearing the lubricant around the lips of her sex and then working it deep
inside.

"Easier for you," said Xero, in her halting Xendrian.

The fire drink seemed to be working already, because Alasha found
herself trembling at the girls' touch, and she had no desire to resist
Zanya's exploring fingers.

Xero fingered the rings that pierced Alasha's nipples for a while,
and said something to Zanya. Both girls collapsed into fits of giggles.
Zanya placed a spare flask next to Alasha's head, pointed to it, and said
something incomprehensible.

The girls giggled together again and then left her alone, lying
naked on the furs.

Alasha wriggled over to the side of the wagon. By straining at the
limit of the chain, she could just see through a crack between two
warped boards.

The Arbians had pushed a row of flat carts together, forming a
crude stage. They had surrounded this on three sides with the rest of
their wagons; Alasha was at the left side of the stage, where the customers would be able to reach her easily. It was only just getting dark,
but enough of the men had already glanced in her direction to tell her
that the wagon was marked.

Or perhaps it was the soldier who lounged nearby with a slotted jar
cradled in one arm, waiting to collect the payment required from those
who wished to visit her.

Xero and Zanya appeared on the stage, bowed to the audience and
then stood motionless for a while, gazing out into the gathering darkness. There were a few catcalls, and a smattering of applause. The only
motion on the stage was the breeze rippling through the silk garments
of the dancers, and the flickering torchlight that illuminated their bodies.

Somewhere out of sight, a slow drum began to beat.

Both girls rose to their toes and approached the center of the stage
with a patter of bare feet and a jingling of ankle bells that flirted around

the drumbeats. They linked arms for an instant as they passed each other, and thus swung one another around so that they returned to their original positions.

Alasha saw that each girl now had a veil in her hand, and each had lost part of her garment; the layers of silk that covered the girls' legs were a little more translucent and a little briefer than they had been.

The warmth of the fire drink was spreading through her body again, and she understood why the men in the audience might want to visit a girl after a display like this. Her wrists strained against the thongs that secured them, in a vain attempt to reach her sex.

Even in her agitated state, Alasha understood why they had bound her hands: not to stop her from resisting, but to prevent her from spending the drink-lust by touching herself, to make sure the customers were served warm and willing flesh.

The drumbeats came faster now, and the dance was more urgent. Most of the dancers' clothes were gone, discarded on the stage or thrown into the crowd. The girls had merged into a whirling tangle of dark locks and supple limbs.

The drum beat faster still, and the final scraps of silk vanished into the darkness. The dancers were now clothed only in shadows and torchlight.

The audience had fallen silent, as if mesmerized by the relentless rhythm and the quicksilver dance.

Zanya rose on tiptoe and stretched her fingertips to the stars, while Xero fell abjectly to her knees and offered her companion a long and intimate kiss. Zanya held the pose and then bowed, still clasping Xero's head to her loins. Both dancers remained perfectly still through the final flourish of the drums. On the very last beat, the torches hissed and died.

Even inside her wagon, Alasha heard the collective release of breath from the audience, a long sigh in the darkness. When the torches were lit again, she saw a knot of men drifting towards her from the crowd, with silver coins glinting in their hands.

The first customer arrived. Alasha watched through the crack, heard the clink as he dropped his payment into the guard's jar, and then he was climbing into the wagon.

He offered her a snaggle-toothed grin as he unfastened his breeches. Alasha felt nothing but revulsion: no lust, no desire. Perhaps the drink had worn off; perhaps she was supposed to have been sipping from the flask Zanya had left behind.

It didn't make any difference, anyway. She was naked and chained, and this man had paid his silver piece. All she could do was to lean back on the furs and close her eyes, distancing herself as much as she could from what was happening. She flinched when he touched her knees, urging her thighs apart, but she didn't resist.

He crawled onto her, and his unclean breath wafted over her face. She shielded herself with her hands; at least the tether was long enough to allow her that. He gave an impatient grunt and forced her wrists apart so that he could plant his mouth on hers.

The bile rose in Alasha's throat at the taste of him, but the desire was rising too. *Perhaps the firewater isn't spent, after all,* she thought. *Or perhaps there is no need for it. Perhaps the ingredients are all within me, simply waiting.*

His hand was between her legs, testing the wetness that was growing there. It still hurt when he entered her, and the thought came into her mind that a man such as this might be carrying the unwashed evidence of a dozen ruttings.

Or worse.

At least it wasn't long before he was done.

When he had gone, Alasha looked at the flask that stood nearby. It would make things easier, but she decided not to use it: she wanted to remain alert, to understand what was happening. If she allowed herself to take comfort the arms of the drug, she knew that she would be perfectly satisfied to spend every night of her life like this, chained up and being whored out to one customer after another.

She unstopped the flask and let its contents run between the floorboards, so that they would think she had taken the drug, and so that she wouldn't be tempted to change her mind later.

Outside, she heard another clink of silver, and another set of footsteps approaching the wagon.

After a while, the drumbeats started again.

8   stalker

Alasha woke up stiff and sore the next morning.

The entertainment had continued for far longer than she could bear, but at least there had been respites during the performances: Mussuf kept a whole string of dancing girls, and Alasha thought that each must have taken a turn on the stage.

As she washed herself in the stream near the camp, she found several bruises on her shoulders and around her nipples, and a slick of still-wet oil on her thighs. There were other stains between her legs, too; she'd been too exhausted to wash herself the night before.

The camp was filled with a tense edginess that seemed new to Alasha; the Arbians appeared harassed and almost fearful, glancing around the clearing as they hurried about their morning tasks.

Something must have happened while she slept, Alasha decided. After the previous night, she knew she wouldn't survive long without allies and information, so when Zanya came to fetch water, she smiled and nodded, trying to pretend that nothing had passed between them.

"What's going on in the camp?"

"Camp in bad place. Two warriors dead in night."

"Two of the guards died?"

"Yes. Very bad place."

"Very bad place indeed," said Alasha, with feeling.

Mussuf came out of his tent, shouting orders in Arbian. The soldiers started striking the tents and hitching up the mule teams, while the dancers busied themselves with loading the wagons.

The caravan master turned to Alasha. "Help pack, girl, and then get back in the wagon. Hurry. We move within the hour."

As he turned away, there was an outcry at the edge of the clearing. Two soldiers were returning, bearing a comrade between them. Alasha saw a black-feathered arrow embedded deeply in his back; there could be little doubt that he was dead.

When she saw the arrow, she felt hope in her heart for the first time since Aric had fallen: someone was killing the Arbians with their own weapons. What if Aric had survived, somehow? Yet she'd seen him slain, with the head of an identical arrow buried in his chest. She'd seen the blood that stained his robes as he toppled from his horse.

Her pulse raced a little faster anyway; who could be shooting these people with their own arrows? They would hardly be killing one another. Would it be better to keep silent, or to sow fear and confusion by announcing what she hoped? If she spoke, panic among the Arbians might help whoever was slaying them, and she had other reasons for telling, too: if her lover was indeed dead, teaching them to fear him would be some sort of revenge.

She decided to speak. "Aric is coming for me. He will kill you all."

Mussuf turned towards her with narrowed eyes. "What do you mean?"

"He is a master of stealth and sudden death. I am his favorite possession. You have harmed him, and me. Now you will pay with your lives."

"Nonsense, girl. The man is dead. I saw him fall myself."

Alasha cast her mind back over her schoolbooks. One of the things she remembered of the Arbians, besides their skill with alchemy and potions, was that they were a superstitious race.

"He has had many enemies," she said. "Many have believed him slain, yet each time he has returned to take his revenge, turning his foes' own weapons against them."

Mussuf's glance strayed to the Arbish arrow that had killed his guard. So did the eyes of two other soldiers, who evidently understood some Xendrian.

"Silence, girl. You know nothing. Your Master lies in a ditch. Wild dogs gnaw at his bones."

"It must be as you say, Lord. Your dead soldiers are nothing more than a co-incidence, such as could happen anywhere in lawless Xendria. I am sure that there will be no more deaths tonight."

Mussuf's eyes showed a flicker of fear and then hardened. He barked some orders to his remaining soldiers, and stalked off towards his wagon.

"You bring bad luck," said Zanya.

Alasha shook her head. "Mussuf killed a fine man, and stole me. He brings bad luck to all of you."

Zanya just spat on the ground and went off towards the wagons.

The Arbians struck camp hastily; it wasn't long before the troupe was underway. Zanya and Xero had tethered Alasha's wrists to her collar once more, and chained her behind a stack of barrels that were strapped to one of the flat wagons. At least they had allowed her to clothe herself in her Arbish slave veils.

Mussuf came up on his horse and rode alongside her for a while. "In a few days we will reach Issing Ford," he said. "There are plenty of brothels in the town, places that will take a bitch such as you. I will sell you to the first one we pass, and buy a new whore."

"He'll still come after you."

"Dead men take no revenge. Even if the gods willed that he was spared, he will never find you. You will spend the rest of your youth chained to a stinking pallet, fighting against the shackles that hold your legs apart until you are too worn out to be of further use." He spat on the ground. "You would have done better with us, girl."

"You have yet to reach Issing Ford."

"Oh, I will reach it. You may not, though." He half drew the jeweled dagger that he wore at his side. "My men whisper that you bring us bad luck already. It would be no great hardship to forfeit the price you would bring."

Alasha fell silent at that, and after a while Mussuf gave a sour laugh and rode back to the head of the caravan.

In the middle of the afternoon, a baggage cart broke an axle at a river crossing; the whole caravan had to stop while the spilled load was transferred to the other wagons. The dancers lit a fire to prepare a meal, but no one released Alasha, or brought her any food.

"Please could I have something to drink?" she called when Xero came to fetch water for the bitter brew that the Arbians called khavé.

Xero wouldn't meet her eyes. "Sorry. Mussuf say no water."

Alasha licked her dry lips and leaned against a barrel, watching the river bubbling through the spokes of the broken wagon, wishing her chain were long enough to let her reach down to quench her thirst. After a while, Mussuf returned.

"I suppose you have been hoping that this breakdown would delay us," he said. "It would have meant one less night in Issing Ford for you, would it not? Alas, I regret to inform you that we will be pressing on. The wagon can catch up later."

"I need water," said Alasha.

"You will have plenty to guzzle, later on."

There could be little doubt about what that meant: more of the fire drink from his stock of flasks. Alasha was already so thirsty that she would have swallowed as much of the potion as he cared to offer; she wondered if there was enough water in the stuff to keep her alive.

"I see that you understand," he said. "You shall have as much as you can drink, at the end of the day. Understand how privileged you are: the firewater is a closely guarded secret with us, one that we seldom waste on unbelievers."

Alasha's thirst forced her to speak. "Then give me water instead."

"It is a great sorrow to me that we have none to spare." His eyes flicked towards the river and he gave a thin smile. "Concerning the potion, you should know that with excessive consumption the effects become permanent; the agony of withdrawal is most unpleasant. You are already entwined among the drug's first coils. The rest of the gift is yours to embrace or not, as you will."

The caravan moved on, leaving three men to repair the broken axle and escort the empty wagon back to the main group. Mussuf's nervous glances towards the trees on either side of the road told Alasha how vulnerable he felt now, with only four guards to protect the caravan.

The one who had shot Aric was among them. He hadn't even glanced at her in the two days since her capture.

All day, Alasha was tortured by thirst, made even worse by the memory of the river where she'd washed but neglected to drink, and by the sound of water sloshing inside the barrels close by. Every hour or so, Mussuf rode back to check on her, and to gaze back along the road as if searching for signs that his broken wagon and its escort were catching up.

The stragglers had still not appeared when the troupe stopped for the night, but Alasha was in no condition to feel any satisfaction about that. Her head ached and her flesh felt parched and hot, as if her body's moisture was being slowly leached away.

The campsite was to be a broad clearing that showed evidence of having been used as a resting-place before. Alasha heard Mussuf give some muttered instructions to his soldiers, who drew the wagons into a tight circle and prepared several fires outside the protective ring, in the space between the encampment and the trees. Alasha saw that anyone approaching the camp after dark would be silhouetted against the flames; an easy target for the defending archers.

While the men secured the encampment, the dancers stayed within the circle of wagons, preparing the evening meal. Mussuf came to Alasha and gave her a flask of the fire drink. He said nothing, and her mouth was too dry to let her speak; she knew she had to accept the drink no matter what it might do to her.

She put the bottle to her lips and let some of the liquid run into her mouth.

It was cloying, closer to honey than to the water that she craved, but it was much better than nothing. She swallowed the first mouthful and felt the slow fire that kindled in her loins, took a second pull and felt the potion's intoxicating fingers reaching into her brain.

By the time the flask was empty, she found herself looking up at Mussuf with a mixture of hatred and desire.

A single measure wasn't nearly enough, though. She was still thirsty. She reached out to Mussuf and he gave her a second flask. Alasha drained that too, and Mussuf offered her a third.

Now her stomach was full and her nerves were tingling, but her body was still parched. She took a sip of the liquid and ran it around her mouth before swallowing it.

"It is good, no?" asked Mussuf. "Keep taking a little at a time. That is the way to feel the benefit."

Alasha ran her still-dry tongue over her lips. Almost against her will, she found herself brushing her hair away from her face and arranging her limbs in a way he might feel pleasing. "Please give me some water, and then take me," she said, her voice sounding pitifully hoarse and cracked in her own ears. She knew he wouldn't want her, not all dried up and sounding like an old crone, but she couldn't help herself.

"Time enough for that later on. Enjoy the drink while you can, girl. The time will come soon enough when you'll wish your new owner knew the recipe. Still, at least the anguish of withdrawal will distract you from whatever else is happening to you … assuming you survive it."

The drink-lust was close to overwhelming her, but she forced the feelings down for a moment to concentrate on what he'd said. "Survive it?"

"You have just guzzled enough to become a slave to the drink, as well as to me. When you are unable to obtain more, it will be most unpleasant for you. The last girl died on the fifth day after much suffering; I believe she was glad to have an end."

"Then keep me. I'll do whatever you wish." Alasha's words sounded thick and strange to her, as if they were spoken by someone else, but she knew they were true: if he kept her supplied her with this drink – and provided men to quench the flames it kindled – she would serve him faithfully.

Deep inside, a small and bitter part of her hated what was happening, and knew that Aric should be the one standing before her when she was consumed with this fire. The thought of him pushed her over the edge, and she strained against her chains, reaching for the hungry void between her legs.

Mussuf's mocking laughter seemed to come from very far away.

She returned to an acrid smell of burning and hoarse cries of alarm. The dancers were beating at flames that were threatening to engulf the store wagons, and the guards were sending arrows towards one of the watch fires.

Mussuf loomed out of the night. "Your ghost shall not have you back, and he shall not have me."

Padlocks clinked in the darkness as the man unchained Alasha's collar and wrists, and then her arms were bound again, this time with loops of rope that he pulled cruelly tight behind her back.

"Come."

Alasha followed obediently, still befuddled and able to think of little except for the possibility that he was taking her somewhere dark and private, where he might give her more of the drink and spend the rest of the night fucking her.

"Mount the horse." He was guiding Alasha's bare foot into the stirrup and boosting her into the saddle. Deprived of the use of her hands, she wobbled for a moment before her fingers found the cantle and she managed to steady herself. She felt the stirrup leather brushing her ankle, and followed it down until her toes encountered the other stirrup and slid into place. Then she squeezed her thighs together, holding herself in the saddle as securely as she could.

Mussuf was already on his own horse, with the trailing reins of Alasha's mount held easily in his hand. He glanced back at her and urged his horse silently between a narrow gap between two wagons, moving away from the disturbance at the other side of the camp, and towards the tree line.

Alasha glanced back one last time. The flames seemed to be spreading through the camp; most of the defenders had either fled or been killed. The high-pitched wailing of the dancers mingled with the clash of steel on steel: there seemed to be two guards left, matching blades against a lithe shadow that danced among the flames.

Then they reached the darkness under the trees, and she could see no more.

They rode through the forest for what seemed like hours, picking their way with the aid of the pale moonlight that filtered through the branches. At last, the night grew old and they came to a clearing where the quality of the darkness was different. Birds began to sing all around them, quietly and few at first but soon becoming a full chorus. Mussuf reined his horse in and swung himself out his saddle, and then helped Alasha dismount.

The winter's dried leaves were cool and brittle under her feet, and they rustled crisply as she moved, stirring up the earthy woodland aroma of previous falls.

"I told you that your ghost would not have us," said Mussuf. "We are deep in the forest now. He will never find us here."

The fire-lust had evaporated with the night, leaving Alasha feeling nothing but hatred for her captor. "He wasn't going to kill your people and burn your wagons either," she said, as sweetly as she could. "It would be best for you to let me go. You'll have a better chance on your own."

Mussuf glared at her and placed his hand on the coiled rope that hung from his saddlebag. "Hold your tongue, bitch, lest you provoke me into renewing your welts. Your next owner will certainly prefer your body to be a blank parchment on which he can inscribe his own message, so do not test my patience."

She looked at the rope and fell silent. As long as her wrists were tied, there was nothing to be gained by arguing with the Arbian. It would be best to wait until she was less helpless.

He stared at her for a while, and then turned to his saddlebag and removed one of the flasks. "We must rest now. You may drink this."

Alasha's body was already craving more of the drink, and she accepted the scant mouthful that remained in the flask eagerly, wishing there had been a few drops more even as the potion spread into her blood and kindled every nerve with desire.

She looked at Mussuf, caught between lust and loathing. Half of her hoped his life would come to a brutal and sudden end; the other half, that he would have his way with her before he slept.

He cast the drained flask aside and smiled. "Now you will not be tempted to stray far from your sole supply, or from me. But it is always best to make doubly sure."

He took the rope from his saddlebag and tied one end to her collar before making a loop that he slipped over his own wrist. "That will teach you wisdom, and keep you close at hand," he said, and then settled himself under a tree.

Before long, Mussuf's deep snoring filled the air, drowning the singing of the birds and the sighing of the breeze among the branches.

Alasha pretended to fall asleep, distracting herself from lustful thoughts of the Arbian by keeping an image of Aric in her mind. She was almost sure now that the arrow had been fatal, and that it must have been someone else who attacked the camp, but her heart couldn't help hoping against hope that somehow her lover might be alive, and not far behind.

After all, who else could it have been?

When she was certain that Mussuf was truly unconscious, she opened her eyes and glanced around the clearing, looking for anything that might help her escape.

The horses were tethered out of reach. The only thing she could see, apart from rocks and roots and fallen leaves, was the bottle that Mussuf had thrown away so carelessly.

Perhaps she could reach it.

She shuffled a few inches away from Mussuf and then paused, checking for any reaction from the man. His regular snoring continued, and she moved again. Eventually, she came close to the rope's limit, and dared to go no further.

The flask was still out of reach.

She moved backwards a little, to put some more slack back in her tether, and then swiveled so that her legs were pointing towards the bottle. Now, when she shuffled forwards again, her toes made contact with the neck of the flask. Carefully, gently – terrified that she might slip and push it further away – she gripped it between her feet and eased it towards herself.

A few heartbeats later, she was clutching it in her bound hands, between her arched back and the forest floor.

She waited, concentrating on Mussuf's snores, hoping that she wasn't about to open an artery.

At his rumbling reached a peak, she brought her weight down on the flask, and heard it break into several shards. Instantly, she started to saw her bonds against one of the sharp edges, praying that the wetness she felt was nothing more than the last dregs from the bottle.

She sensed the ropes parting, strand by strand, and the pressure on her wrists eased.

The forest was peaceful again. *Please don't let him wake up yet*, she prayed.

Although her hands were loose, her fingers were still too numb to work the knot at her throat. Instead, she picked up the broken neck of the flask and sawed through the tether.

At last, she stood free, close to the edge of the clearing. Mussuf had rolled over onto his side. She looked at him, and then at the shard of glass that she held.

I should slay him while he sleeps, for what he has done, she thought. *At least I must take his supplies of potion.*

Mussuf started in his sleep and sat up, almost as if she had spoken aloud. He rose to his feet and drew his dagger in a single fluid motion.

Alasha turned and fled into the forest.

Behind her, she heard the Arbian cursing and crashing through the undergrowth as he came after her.

Alasha ran easily at first: she was young, lightly dressed, and fleet of foot. She also took comfort from the knowledge that Mussuf was used to riding, not running, and that his heavy-set strength was likely to tell against him in a long chase.

Even so, she hadn't eaten or drunk properly for days, and all too soon she found herself flagging. She staggered on, heading downhill because the going was easier, and because she hoped to find a stream where she could quench her thirst.

She tried not to think of her other needs: for food and shelter, and for the Arbian's fire drink.

At last, Mussuf seemed to give up the chase. Alasha paused, too, her lungs working like a pair of Marlish steam pistons, and listened for sounds of further pursuit.

Instead, Mussuf's voice came booming through the trees. "Hide if you wish, girl. You will return to beg for my charity and my punishment, when the thirst comes on you. For what other merchant will you find in this wilderness, to supply your need?"

Alasha collapsed against the trunk of a tree as she listened to the cruel, confident laughter that came echoing down the hill.

Later that morning, she found the river she sought, and knelt at its bank to quench her thirst. The water was icy cold, reminding her of the winter snowmelt from which it sprang, but it still tasted sweeter than the finest wine in the cellars of Malkenstorm.

Alasha saw dappled fish gliding through one of the deeper pools, and tried to catch one with her fingers, copying the technique her mother's gamekeeper had shown her when she was a girl.

She'd never been able to manage it then, either, and she couldn't keep her arm submerged in the freezing river for long.

Her stomach was growling constantly, making her wish it was autumn, because then at least there would have been nuts and berries to eat. As it was, she had nothing except for her Arbian slave garment and the glass splinter that she still clutched in her hand.

The dress, she thought. *The veils are little more than wisps of silk; surely I can fashion a fishing net from them?*

By the middle of the day, she had a framework made from vines and a long Y-shaped sapling, whose branches she lashed into a hoop and draped with one of her veils.

Shortly before sunset, she managed to land her first fish.

Alasha had no wish to show light or smoke, and no way to make a fire in any case, so she sliced her catch open and cleaned it in the water, and then carved it into two fillets that she ate raw.

No fish had ever tasted so good before, not even when fresh-caught in the castle lake and poached in the most exquisite sauces that her mother's chef could contrive. Alasha licked her fingers clean and returned to the riverbank, wondering if she might catch another before it got dark.

But the sun was already going down, and now that one appetite had been partly satisfied, others were making themselves known.

The forest was growing cooler as the shadows deepened. She felt the goosebumps rising on her skin, and a sudden fit of trembling racked her body.

It wasn't just the cold that made her shiver. It was her own body, telling her that it needed more of the firewater. She had no choice but to steal the rest of Mussuf's supply, and hope it would last her to Issing

Ford. There, she might find a leech or an apothecary to help her.

She hid her improvised net under a bush and started up the hill, back towards the place from where she'd last heard her tormentor's voice.

The light of the Arbian's fire showed long before Alasha got back to his camp. She dropped to her hands and knees and crept closer in the darkness, testing the ground for treacherous twigs and branches each time she moved.

At the edge of the clearing, she flattened herself among the tree roots, striving to cover herself with shadow. Mussuf was reclining under a blanket near the fire, his head resting on his saddle.

He seemed to be asleep.

She could see the horses, tethered at the other side of the clearing. Near them, Mussuf's belongings were stacked under a tree.

That was where the flasks would be.

Alasha started to skirt the clearing, working her way closer to the saddlebags.

"Are you out there, yet?" asked Mussuf loudly, addressing the stars. "Are you ready to beg for a sip of potion, and for whatever treatment I have in mind for you?"

She shrank fearfully into the darkness and crept away, back down the hill.

Alasha spent a cold night in a drift of dried leaves, and when she awoke the next morning, she was shaking with fever.

It had been two days since she'd drunk her fill of firewater; the few drops from the broken flask had been almost worthless. Now, she was beginning to understand more truly what it meant to be enslaved.

She managed to catch another fish, and forced herself to eat its flesh despite the fact that her appetite for food had gone, subsumed into a different hunger.

The rest of the day passed slowly, with Alasha dozing fitfully and shivering in her pile of leaves. Her sickness brought hot, bright-edged dreams, in which she often saw Aric Albigenses wandering in the woods, but when she called his name, it was always Mussuf who turned to her with his stony eyes and empty smile.

When darkness fell at last, she waited as long as she could bear and then made her way back up the hill. She found Mussuf's camp just as she'd left it, except that tonight he was snoring.

Alasha circled the clearing, working her way closer to his saddle-bags. She crept out from the shelter of the trees, praying that the horses wouldn't grow restless or whinny in greeting, and that Mussuf was truly asleep.

Her heart was pounding so loudly that she was sure he must hear it, and her shaking hands could hardly unfasten the buckles of his bag. At last she managed to fumble them open, and exulted silently as her fingers closed around a cool, smooth flask.

Alasha couldn't wait. One bottle, she promised herself, and then she'd feel strong enough to carry the entire bag away. She uncorked her prize and raised it to her lips, imagining how good it was going to feel.

A single mouthful, and she froze with dismayed surprise: the flask contained nothing but water.

Whimpering softly, she scrabbled another bottle out of the saddle-bag, heedless of the clinking sounds she made. That one contained water, too.

The cursed Arbian had tricked her. *Where can he have hidden the stuff?* she wondered, and glanced around the camp, and that was when she saw that Mussuf wasn't asleep at all.

He was standing close by, lit by firelight with his arms folded across his chest and a triumphant smile on his face.

"I believe this is what you are looking for?" he asked, showing her the flask he held.

"Please, I must drink."

"And what are you prepared to do to earn it?"

Alasha hesitated, pride struggling with need. Pride yielded, as she knew it must. "Whatever you want."

Mussuf's voice hardened with anger. "I want my girls and my wagons back, and to be rid of all scheming vixens. Perhaps I shall kill you later, when I am done with you."

The threat scarcely penetrated Alasha's consciousness; she was completely consumed by the need for the drug he held. "Please," she heard herself whisper.

"Be assured that I shall seek a very special buyer for you, someone who will delight in working you to death slowly. An insatiable minx such as you should fetch a good price, if I dose you with as much potion as you can drink before the sale. Perhaps there will even be enough gold for me to start again."

Alasha reached towards the flask. "Please," she said, again.

"Go closer to the fire, and undress."

She hurried to obey, glad of the warmth of the flames. As soon as she was naked, Mussuf tossed the flask to her. She caught it and drained it eagerly. Her sickness disappeared almost instantly, to be replaced by a different sort of fever.

The Arbian came closer. "Get on your hands and knees, and stick your arse in the air."

Alasha dropped to the ground, and presented herself as instructed, lascivious fumes flooding through her body. She had almost stopped caring about what would happen next, was almost looking forward to it.

Almost, but not quite. Not yet. She hadn't stopped hating Mussuf, yet.

She sensed him moving behind her, heard the whisper of his breech lacings, and fought to hold her body still while more fire rushed into her brain, urging her to welcome whatever came.

It wasn't long before she felt his hand on her: fingers probing between her legs and teasing the tiny jewel that Aric had discovered so delightfully. Mussuf's moistened thumb rested lightly on her other, more shameful entrance.

Within a few heartbeats of his first touch, her will to resist was gone.

The fingers played with her for a while, testing and developing the heat and the wetness they found. Their rhythm became faster, and the pressure between her cheeks grew slowly until she felt herself give way, as if she was a bubble that had been popped by some irresistible thorn, and his thumb was inside her.

Another hand snaked around her flank, reached for her breast, and began to toy with her nipple ring.

Alasha became an instrument in the Arbian's hands, repeatedly building towards a crescendo and then backing off as he reduced the tempo. Her revulsion was gone now; all that remained were the man's searing fingers and the animal sound of her own whimpering.

Then she was moaning even more loudly, because he'd stopped, but it was all right: his cock was pressed against her pussy, guided there by the hands she could feel between her thighs.

He pushed her forward, pressing her face against the ground, so she was blind to everything that was happening, but she saw his manhood in her memory, and imagined it sliding into her again as it had before. Only this time, there was no gentle pause, no time for her to expand to accommodate him, no slow pouring of wine to keep from overfilling the glass.

He sheathed himself in her body with a single brutal thrust; she felt his belly strike her proffered rump as he buried himself deep inside her. Alasha's pleasurable moans were cut off abruptly, replaced by a gasp of surprise and pained arousal as he filled her to bursting.

Then he was sliding out of her, and it was relief filling her instead of his flesh: relief that she was empty again, and hadn't split asunder.

Then the fire roared up and overwhelmed her utterly, and she wanted nothing more than to feel herself mastered and transfixed by his overpowering cock once more.

She didn't have to wait for more than a heartbeat before he was inside her again, and this time he carried some of her wetness further inside her so that his entry was easier than before.

With his third thrust, Alasha started to come. After that, she lost track of what was happening: before she could find her way back from one climax, the next was upon her, until her whole body was quivering in time with his strokes.

He withdrew without warning and before she could comprehend it, the head of his cock was pressed between her bottom cheeks, nestling wetly against her arsehole.

He pushed past her resistance quickly, still so slick from her juices that she couldn't have denied him even if she'd had time to consider the matter. The pain was even stronger than before, but it mingled with the afterglow of the fucking he had given her, and became good. Alasha heard herself cry out so loudly that the dawn's first tentative birds were silenced for a while, heard her anguish and her ecstasy echoing through the forest, and felt her bowels filled to bursting, just as her womb had been.

Mussuf made certain that there would be no more escape attempts. Before he slept again, he bound Alasha's ankles and wrists, and leashed her to his belt.

The next morning, he fed her a flask of firewater and then untied her feet and tethered her collar to his horse. Light-headed from lack of food and excess of passion, she remained kneeling while he collected her garment and took the reins of the other beast. When he spurred his mount out of the clearing, she had no choice but to scramble to her feet and follow.

She stumbled along after him, acutely aware of the change from dried leaves to soft pine needles under her feet as they moved into an area of thick evergreens. Sharper needles covered the branches that sprang back from Mussuf's passage, and she soon had cause to wish that she wasn't naked, and that her hands were free.

At last, they left the belt of pines and entered an area of broad-leaved trees that ran down to the edge of a gurgling river – the same one, perhaps, as she had found before. Mussuf dismounted and untied Alasha's leash from his saddle, and then loosed her hands from behind her back.

She stood on the riverbank for a moment, rubbing her bruised wrists.

"I have not brought you here to preen yourself, girl. If you are to please your next owner, and me, you must observe the virtue of cleanliness. There is the river: wash yourself."

Alasha picked her way down to the bank and braced herself against the cold as she squatted in a swirling pool. The most logical part of her welcomed the chilly water, hoping it would quench the embers of desire that still smoldered within, eager to betray her.

She heard Mussuf chuckling as she climbed back up the bank, and saw that he was looking at the branches that hung over the water.

"I have invented the perfect way to repay your little escapade," he announced.

With that, the Arbian took a long rope from one of his bags, and slung it over a low branch that overhung the riverbank. The thrown end dangled into the swirling water, slipping downstream past a sharp, dark stone that jutted from the riverbed below the tree limb.

"Bring it back here," he commanded.

Alasha waded into the water, moving quickly because of the cold, and retrieved the rope, which was now draped over the tree limb, with one dry end – now hitched to Mussuf's saddlebow – and one sodden end, which Alasha held.

"Give me your hands, girl."

She obeyed, wary of whatever Mussuf's spite might bring, but fearing the consequences of rebellion even more.

He tied the ends of the rope about her wrists, pulling the loops cruelly tight. The harsh texture of wet hemp – and the rough handling he gave her – showed all too quickly that the cold water had done little to douse her desire.

"Now go to the rock, and mount it as if it were a horse."

Alasha looked at the depth of the water around the rock and hesitated. She turned to Mussuf, hoping he would reconsider. He simply took his horse's bridle and urged it along the riverbank, tautening the rope at her wrists.

"It makes little difference to me whether you wade, or swim, or are dragged," he said.

Alasha stepped back into the river and picked her way towards the rock and the overhanging branch. She felt gravel and rounded pebbles shifting under her feet, and saw the dark plumes of silt that she sent flowing downstream. The water soon rose to her calves, then to her thighs. It seemed even colder than before.

As she plunged deeper into the stream, Mussuf walked his horse along the bank, keeping the rope tight so that it was impossible for her to do anything other than move in the direction he chose. She glanced back at the riverbank, wishing she could return to it. The sense of being trapped in the freezing river, so close to the sun-dappled carpet of dry leaves, made her feel even colder. She started to shiver.

It didn't take long to reach the rock she was to climb. Now that she was close to it, she could see its nature more clearly: it was a smooth, dark outcropping of the riverbed. Eons had carved the upstream end to a knife's edge that parted the water smoothly and silently, without any fuss.

The top of the rock was less sharp, but it was still very narrow, being little more than the breadth of Alasha's thumb.

Mount it as if it were a horse, he had commanded.

She put her bound hands on it and pulled herself out of the water. A wave of relief flooded through her as her legs and feet came clear of the icy flow, and the sun-warmed stone started to revive them. She managed to swing herself astride the rock, and perched on it with her knees bent and the water just kissing her toes. She kept her arms straight, with her hands between her legs and holding most of her weight.

It didn't seem too uncomfortable, and she couldn't help wondering what her tormentor hoped to achieve by ordering her into this position.

She found out as soon as she glanced at Mussuf. He had been watching her as she climbed onto the outcropping, and once she was securely in place, he urged his horse further along the bank. The rope at Alasha's wrists tightened and pulled her hands away from the rock.

Now her whole weight was supported on the narrow ledge of stone between her legs. She pulled down against the rope with her wrists and managed to relieve the pressure for a moment, but Mussuf kept backing the horse away.

Before long, her hands had been forced up to the level of her face. Her upper arms started to tremble, and then to ache from the unaccustomed strain, and she lowered herself back onto the sharp edge. The rope kept tightening, hoisting her arms further up until they were held taut above her head, with her fingertips just able to brush the smooth bark of the bough from which she hung.

She pulled herself off the rock again, until her wrists began to hurt from the abrasion of the wet hemp. She fished for the rope with her fingers, but her wrists were tied so tightly that she couldn't grip it. Her shoulders were starting to hurt horribly.

Alasha lowered herself back onto the rock and twisted her neck until she could see Mussuf.

He seemed happy with the length of the rope; he was hitching it to a tree limb. Once it was secure, he put his hand on it and plucked it like a harp string, sending a vibration along its length that Alasha felt through her whole body.

"I am weary after the work of raising you to that position," he called. "I will sleep now, leaving you to reflect on the folly of seeking to escape, and of prophesying doom – most particularly when your words come true."

He tethered the horse again, and then he lay down under a tree and covered his eyes with his arm.

Alasha looked up at the rope and the tree limb from which it hung. Perhaps she could lift herself up and stand on the rock ... it might be less painful against the soles of her feet than against her groin. She bent her arms as far as she could, managing to pull her face up to the level of her wrists.

"I told you to mount the rock, not to stand on it. Don't make me weight your ankles, girl."

Mussuf wasn't asleep yet. Alasha lowered herself again, holding her crotch away from the rock at the expense of her aching wrists. She knew that she wouldn't attempt to cheat this punishment a second time: even if the Arbian fell asleep, he could wake up at any moment, and things would surely then be even worse for her.

She pushed her legs back down into the freezing water, bare heels scrabbling against smooth rock. The water came up to her thighs, but she managed to find some purchase and the pressure on her wrists eased a little.

The movements of her legs had opened her sex slightly, and she found herself pressed against the smooth stone even more intimately than before. It was hard and cold, but it was quite bearable in a perverse way, as long as she didn't rest her full weight on it.

If only the rock were wet, perhaps I could slide myself back and forward along its length.

She raised one thigh abruptly, trying to splash some water onto the outcropping. It didn't work, so she tried again with her other leg. That didn't work either, but it didn't matter any more: the jiggling of pussy against stone had achieved what she wanted, and she was sitting in a slick of her own juices.

Her calves and feet were becoming uncomfortably cold, so she released her heel-grip on the rock and bent her legs up and out of the water, taking her weight on her arms again. The sudden sensation made the rock beneath her even wetter, and she squeezed her thighs together to lift herself away from it slightly, and then lowered herself again, sending a bolt of pleasure through her body to mingle with the discomfort of her constricted wrists.

Alasha's world closed in until it contained nothing except for harsh rope, rushing water, and the slippery hardness of rock against pussy. She pushed herself up again and let herself back down. A tiny rogue orgasm caught her by surprise, and she found herself with her legs trailing in the icy stream again, scrambling for a foothold as the pressure of the rock against her intimate parts became too intense.

She tried to judge how long she remained on the rock by watching the angle of the sunbeams that slanted through the trees. As far as she could tell, Mussuf slept through the entire morning. Alasha spent the hours alternating between abusing her wrists, forcing her legs into the cold water to take her weight, and torturing her pussy against the rock in a delightfully painful way. The morning settled down into a series of long build-ups during which the condition of her arms and legs grew steadily more intolerable until the suffering climaxed in an uncontrolled wriggling that would send another orgasm shooting through her body.

Each time she came, the cold and the constricting discomfort receded for a while: she seemed to be floating in the warmth of afterglow instead of hanging above the swirling water. But the warmth never lasted long enough; all too soon she came back to reality and found that her arms were hurting more than ever, or that her feet were becoming numbed by the icy stream. Then the slow, firewater-fueled journey from pain to pleasure would start all over again.

When the sun had just passed its highest point, she realized that someone was speaking.

"You seem to be enjoying your position more than I intended, girl."

Alasha made no reply: she was still panting from her latest orgasm, and only vaguely aware that Mussuf was standing by the riverbank instead of sleeping under his tree.

He loosed the rope very suddenly, so that she toppled off the rock and into the water. The current was strong, and she was unable to plant her feet firmly on the riverbed; the torrent swept her downstream until the rope went taut again, and then Mussuf was hauling her back to the river bank.

She lay for a while on a pile of leaves, shivering as much from the heights she had discovered suspended from the tree as from the depths of the icy river.

Mussuf let her dress herself and sleep in the sun for a while, and then he gave her a swallow of firewater and a strip of dried meat to chew. The heat of the liquid made her craving for the stuff recede for a while, and the meat brought some strength back to her limbs.

The hours spent on the rock had sated her for a while, but now Mussuf's drink was running through her veins again, raking the embers of her desire. In a perverse way, she was glad that he hadn't allowed her more than a sip: her enslavement to the potion was such that she would have emptied the flask if he hadn't snatched it away, and then she would have been desperate to have him take her again.

They followed the stream down through the woods: he told her that this was a tributary of the River Issing, and that they would reach the ford in a few more days. When they came out of the woods, they called at a post inn, where Mussuf sold Alasha's horse for a purse of silver that he stashed in his saddlebags. After that, she followed behind him, tethered to his saddlebow by her wrists as he rode along the side of the road.

Alasha knew that every step brought her closer to Issing Ford, where Mussuf would certainly sell her for as much silver as he could get. She tried not to think about that, or about how she would manage without firewater, once he departed with his dwindling stock of bottles.

Instead, she retreated into a world of daydreams where she summoned Aric back to life and placed him at Issing Ford, waiting to rescue her. If she made herself deny that she had seen him slain, she could almost believe that it had been him harassing the wagons, killing the guards, coming to claim her. Each time, though, she ended up seeing his last moments in her memory again, watching as he fell from his saddle with the black-feathered shaft piercing his breast. Then, she knew that the pursuer must have been no more than a bandit, a random attacker who happened to match the tale she wove for the discomfiture of the Arbians.

Whoever the mysterious warrior had been, she couldn't help but be impressed by his fighting skill – but she also couldn't deny that he'd missed the trail and allowed Mussuf and herself to escape. For all she knew, the man had fallen to the Arbians' arrows and blades, and died in the circle of burning wagons.

Even if by a miracle her lover truly lived, how would he find her once she had been sold to the keeper of some squalid whorehouse? Aric Albigenses had hardly seemed to be the sort of man who would frequent such places.

Issing Ford was a small town in the process of becoming a big one. The bustle of construction and trade was everywhere, yet the roads were still no more than muddy tracks. As Alasha followed Mussuf's horse across the ford, she saw dozens of pine trunks stacked near the water, surrounded by huge coils of rope, piles of wooden pegs, and great barrels of pitch. It was plain that they were building a bridge, and that the name of Issing Ford would soon be outdated.

They stopped at the first tavern they came to. The place was little more than a shack: built of fire-blackened timbers that might have been salvaged from some conflagration, roofed with sprouting sods, and surrounded by a sea of mud.

"The taverns and brothels near the ford are often unpleasant," said Mussuf, "because they serve the scoundrels and vagabonds who dare not venture further into the settlement. I judge that you will enjoy dealing with such men, so perhaps I am doing you an unintended service by selling you here."

"Then let us go further into the town," said Alasha, praying that if she was to be sold, it would at least be to a better establishment than this.

"No. The men who use this place have nowhere else to go, so the prices are higher. Which means I will get the most silver for you here."

"But you do not have my papers…"

"Documents mean nothing in a place like this. You are collared and leashed by my rope. That is enough."

He hitched his horse to the rail that stood near the door, took the tether that was still fastened to her wrists, and led her inside.

The air was thick with pipe smoke and the reek of unwashed bodies, but at least the room was warm. Most of the windows were tightly shuttered, and the few that had glass panes were filthy from years of neglect, so that the atmosphere was gloomy and stifling.

A dozen or so men sat around crude tables and along a counter made of rough-hewn logs, dressed for the most part in filthy smocks and badly cured skins. Their accents were harsh and guttural in Alasha's ears: she could barely understand what they were saying. Every head turned as Mussuf urged her through the door and led her across the room to a vacant table.

"A bottle of wine," he called to the tavern keeper.

The man brought a pottery flask and a cup of darkly aged leather, and set them on the table. "Two silver pieces for the wine, and a copper for the cup."

Mussuf counted out three of the coins he'd received for Alasha's horse, and looked around the room.

"This one is for sale," he announced, nodding at Alasha. "I understand there is a back room, where it is customary to sample the goods before buying. Anyone may use it before making a decision, at the cost of five silver pieces."

"Five silver for a quick roll on the floor?" asked one of the men.

"I wish to discourage all but genuine buyers," replied Mussuf with a broad smile. Alasha noticed that he had only sipped his wine, and that his hand never strayed far from his dagger.

One of the men approached the table and pulled up a stool. As he sat down, Alasha saw that his clothes were of finer quality than most, even if they seemed much mended and seldom washed. His cheeks were ruddy and his close-cropped hair was flecked with gray. His eyes were of piercing blue.

"I'll take her to the back room," he said. "But then I want first option on buying her. What's your price?"

He didn't take his eyes off Alasha as he spoke, as if the Arbian held no interest for him at all. She saw the man's gaze travel from her face down to her breasts, which were barely concealed under the gauzy costume she wore, and then move on to her legs and ankles. He ended up staring at her feet, or perhaps at the ground, and that was where his attention stayed while he waited for a reply.

"You may have her for two hundred silver pieces, friend," said Mussuf.

The man looked back up at Alasha's face, and then dropped five coins onto the table. "You will untie her wrists."

Mussuf drew his dagger and sliced through Alasha's bonds, and the man took her by the hand. Alasha rose to her feet and followed him to the door at the back of the tavern.

"What is your name?" he asked.

"Alasha."

"I am called Merik."

Alasha couldn't think of anything to say. She was sitting on a pile of dirty sacking, leaning against the wall. He squatted opposite her with his eyes downcast, as if unwilling to meet her gaze.

"Alasha is an unusual name for a slave girl," he said at last.

"I was not born to this."

"I knew it! I could see your blood was noble, from the way you walked. Even with your hands bound and following a leash, you moved with such aristocratic grace..."

"Thank you."

"Then my suspicions are right? You are high born?"

"My mother was Matriarch of her own lands. I was tricked into signing a document of indenture by my stepfather." Even as she spoke, she wondered why she was sharing this information with a stranger, but she was too weary to keep it secret. It hardly seemed to matter any more.

"Would it please you to be treated as a Lady again? Perhaps by a man such as myself?"

She studied him more carefully, and the pieces of his male puzzle started to fall into place. Under the ragged clothes, he seemed clean and well muscled, and if she understood him correctly, he represented a much better chance than she would be offered by any of the men beyond the door.

Alasha decided to risk everything on being right. She made her voice hard and cold. "What makes you imagine you could possibly deserve to serve me?"

His face told her that her boldness had paid off, and that her guess had been a good one.

"Nothing, Lady ... but if it was permitted to hope..."

Alasha's mind raced, seeking the unfamiliar words that would give her what she needed – and him, too, if she judged correctly. After a while he shifted and raised his eyes, and she dared delay no longer.

"Hope is always permitted," she said. "Fulfillment is more difficult to come by."

He was speechless for a moment, which Alasha found very satisfactory. Then he jumped up and offered her his hand again. "If you would follow me, Lady, while I settle some business, and then if I might have the honor of escorting you home?"

"I believe I can allow that, if you continue to behave yourself," she said, as she accepted his hand and permitted him to help her to her feet.

A gray-haired woman opened the door of Merik's house.

"Lady Alasha, this is Marla, my housekeeper. Marla, the Lady Alasha will be staying with us. Please will you see she has everything she needs?"

"Aye, my Lord." Marla's words sounded humble enough, but the look she shot at Alasha was full of resentment. Her gaze traveled up and down Alasha's body, and her sneer made it very clear what she thought of her visitor's bare feet, inadequate dress, and evident station.

She held the door open while they entered the house, and then stalked away, muttering something about unexpected guests and more work for her poor tired hands.

Alasha had no experience of dealing with men like Merik, but she knew she had to learn quickly. His desire to please her was the first good thing she had found since the death of her lover, and she pondered long and hard on how to make the most of it.

"Is there anything you require, Lady?" he asked, when they were alone in his parlor.

"A bowl of hot water would be welcome, so that I can warm myself and clean the muck of the road away."

He glanced at her feet, which were filthy after all her barefoot wanderings, and hurried away. She was expecting the grumpy housekeeper to return with the water, but Merik brought it personally, together with soap, towels, and a bottle of fragrant oil. He laid these down in front of the couch where she sat, and then to her surprise he knelt on the thick carpet of his parlor and started to bathe her feet.

"So exquisite," he whispered as he applied the soap. "Such delicate ankles, such shapely arches…"

Alasha smiled to herself as she stored this information on his interests away: another piece of knowledge that she could use to strengthen her hold over the man.

When he had finished washing her, he took the warm towel and dried her carefully, and then he picked up the flask of oil.

"Would you permit me to anoint your feet?"

Alasha leaned back in her couch and stretched her legs towards him. She remembered how the Arbian dancers' legs had looked longer and more elegant when they pointed their toes, and did the same.

"You may anoint me," she said, "but not while you are so over dressed. And if you tickle me, you shall suffer the consequences."

"Of course," breathed Merik, and scrambled out of his clothes with a haste that was almost comical. The body he revealed was hard and lean, and his bobbing cock showed how much he was enjoying this experience. Alasha found herself watching him with critical approval. As soon as he was naked, he poured a slow stream of oil into his hand, and warmed it carefully before taking her foot in both hands. He started to work the scented ointment into her sole and between her toes.

Alasha relaxed and let the comfort of warmth and intimate attention wash over her. It did tickle a bit, and she decided to have words with him about that later if it seemed useful, but it was also most pleasant – in part, perhaps, because her final sip of Mussuf's potion hadn't yet worn off. She knew she'd be desperate for more of the stuff in a day or two, but for now, the worry of how to get further supplies disappeared under the skilful ministrations of her new owner's hands.

If that was the right word for him. It seemed that he was her slave as much as her owner, or at least that was what he desired.

"The other one, now," she commanded.

"Thank you, Lady. I pray that you never fear to order what you desire from me."

He poured more oil into his palm, and attended to her other foot with infinite patience.

Alasha was beginning to find the sensation completely delightful. She allowed him to continue for as long as she could stand, and then she decided to reward him – and herself.

"Now you may kiss me," she said. "Start with my feet, and work your way up. Slowly. If you miss a single part, you shall pay for it dearly."

Merik went completely still, and Alasha wondered whether she had misjudged him, whether his desire went no further than kneeling before her and bathing her feet. Then he stooped, very slowly, and she understood that he had simply been unable to believe his good fortune.

She felt the touch of his lips on her toes, and then his warm tongue flicked out to taste them. It tickled more than his hands had, but Alasha was now so relaxed that it hardly mattered. Merik seemed hesitant at first, as if fearful that she would flinch from him, but soon his tongue was exploring her lovingly, pushing moistly into the delicate clefts between her toes.

"That's good," she murmured, and hooked her other foot behind his neck to let him know he should linger there for a while. "Do it again."

He withdrew his tongue for a moment and then it returned, freshly moistened, to probe her once more. This time, he spent longer in each place, flicking into and out of the spaces. Alasha was aware that her soft sighs were turning into deeper moans. The sensation was exquisite, but it had more to do with teasing than with satisfying. She wanted more.

"Suck me," she gasped.

Instantly, his lips were around her big toe and he was rocking his head back and forward as he suckled her. Barbed shafts of pleasure ran through her foot and up her leg and found their target somewhere near the pleasure bud that she intended him to reach before the end of the evening – but only after a long, drawn out journey of delight.

The sensation was too intense to bear for long. "The other one," was all she could say, and he instantly switched his attentions to her other foot.

Alasha felt the wetness that was soaking out of her, and briefly wondered how costly the couch was. She scooped up the towel from where he'd dropped it next to her, and arranged it on the seat between her legs. After that, she relaxed completely.

"Start moving up now," she said.

Merik began to pay attention to the rest of her feet, covering them thoroughly with tiny kisses and tasting each part with his tongue. Then he moved to her ankles and her calves, except that he seemed eager to proceed more quickly now, and she had to reprimand him several times to make him pause long enough to give every part its proper due.

Finally he reached the tops of her thighs, and there she made him delay for longer than she – or he, going by the noises he made – could really bear, because she was learning that delaying things made the eventual reward all the more explosive. So, when she finally told him to "Do it!" it seemed only a few heartbeats before she was riding the wave of her first orgasm, and forcing his mouth hard against her sex with her fingers twisted tightly in his hair.

10 merik

When Alasha was finally done with him, Merik remained kneeling before her, looking up at her as if waiting to be told what to do next.

"Is there any other task I may perform for you, Lady?"

"You may show me the house."

"Very well, if you would follow me?"

First, he led her upstairs to the sleeping quarters. "This will be your chamber, if you will have it. My pallet is in your antechamber. Thus you may summon me should you require anything, yet have privacy if that is your desire. I trust that will be acceptable?"

Alasha looked at the man, wondering if he really wanted to sleep on the thin mattress in the tiny entry hall, or if he hoped to be invited to share the comfortable quarters he had provided. *Probably a bit of both,* she decided. *Perhaps I should leave him out there for a while, and then take pity on him and order him to bed.*

In truth, although she had delighted in his attentions so far, and although she was beginning to enjoy the sense of power that his eager subservience brought, in some ways her new position was no less disturbing than her old one had been.

I suppose I'm more comfortable as a slave, obeying orders, than as a Mistress giving them, she thought. *Still, it makes a nice change.*

Above all, she knew she had several tasks – such as obtaining more firewater, and finding out what had happened to Aric – for which the services of such a devoted servant might be indispensable.

From the bedroom, he led her into a bathroom with marble tiles and a deep tub made of smooth, black stone.

"I shall heat water whenever you desire it, naturally," he said. "And this will be your private bathroom. There is a cistern room in the old servants' quarters that I will use."

"I'm glad to hear it," said Alasha, "though I might require you to attend me here on occasion, if I judge that you deserve such favor."

The look of gratitude in the man's eyes was almost too much, but she controlled the urge to laugh. Something told her that open mirth would ruin everything, and bring this entertainment to an abrupt end. Instead, she decided to ask him about the household.

"You mentioned the servants' quarters. Won't Marla and the others remark on you using their facilities?"

"Oh no, Mistress. I live in this house alone. The servants have lodgings elsewhere in the grounds. They are few, and very discreet."

"I see. Well, let us continue."

He took her down to the kitchens.

"Not that you'll ever need to come in here, of course, unless you wish to inspect anything. When Marla has left for the evening, I shall do the cooking and the cleaning."

"Naturally," said Alasha. "I trust you'll perform these tasks to my satisfaction."

Merik gulped. "I shall try my best."

"What other rooms are there?"

"Well, apart from the floors you have seen already, there are only the cellars."

"Show me."

He lit a candle and led her down the stone steps, and Alasha understood what a man can achieve when he tries to build his dream.

There was a tall cage in one corner, and manacles hung from the walls. Braziers and whipping posts were set in the floor, and an ancient-looking rack dominated the center of the room.

Alasha looked at her host, understanding a little more of his nature.

"Very impressive," she said. "I have noted several things about your performance so far that have been less than satisfactory. Unless you find a way to redeem yourself, I fear we shall be testing some of these devices before the day is out."

The blood left Merik's face, and he moaned – perhaps from fear, perhaps from desire. Most probably, she decided, from a mingling of both.

"Please let me know what I can do to make amends," he stammered at last. "If there is anything."

Alasha pretended to consider for a while.

"I desire something from the man I was with before."

"Yes, Mistress?"

"He took many things from me, and he still has some things I need. Have you the skill to recover them for me? Answer truthfully, now. I cannot command you truly unless you are honest with me."

"I am not inexperienced in such matters. Name the missing objects, my Lady, and I shall obtain them."

"I require some bottles that he keeps in his saddlebags. It would also please me to interrogate the man himself, in a place such as this. Can you arrange these things for your Lady, slave?"

"Mistress, it shall be done."

"Good. If you manage everything to my satisfaction, I might be merciful, and perhaps whip you slightly less severely than I had planned."

"Thank you," he said hoarsely. "If it is permitted for me to go and make the arrangements?"

Alasha gave a single nod to indicate that he had her assent to leave, and Merik fled from the room.

At breakfast the next morning, Marla the housekeeper bustled in and out, piling Merik's plate high, but scarcely bothering to serve Alasha at all. Merik kept apologizing and transferring food from his plate to hers, and in the end Marla relented, providing Alasha with toasted bread, poached eggs, and a steaming cup of tisane.

Alasha didn't ask how he achieved it, but once Marla had left, Merik informed her that there were a dozen bottles of firewater on her bedside table and an extremely angry Mussuf chained in the cellar, stretched out on the rack and awaiting her pleasure.

Alasha finished her breakfast and hurried back to her bedchamber, eager for another dose of the potion.

She'd been worrying about the instructions she'd given to Merik, and she was relieved that the business seemed to have gone well. It wasn't as if he understood the reasoning behind them, or the importance of the drink to her, yet she'd expected him to follow her orders without question. Which was exactly what he seemed to want to do, but still…

There had also been the question of his ability to complete the task without problems. Despite his assurances, she knew that such things could not be accomplished without risk. Alasha would hardly have been able to live with herself if her helper been harmed while following her orders. Only the urgency of her need had led her to assign him such an errand.

Alasha pushed such thoughts aside. Her craving for the drink was growing stronger by the hour; during the night, she had woken to find herself shaking with the beginnings of a fever. She felt better once it grew light, but she knew that it was only the beginning: another ominous warning of the changes Mussuf's drink had wrought in her, and of the price she might have to pay for the rest of her life.

Unless I can wean myself off the stuff slowly, she thought. *Perhaps if I just take a sip...*

No sooner had the first drop touched her tongue than she was greedily swallowing more; by the time she mastered herself, the bottle was half empty, and she understood that breaking this enslavement would not be so easy.

At least the craving had subsided, and she felt warm inside again.

Merik had provided several costly gowns and an array of other clothing that he seemed to hope she would wear. As she flicked through the wardrobe, examining the silver-studded leather and figure-hugging corsets that hung there, her eye caught a remarkable pair of shoes at the bottom of the closet. They were like nothing she'd ever seen before: made of fine-grained black leather, but with a rigid shape that would force the wearer to stand on tiptoe, with her heels supported by wicked-looking spikes that curved down to sharp points. Alasha had little doubt that they had come from some Marlish workshop, and couldn't help wondering how anyone was supposed to balance on such things without instantly toppling over.

Cruel and impractical they might seem, but their shape was strangely seductive, more elegant than any footwear she had ever imagined. She scooped them up and slipped them on, steadying herself against the bedpost and watching her reflection in the long dressing mirror.

Alasha understood immediately why Merik had given her the shoes: they made her look utterly ravishing. She was already blessed with long, shapely legs, but these shoes transformed them ... she took a small step, still clutching the bedpost, still watching herself.

The shoes transformed the way she moved, too.

I'm going to have to learn to walk in these, thought Alasha. She released the bedpost and wobbled closer to the mirror, balancing precariously on the spikes. The shoes were uncomfortable but not painful, and Alasha found the sensation of wearing them – of sacrificing comfort and ease in the name of feminine elegance – to be astonishingly arousing.

Perhaps the fire drink was filtering her perceptions again. It didn't matter. She went back to the bed and practiced walking around it for a while, in order to be close to something soft and forgiving in case she had to sit down quickly.

When Alasha visited the cellars, she found Mussuf in an unhappy mood.

"I'll see that you pay for this, you Xendrian bitch." He glared at her and rattled his chains, twisting his body against the rack. "I suppose you're going to stretch me, now."

"Perhaps," said Alasha. "Though I won't tire myself by turning the wheel personally. My slave is here to handle that."

Merik was standing close by, watching Mussuf and waiting for orders. His eyes were almost popping out of his head, and she smiled to herself, wondering whether she should order him to undress: the cellar was cold and he'd probably enjoy being stripped and left to shiver.

She shook her head: she had a job to do. Perhaps she'd indulge him with such attentions later.

"You're not stupid, Mussuf," she said. "Tell me the recipe for the fire drink; then I'll have no need to hurt you."

"But–" said Merik, his disappointment showing in his voice.

"Silence, slave. Well, Mussuf?"

"You have no right," said the man. "I did nothing that you would not have chosen for yourself, if you spoke truthfully."

"Apart from having Aric killed, and forcing me to take your fire drink, and every other thing that happened while I was in your hands."

"You would have desired it anyway, firewater or no. I have owned sluts like you before, constantly in heat from morning 'til midnight; I recognized your nature straight away. You should be grateful that my potion gave you the excuse to rut like the bitch you are."

Alasha put a gloved hand on the rack wheel and toyed with the spokes for a moment.

"Perhaps we should begin, then."

"Break my body if you will, but I shall never give up the secret of firewater. You northerners know nothing of the art of torture: the worst pain you can inflict here is less than a pale shadow of what my brother Arbians do to those who sell their secrets. I will never speak. At best, you will consign my knowledge to the darkness of the grave."

Alasha looked into his eyes and saw that his words were true: he feared his own people far more than he feared her. She didn't intend to break him in any case: she wanted to repay the pain he had caused her, but not at the cost of killing or maiming him.

She made a decision. "Very well, we will do this another way. Slave?"

"Yes, Mistress?"

"I require four of the bottles that you brought to me, from my bedroom."

"I hear and obey." Merik padded from the room.

By the time he returned, Mussuf's teeth were so tightly clenched that Alasha had to prize them open with a steel spike. At last, she forced the neck of one of the Arbian's flasks into his mouth, and heard its contents gurgling down his throat.

"How many do you suppose it will take to bring you to the place where I am now?" she asked.

He made no answer except to swear at her, so she fed him another bottle, and then a third.

"One more, I think," she said. "It's more than it took for me, but you're so much bigger; four should be enough, don't you think? That will leave a few flasks to keep me going while you consider where your future supply is to come from."

The fourth bottle emptied into Mussuf's throat, leaving him snarling and swearing even as he jerked his hips up and down against the chains.

Alasha watched him for a moment and then sent Merik to fetch one more bottle, just to be sure.

Mussuf still showed no inclination to co-operate. Alasha hadn't expected him to, not until the thirst and the fever started. In the meantime, she picked up a riding crop and led Merik back upstairs, leaving her former captor to his own devices. The man's shouted orders for someone to release him and bring him a woman echoed up the passageway after them.

Back in the parlor, Alasha turned her attention to Merik. He had been most helpful in obtaining the firewater, not to mention kidnapping Mussuf: she hadn't realized how resourceful he would be.

Or perhaps he held more power in this town than she imagined.

"What is your profession, slave?"

"I am a trader, Mistress. My ships sail to other lands, laden with our Xendrian produce, and then return with more exotic cargoes."

"Such as these pretty shoes." Alasha stretched her leg out from where she was sitting on the couch, and flexed her ankle so that he – and she – could admire the workmanship.

"Indeed. They were made in a Marlish factory: the tinkerers have perfected a technique of forming the sole into the required shape, and making the heel strong enough to bear a lady's weight."

"Then the tinkerers are even more to be admired than I imagined," she said. "I am pleased with them, and with you, and in token of this I will deduct two lashes from the tally you have earned."

"Thank you." Merik paused for a moment, and gulped. "Mistress, may I know how many strokes now stand on my account?"

"You may not. You will trust me to keep this reckoning, and if I should make any errors and assign you extra lashes, you will accept them humbly and gratefully."

"Of course, Lady. Thank you."

In truth, Alasha was simply concealing the fact that she had no idea how many lashes would be appropriate for the man. As far as she was concerned, he had served her well, and his coming thrashing was more of a reward than any kind of punishment. Still, she feared that the magical effect she had on him would be spoiled if the truth became clear, so she worked to keep her voice harsh and her methods mysterious.

One thing was certain: Alasha couldn't help wondering how it was going to feel to have a riding crop in her hand, and a man's bare backside in front of her, all hard and dimpled and wriggling. She remembered exactly what it was like to be on the receiving end of such treatment; part of her was curiously eager to taste that exquisite blend of pain and excitement again.

For the moment, though, she was even more fascinated by the thought of being at the other end of the whip.

"You are wearing too many clothes," she said.

Merik undressed hurriedly.

"Can you hold still for your punishment, slave, or will it be necessary to bind you?"

"I will submit to whatever you desire, Mistress."

"Then I will bind you. Fetch rope."

He hurried away, and returned with several lengths of thick cord.

"Bend over that chair," said Alasha. "Put your rump in the air and your hands on the floor."

She stooped and bound his wrists to his ankles, so that he was bent double over the back of the chair.

"Now. You must try to keep still."

"Yes, Mistress."

Suddenly, Alasha was seized with doubt. The bare bottom in front of her looked so fragile, and she hated the thought of hurting its owner and of raising the red welts that she knew would come.

Merik had closed his eyes, and she saw that he was trembling, as if awaiting the first blow with religious anticipation – or dread.

I have no choice, she thought. *I cannot disappoint him now.*

She raised the crop and brought it down hard on the man's rump.

He yelped and wriggled, and Alasha paused, horrified by the livid mark that sprang across his buttocks.

"Thank you, Mistress," said Merik.

That reassured her slightly, although she was still dismayed by the thought of striking him again. She paused, trying to think of a way to buy time, to find out how much of this he could bear.

"So, slave, you have tasted the first blow. How many more do you think you deserve? If you come within three strokes of the number I have in mind, I might permit you to attend my feet again afterwards. Otherwise, I will add further lashes to your tally."

"Ten, Mistress. I deserve ten more strokes," he gasped.

Alasha could see that Merik's cock was still hard, forced against his belly through the slatted back of the chair. That comforted her: it would be obvious if she went too far, in which case she could ease back on the force of the blows, or even stop for a while. In that case, she would say that she required the services of his hands and mouth – and from the tingling warmth she was starting to feel, there would be little need for pretence.

She decided to punish him a little more severely than he had suggested.

"The total I had in mind was twelve. That means your guess was close, slave. Perhaps I will reward you for that."

She cut him with the crop again, and heard him yelp and watched his naked haunches quiver under the blow.

As the beating went on, Merik cried out ever more loudly, but his cock stayed hard and he thanked her for every stroke. By the end of it, his rump was criss-crossed with a dozen angry weals, and Alasha's pussy was soaking wet.

She set the riding crop aside and untied Merik's wrists. He stayed bent over the chair for a moment before straightening, and even when he stood up he kept his gaze firmly on the floor.

Or perhaps he's staring at my shoes, thought Alasha, as she spread a cloth on the couch and sat down again. "Why are you still on your feet?"

He dropped to his knees, instantly.

Alasha decided that she didn't want to be bothered with giving him detailed instructions. "Tonight you are to please me in your own way," she said. "I simply wish to take my ease and enjoy your attentions. You may clothe or unclothe me, and attend me as you will. Simply remember that it is in your own interest to give me complete satisfaction."

"I understand, Mistress."

"Good. Then proceed, slave."

"Then may I remove your gown?"

"I have placed myself in your hands, for now."

Merik went around to the back of the couch, unfastened her gown, and eased it gently down past her shoulders before returning to kneel before her. She raised herself slightly so that he could slide it down over her legs, and then lifted her feet, taking care to keep the sharp spikes of her shoes clear of the delicate fabric.

She felt his hand trembling between her breasts as he undid the lacings of her underbodice, and then he was helping her out of that, too.

Now she was as naked as he was, apart from her shoes and her collar. She heard him gasp as he saw her piercings.

"Why?" he asked.

"I bear them because they are mine, slave. Do you not find them pleasing?"

"Oh, yes."

"Good. Then continue."

"I would ask you to lie down," he said.

Alasha swung her legs up onto the couch and leaned back. Merik turned her onto her face with gentle hands, and placed a pillow under her head.

Then he climbed onto the couch and carefully straddled her.

She heard the soft popping of a cork from a flask, and a slow splash of liquid. There was a short pause before she felt his slick, warm hands between her shoulder blades, and then he was pressing with gentle strength along the length of her spine.

Alasha gave a sigh of contentment to let him know he was pleasing her, and abandoned herself to the warmth of Merik's massage as his fingers sought out tense muscles and weary bones.

Before long, his touch became as arousing as it was relaxing, and she had cause to be glad of the cloth between her loins and the couch. Merik seemed to sense her excitement too, because he moved his attention downwards: first to the small of her back, and then to her buttocks.

After so many occasions when nakedness had meant nothing more than vulnerability, the comfort of his oiled hands on her bare skin was utterly delightful.

The touch of his lips at the base of her spine, when it came, was even better. "Mmmm. That feels really good."

That seemed to encourage him: he pressed his tongue against her flesh as well as his lips, and kissed his way down into the cleft between her buttocks.

Surely, he didn't mean to…

"If it is permitted, Mistress?" he asked, almost in a whisper.

Alasha hesitated for a moment. *Why not? It won't be the worst thing that's ever been there, and it might even feel quite nice.*

"It is permitted," was all she said, and then his tongue was circling the entrance that nestled between her bottom cheeks.

It felt much more pleasurable than she would ever have expected, and when at last he pointed his tongue and darted it into the opening he'd been caressing, it became even better.

"Mmmm. Keep doing that for a while."

He was as good as her word. Within a few heartbeats, Alasha felt herself stiffening against the couch and thrusting her bottom harder against his face as he brought her to the first climax of her evening.

As soon as she came down, he urged her gently onto her back, and knelt next to the couch again. He spent some time kissing her fingers and then her hand, and slowly moved his way along her arm until he reached the hollow of her neck.

Then he moved down to her breast, and circled his tongue around her nipple before sucking it into his mouth and biting it very gently. Too gently, Alasha decided.

"Harder, if you want me to feel anything," she said, and he bit down on her more firmly, sending jangling spasms of pleasure directly to her brain, and opening up another tingling pathway down through her belly to her secret pleasure bud.

Alasha waited for as long as she could before she seized him by the hair and thrust his mouth down against her pussy. He spent some time cleaning up the juices that had soaked her intimate curls and run over her thighs, and then his tongue was lapping at her hidden pearl, and she was coming again and again.

It took two days for Mussuf to fall ill. Merik had transferred him into the cage, and he sat in one corner glowering at her with bloodshot eyes. His face was pale and covered with sweat, and his garments were stained. From the way he kept shifting his position and adjusting his breeches, it was clear that his monstrous cock was painfully stiff.

"I am sick," he said. "Give me one of the bottles, or I shall die." He groaned extravagantly, as if to underline his point.

"I require them for myself. Tell me the recipe, and you'll get what you need."

"Give me a bottle and swear to tell no one. Only then will I divulge the secret." As Mussuf spoke, his hand moved to his groin and he started to rub himself.

Alasha looked away. "I will need to verify your recipe before you receive any of the drink. It would be better for you to co-operate now, otherwise it might be too late. Think on how long the preparation takes, because that is how long you will wait between telling what you know and receiving what you need."

Mussuf slumped back into his corner, defeat showing in his eyes, along with a hint of fear. "Fetch me pen and parchment, then. I will write you the recipe we use in Xendria, since the Arbish spices are unobtainable here. I warn you: it is less sweet than the true potion you tasted before, but it works in the same way."

Alasha took the bundle of paper and the quill that were standing ready, and pushed them into the cage.

Mussuf started to write as she watched.

It was late evening by the time she finished with the first batch and set the bottles to cool. They smelled authentic enough, but she had no intention of tasting them. That would be a task for Mussuf, the following morning.

In the meantime, it was long past time to retire to bed.

Merik was waiting in his antechamber, in case there was anything she wanted before she slept. He was naked, and Alasha chided herself: she had forgotten to instruct him to dress after stripping him earlier in the morning, and he had spent the whole day unclothed. It didn't matter, though: he seemed happy enough with his condition, judging by the state of his cock.

She regarded him in a way she hoped was cold and commanding. It seemed to work: he was unable to meet her gaze, instead keeping his eyes directed firmly at the floor.

"Well, slave, were you comfortable on your pallet last night?"

"Indeed I was, Mistress. Thank you for asking."

"Have you folded my clothes? Polished my shoes? Cleaned my bathroom?"

"All is done and ready for your inspection, Mistress."

"Good." Alasha looked around her bedchamber and then walked into the bathroom, checking that all was neat and clean. "Everything seems to be in order. So tell me, slave. You endured your beating like a man two nights ago, and you services since then have provided me with sufficient satisfaction. Do you believe that you deserve to be rewarded?"

"I leave that in your hands, Mistress."

"Then my hands are what you shall have." She stepped before him and brushed her fingers over his cock. "Did you believe you deserved more?"

His whole body sprang to attention, imitating the response of the part she had touched. "No, Mistress. Your hands are far beyond anything I expected."

Alasha slid her fingers fully around him, and twisted her hand up and down a couple of times. Merik started to whimper.

"It needs some lubrication, I think," she said. "But first, this gown is constricting me. Help me off with it."

He worked with nervous haste, unfastening the little hooks and eyes that ran down the back of her dress. Once it was open, he lifted the garment off her shoulders and hung it in the wardrobe. Alasha removed her under-shift while his back was turned, and dropped it on the floor. Merik kept his eyes averted from her body as he scooped the shift up and folded it over a chair.

She approached him and dropped her hand to his groin again. This time, she fastened her fingers around his balls and grasped them so tightly that he winced.

Alasha leaned close to his ear. "You see, it's not all about pleasure, is it?"

"No, Mistress."

"Come." She kept her grip tight as she led him to the bed and guided him down onto the sheets; then she settled down next to him. There was a bottle of oil on the bedside table, and she poured some into her palm and started to massage him.

The familiar sensation of firewater soon filled her blood, and she was tempted to take him in her mouth, or to mount him and ride him, but she knew that was not part of this game. He already believed he was receiving more than he deserved, so she must restrict herself to caressing him with her hands.

Or with my feet, perhaps, she thought. *He stares at them so often, and he seemed very interested in them on the first night, and then there were the beautiful shoes...*

She bent one leg onto the coverlet and pressed her toes against his cock. She was rewarded by a gasp of surprise: his whole body shuddered, and she half thought that he would explode on the spot.

Alasha placed her other foot on his body, between his belly and his straining shaft, and pressed down with so that his manhood was trapped between the top of one foot and the sole of the other.

Merik went completely silent. His eyes were closed, and beads of sweat stood out on his forehead.

She started to move the arch of her foot up and down his shaft, and then snaked her free hand between his legs to seize his male jewels again, squeezing them roughly. As if in response to the pressure, a single droplet of clear fluid oozed from the tip of his cock and dripped onto her ankle.

She could see that he was struggling very hard to keep from spending himself.

Perhaps he was waiting for permission. She kept rubbing him between her oil-slicked feet for a few more heartbeats, and then she took pity on him. "You may come, slave."

He gasped again, and the drop was followed by a gout of hot seed that arced through the air before splashing across the foot that she had pinned across his belly.

Merik opened his eyes and gazed down at what he had done, his face a mask of horror.

"I'm so sorry, Mistress. That was unforgivable … I fear I lost control. Please let me make amends."

"When I order you to come, I expect you to come. If I choose to have you come on my feet, I expect you to do so. Is that clear?"

"Yes, Mistress. Thank you."

"Good. Now, fetch a bowl and a towel and clean me up."

While he was gone, Alasha pondered the question of where he should sleep. She would have liked him to warm her bed, but she suspected that he would be happier banished to the pallet in his ante-chamber, possibly to be recalled to attend her later.

Alasha sighed. It seemed that every man in the world – apart from Aric – was either obsessed with worshipping her, or with abusing her.

Mostly the latter, she thought. *At least this is less painful, and there's no denying it makes a pleasant change. Still, there is something to be said for the other, as Merik would plainly testify. I wonder how Aric and I would have fared in truth, if he had no desire to play these games? He had every opportunity to command my service, yet he showed no interest in such things…*

In the end, she sent Merik back to his lonely bed, and resolved that she would summon him again as soon as she woke the next morning, in order to compel him to pleasure her with his mouth.

After that, she hoped she might persuade him to step outside his role for an hour or two: to spend some time beside her on the pillows, simply holding her.

11 brotherly love

"I fear I must depart on business, Mistress. With your permission, of course."

Merik was regarding her nervously over the breakfast table, and Alasha wondered what would happen if she refused.

"Explain yourself."

"I am in partnership with my brother. We take turn and turn about, staying at Issing Ford to look after our trading affairs here, and journeying around the land to oversee our enterprises elsewhere."

"Then your brother will be here while you are away?"

"Yes, my Lady."

"What manner of man is he?"

"He is unlike me, Madam, but he will surely take good care of you."

"Very well. You must not neglect your affairs, Merik. You have my leave to depart. I trust you will keep your eyes open for suitable gifts for me?"

"Naturally. Thank you, Mistress. I must leave this morning. I was hoping to see Ensis before my departure, but I cannot delay any longer: I must inspect one of our ships before it sails. Perhaps my brother is tarrying at one of the post inns, and I will meet him on the road."

Alasha smiled at him. In the few days that she'd known him, she'd grown fonder of the man than she would have believed possible, both for his services and his company – even if his nature stopped him from satisfying every aspect of hers.

"I hope it will be so. I wish you a safe journey and a swift return, Merik."

Merik blushed and stammered his thanks, and then hurried from the room.

Alasha went to her bedroom window as he rode away from the house, and watched until he was out of sight. She hadn't expected to miss him so soon.

After a while, she decided to distract herself by considering what to do with Mussuf. *Perhaps it would be best to discuss the matter with the man directly,* she thought, and carried two bottles of freshly made fresh fire drink down to the cellars.

Mussuf was exactly as she had left him, except that he looked even worse. He had hardly moved since the day before. The plate of food that waited just inside the cage hadn't been touched. His head swung up as she came into the room, and she saw his eyes fasten on the flasks she bore. He licked his lips.

"Please," he said.

She pushed a flask between the bars. Mussuf's hands trembled as he uncorked the bottle and drained its contents in one long swallow.

"Ah. That feels better."

"Then your recipe was good."

"Of course it was good, girl. I knew I would be your poison tester. Do you take me for a fool?"

"No, Mussuf. I would never take you for that. A brute, but not a fool."

"Well, you are wrong on that count as well. All I am is a dead man, once my brethren hear of my treachery."

"Is there nowhere you can hide? No one who will help you?"

"Who will protect a penniless Arbian abroad in Xendria, where we are treated no better than dogs?"

"You might find protection here," said a strange voice. Alasha turned and saw an older version of Merik standing at the bottom of the cellar steps: almost his twin, except that he was perhaps a little taller and had more gray in his hair.

"Welcome," she said. "You must be Ensis."

"And you must be Merik's new plaything. He told me all about you when we met on the road."

"Plaything is not a word I would use," said Alasha, carefully.

"I honestly don't care to bandy words with a slave girl. I understand my brother paid for you, and I see he neglected to remove your collar. Your status is clear."

Mussuf sniggered behind her, and she turned to face him.

"At least I am not the only one with problems, it seems," he said.

"Indeed," said Ensis. "Perhaps your problems may be solved more easily than hers."

"More easily than hers? What do you mean?"

Ensis picked up one of the flasks and studied it for a moment. Then he opened it and sniffed its contents. "My brother tells me that these vapors hold your soul in thrall, Arbian. Is he right?"

Mussuf just nodded and glowered.

"Then you cannot travel easily, and you have nowhere to go. Even your own people would hunt you down as a renegade. Only I am prepared to protect you."

"Really? I have no doubt your protection would carry a high price."

"My price is simply that you sign a piece of parchment and swear an oath, undertaking to serve me faithfully."

"In other words, you wish to make me your slave, as she is."

"There are many kinds of slave, Mussuf. There are worse alternatives, as you will discover if you choose to leave this house, for I will not detain you against your will. I understand you were master of your own caravan once; do not think that your skills would go unused."

The Arbian hesitated, visibly weighing his options.

Ensis came further into the cellar and stood close to Mussuf's cage. "I am offering you protection and status in this household, man. I'm offering you a supply of the drug that you need. I ask only for your oath of loyalty to me and mine."

Mussuf scrambled to his knees next to the bars, and extended his hand. "I accept your offer, my Lord."

"Good. Let him loose, girl."

As Alasha moved to unlock the cage, Mussuf met her gaze and gave a twisted smile. What she saw in his eyes was the glitter of triumph and the flame of desire, fanned by the fire drink.

"Why is my brother's room full of your things?"

"This is where he placed me."

"You will address me as 'Master', or 'my Lord'."

"Yes, my Lord."

"I suppose Merik slept on that pallet in the antechamber?"

"He wished it so, my Lord."

"Well, I do not wish it so. Find a bed in the servants' quarters. That gown isn't fitting for your station, either. You may leave it here."

Alasha stripped to her shift and hung the gown in the wardrobe.

"That's better. I see he bought you some shoes."

"Yes, my Lord."

"And you enjoyed them."

"Yes, my Lord."

"Good. Why aren't you wearing them now, then?"

Alasha looked down at the comfortable slippers she had put in that morning. "I wore them for him in the evenings, my Lord."

"You wore them for him in the evenings." Ensis reached into the back of the wardrobe and pulled out another pair of spiked shoes, equipped with silver chains to adorn the wearer's ankles, and even higher than the pair Merik had given her before. "I love my brother," he continued, "and I would have his gifts of love used to the full. Put these on."

Alasha took the shoes from him and sat on the bed while she pulled them on.

"Put your legs up on the bed."

She obeyed, and Ensis sat next to her and fastened the ankle chains. Alasha saw that they were furnished with tiny silver padlocks, and he snapped these closed so that the shoes were tethered to her ankles.

"There. You'll not be removing these soon, will you?"

She stared at her feet, trapped in the impractical shoes. She knew from experience of the previous pair how uncomfortable such footwear could become after a while. How was she to manage this pair, that were so much higher – and impossible to remove?

"No, my Lord, I will not."

"Good. Now leave me, and find your new quarters. Attend me at sunset. Perhaps I may unlock the shoes."

Alasha made to leave the room.

"Or perhaps I may not," he added darkly, as she made her unsteady way out of the door.

The shoes became very uncomfortable, very quickly.

They forced Alasha to adopt a most disagreeable, tip-toed stance, with her arches straining and her calf-muscles protesting. Her body was tipped forward, so she found herself curving her spine and throwing her shoulders back in order to keep her balance – a feat that she could only manage by walking with a wobbling gait, and taking very short steps.

They were far more difficult than the previous pair.

Half way up the winding stairs to the servants' quarters, she slipped and only saved herself by clutching the step in front of her. Her hand twisted awkwardly, and she felt hot tears streaming down her face – as much from shock and anger as from her sprained wrist.

Why couldn't I be satisfied with things as they were? How stupid I was, wishing for something more than Merik could offer, without thinking how it would be if my wish was granted … this is all my own fault.

At the top of the stairs, she caught sight of herself in a tarnished wall mirror and caught her breath. The shoes might be painful to walk in, but there was no doubt about the change that they wrought in her posture and movements.

There was also no doubt that the embers of enslavement, which had lain almost dormant during her time with Merik, were already beginning to smolder again. She thought of Ensis and wondered what he might expect of her later. There was no telling: he was so very like Merik, but so different as well.

Perhaps it would be worth it, after all.

Alasha passed most of the day in the room she had chosen, walking up and down in order to accustom herself to the precarious heels. When she could no longer walk, she rested on the narrow bed, rubbing her calves and trying to squeeze her fingers under her arches so that she could massage her aching feet.

She hoped she would get used to the shoes soon, or that Ensis would take pity on her and unlock the chains.

When the bell from his rooms jangled above her door, she hastened back down the stairs, eager to give him the opportunity to do exactly that.

"Well, girl, you seem to have acquired the knack of making this

Arbish firewater. Mussuf tells me that your product is first class."

"Thank you, my Lord."

"I think we should go into production. There are profits to be made with stuff such as this."

"But, my Lord…" She hesitated, afraid to arouse his anger.

"Yes?"

Alasha decided to risk voicing her opinion. After all, this was Merik's brother: he couldn't be completely unreasonable.

"First, the firewater is dangerous. I have seen what it has done to me, and now to Mussuf. Neither of us can last more than a day or two without tasting the drink, or we fall ill. I think perhaps we would die in the end, without supplies of the potion."

"Agreed. I'm planning to hold the first trials in a business where Merik and I already hold an interest, so that we can control how it is taken. Once it is accepted, we may offer small samples to noble houses, where they will be used with proper care. After all, there's no point in having our customers falling ill and dying, is there?"

"No, my Lord. Then there is also another problem…"

"Well?"

"The Arbians, my Lord. They hold that the secret of this potion is rightfully theirs. I believe they might object to any rivals in the trade."

"Perhaps they will, though we are far from Arbish lands, and merchants who keep their best products for themselves can hardly complain when others offer them to the world. Were there any other objections?"

"No, my Lord."

"Good. Know that I am pleased that you thought this matter through, and that you saw fit to speak up."

"Thank you, my Lord."

"Tomorrow, you are to go to the kitchens and spend the day manufacturing more of the potion."

"I understand, my Lord."

"Good. Then you'd better get some rest. Return to bed."

Alasha looked at him blankly. She hadn't expected to be dismissed so quickly.

"Do you not require anything of me, my Lord?"

"No."

She looked at his face, trying to see whether his eyes contradicted his words, but he turned away.

Alasha pressed on, greatly daring. Even she didn't know whether she was trying to provoke a response, or if she simply wished to be rid of her footwear.

"And the shoes, my Lord?"

"You really are a most persistent slave, aren't you? I feel sure my brother has spoiled you beyond redemption."

She lingered in the doorway, wishing he would summon her back and make some use of her, even if it was only to tie her up, or to beat her, or to take some pleasure from her mouth.

Even if he left her locked in the impossible heels afterwards.

"It will do you no harm to spend a night wearing the shoes. That will be all, girl."

"Good night, my Lord," she said, as she closed the door very gently and made her unsteady way back to her room.

This is how Merik must have felt when I sent him back to his lonely pallet, she thought. *I suppose he was fortunate, wasn't he?*

Alasha teetered into her room, desperate to take the weight off her feet by collapsing into the bed. The last thing she expected was that Mussuf would be reclining on it, waiting for her.

"I have taken the chamber across the passage from you," he said. "Being neighbors will be most pleasant, for old friends like ourselves."

Alasha thought quickly. "Ensis has commanded me to rest, so that I may give my full attention to my work tomorrow."

"And rest you shall, when we are done here."

"Our Master would not wish you to touch me."

"Then why has he housed us on the same corridor?"

There was no answer to that. Perhaps Ensis meant to offer her to Mussuf after all – there could be no doubt of his eagerness to recruit the man, with all the promises of protection and status he'd made.

Perhaps I am part of the deal, thought Alasha.

"Come, girl. Surrender yourself. Your Master plainly wants me to have you. I want you. If you search for the truth in your own heart, you will admit that you want to be had, too."

Yes, I want to be had, but not by you … I want to be had by Merik, or by Aric, or even by Ensis whom I scarcely know. But not by you.

She didn't give voice to that thought, though. Perhaps she simply feared him, or perhaps the vapors of the fire drink were once more seeping into her brain.

Alasha backed towards the door, moving carefully in the heels, cursing how helpless they made her feel. The sound of her beating heart was loud in her ears.

Mussuf rose to his feet. "You will not outrun me in those."

She knew he was right. Outside the room, the corridor stretched in both directions. Even if she made it to the end, he would catch her in one of the stairwells – or, more likely, she would simply trip and fall, to be scooped up like some prize at an Arbish bazaar.

"I'll make you an offer, girl."

"Yes?"

"When the time is ripe, I mean to break my addiction to this stuff." He indicated the flasks of firewater that stood next to her bed. "There are rituals that must be timed according to the stars, and cleansing herbs to be collected under the appointed moon."

"Go on."

"It is not a journey for the uninitiated. You would never find your way through the dark rites alone. But give me what I wish, and I will free you too when the time comes."

"I hardly need ask what it is that you wish," she said.

"Indeed. I wish your co-operation in everything I desire to do to you, and with you. Your obedience to me as if I were your Master, whenever we are here in these quarters. And you must breathe no word of this to our other Masters."

"And why should I trust you to keep your word, or even believe that this sickness can be cured?"

"Do I seem worried about a lifetime's enslavement to the drink, girl?"

It was true. He'd been terrified of the vengeance that his country-men might take, but he'd never shown any concern about his need for the firewater. Perhaps he told the truth, and there was a way to break the chains ... *and anyway he will take whatever he wants, whether I will it or no.*

"Very well," said Alasha, feeling her heart sink as she spoke. "I agree to your terms."

"Good. Then I will begin by having you strip for me."

She pulled the shift over her head, and stood before him, exposing all the smooth skin and feminine parts that she'd thought he would never see again.

"I cannot remove the shoes," she said.

"Then you may keep them. The parts I wish to use are already on display, and the shoes are pleasing enough in their own way. Now, lie on the bed, and raise your knees against your shoulders."

Alasha sat on the bed and leaned back against the thin pillow. The mattress was hard, stuffed with straw, and for a moment, she thought regretfully of the feather comforts in Merik's room. The coverlet was made of roughly spun wool, and it felt harsh and coarse under her naked body.

She pulled her legs up, just as he had ordered, and looked down at herself. She could see her breasts, pert and proud and pressed almost together between her lifted knees, and between them peeped the dark curls of her sex, which she had no doubt would soon be receiving Mussuf's most forceful attentions. Her whole body seemed to be framed between her raised legs, and set off by the black leather of the hateful shoes.

The mattress moved slightly as Mussuf sat next to her, and then he was placing a blindfold over her eyes.

"In a way, I am initiating you into your first Arbish rite," he said. "The ritual of blindness is often performed on our slaves. First with the cloth, and later with hot iron, once the girl has learned to appreciate the joy of the dark."

For Alasha, there was no joy in wearing Mussuf's blindfold. It simply made her feel more naked, more vulnerable, and more helpless in the face of whatever else he chose to do. She lay on the bed, straining with her other senses, trying to guess what would happen next.

Something soft brushed her lips, seeking entry into her mouth. She clenched her teeth against it and twisted her head aside blindly, but the thing followed, pressing harder until she surrendered and parted her lips to accept it. It seemed to be a tightly wadded cloth that expanded as soon as it was in place, drawing her mouth's moisture into itself, leaving her feeling parched and dry. Mussuf kept ramming more of it in, until she feared she'd choke on it, and then she felt him tying something behind her head so that the cloth was held firmly in place, filling her mouth with its dry, musty flavor.

"This is the second ritual," he murmured. "The blinded girl is deprived of the use of her tongue: first with the gag, and later with hot pincers, once she has learned the value of silence."

Alasha squirmed against the mattress, and started to protest. All that came out were small mewling noises.

Now he was working at her collar, and she felt the coldness of iron and the clinking of chains. Her hands were encircled by cold links, and tethered to her neck and then to the bedstead.

Now Alasha was truly helpless. She thought of what she had done to him in the dungeon, and wondered what revenge he was about to take. She started to tremble, even as a familiar warmth reached her loins.

"The third ritual. The girl is blind and mute, and she is deprived of the gift of movement. First with a tether, and then with a sharp blade, once she has learned the joy of remaining close to her owner."

Alasha made a muffled yelp and tried to sit up, but the chain pulled her up short. *What does he mean to do to me?* she thought desperately. *What have I allowed him to do?*

She could smell her own fear, mingling with arousal.

There was more clinking, this time down towards her feet and then at the top of the bedstead. She'd already been holding her legs open and against her shoulders, exactly as Mussuf had commanded, but now they were pulled even further up and further apart, and she realized that he'd attached chains to her shoes somehow, and tethered them to the top of the bed frame.

She tried to wriggle upwards, to relieve the pressure that held her open and bent her double, but her head was already jammed between two iron uprights and she could go no further.

"The fourth ritual," murmured Mussuf. "The girl is quartered and spread wide. First with chains and with the promise of pain, and then by the remnants of her own will, once she truly understands that she is owned."

The mattress shifted again, and she sensed that he was moving into the position where he would be able to inspect his handiwork, and have free access to all the parts that he had spread so wide, so vulnerably open.

She felt his fingers testing the wetness she couldn't control, tracing a pattern outside the lips of her sex, and then slipping inside. She did her best to keep still, but she could not stop herself from bucking under his touch. She knew from Mussuf's chuckle that he had felt it too.

"I think you understand," he said. "I think that this blindfold and these chains are no more than adornments, for you. I think you know that you are owned."

Then his hands left her, and he slapped her on the face.

The gag stifled Alasha's yelp of pain, and all that emerged was a muffled whine.

"This is the first repayment for what you have done to me," he said.

An instant later, his cock entered her. It felt bigger than ever, as if the potion had caused it to swell to an even more unnatural size, and if it hadn't been for the gag Alasha would have cried out in distress.

Judging by the steady rhythm he adopted, the potion had done wonders for Mussuf's endurance, too. At first, his thrusts were stabbing pains that he sent lancing up into her belly, and then they became a throbbing ache, ebbing and flowing with the depth of his penetration.

Somewhere, half-obscured under her discomfort, there was also a slow build of firewater arousal. *Or is it more than that?* she wondered. *Is this a deeper enslavement?*

Alasha tried to push such weakness aside, to hold on to her hatred of this man and his abuse, to resist the easy escape into submissive pleasure.

It was hopeless. If anything, the bondage that blinded her and stopped her mouth and held her body so tautly open was what pushed her over the edge and into her first orgasm.

After that, Mussuf's first climax arrived quickly. She heard the man's deep grunts as his pleasure built, felt the hot splash of his seed invading her womb, and then she was twisting against the chains in panic, because it was like fire; his seed was like liquid fire, burning deep inside her body.

He kept moving in her as her stifled whimpering turned to moans of pleasure, because within a heartbeat the fire had re-lit the smoldering embers of pleasure in her belly, as if Mussuf's seed was imbued with the fiery essence of the Arbish potion itself.

He kept moving, building to a second climax, and then a third, until Alasha's cup brimmed over and ran onto the coverlet, and the fire-potent seed spilled over her naked skin as well as into her womb.

When he was done, she remained on the bed, unable to lift her bruised, abused body even after he'd unchained her. He left her alone in the darkness, left her listening to the door closing behind him, and then to the snores that soon rumbled across the corridor. As she drifted into a fitful sleep, she couldn't help wondering how many flasks she'd need to make once the potion's effect on the size, stamina and productiveness of the imbiber's male parts became widely known.

Alasha held herself stiffly as she regarded herself in the mirror, examining the finger marks that Mussuf had left across her cheek.

She couldn't let Ensis see her like this.

It wasn't so much that she had sworn to keep her servitude to Mussuf a secret. It was more a question of her own embarrassment, of allowing herself to be treated in such a fashion. She knew that Ensis and Merik owned her and had the legal right to do whatever they wished with her, but Mussuf was a slave now, just like her.

She was also mortified by the knowledge that it would happen again, night after night, for as long as Mussuf desired it. Every night of the rest of her life, perhaps. She imagined herself pinned to the bed again, the hapless protagonist in an endless story of blindfolds and chains. The thought turned the blood to ice in her heart, but it also brought the heat of Mussuf's seed back to her loins.

She found some cosmetics in the servants' bathroom, and applied some flesh-colored cream to her face, obscuring the marks. She repeated the treatment on her other cheek, to make both sides look the same. Then she applied powder, in order to disguise the cream.

When she'd finished, Alasha decided she didn't look too bad.

I hope he doesn't hit me every time, she thought. *It seemed to be in revenge for what I did to him with the firewater. But that was no more than what he had already done to me.*

She decided to speak to him. If she submitted to his desires willingly, perhaps she could persuade him not to strike her … even if the man was a complete brute, surely he would understand that Ensis, and most particularly Merik when he returned, would not tolerate their slave girl being damaged like that.

Yes, I will speak to him, she told herself. *The man can be reasoned with, after all.*

By the end of the day, she had prepared eight crates of the fire drink, each containing a dozen flasks. There were two flasks left over: one each for Mussuf and herself. When Ensis came into the kitchens to inspect her work, he seemed pleased.

"You've done well, girl. It's good that you read well enough to follow Mussuf's recipe: perhaps my brother made a better bargain than he knew. Go to my study now, and follow the instructions that await you on my desk."

Alasha wobbled towards the stairs, wincing as she moved. After her day of kitchen work, she was getting a little more accustomed to the shoes, but her body was still stiff and bruised from the night before. Her calves ached horribly from the strain of balancing in the spike heels, too, and her feet were painfully sore.

She didn't turn to look, but she sensed Ensis's gaze following her until she turned the corner into the passage outside.

Please let him follow, and take these shoes off me, she thought. *Then, please let him take me.*

Ensis had his own suite of rooms on the second floor, and Alasha found his study without difficulty. There, on his polished desk, was a folded square of parchment with her name written on it in elegant letters.

So he knows my name after all, even though he only ever calls me 'girl'.

Alasha picked up the note and read the instructions it bore.

Alasha,

Remove your shift, and your shoes. The key that unlocks your ankle chains is in the top left drawer of my desk.

When you are naked, go into my bathroom and bathe yourself. On your return to this study, you will find a second note with further instructions.

Ensis

Alasha shrugged the shift over her head, then folded it carefully and laid it on a chair. The key was in its appointed place. She sat in Ensis's chair, shivering slightly at the cold touch of the leather upholstery, and lifted her right ankle onto her left knee.

The silver padlock was tiny, and it took a while to coax the key into its slot, but eventually the lock snapped open and the chain fell away from her ankle with a light tinkling sound.

She slipped the shoe off, then set about freeing herself of its partner. As soon as she was barefoot, she rose from the chair with a sigh of relief, glad to be standing on deep, yielding carpet instead of cruelly curved, unforgiving leather.

Her legs and her spine relaxed gratefully too, though there was a tight ache in her calves, as if muscles and tendons that had become accustomed to the spike heels were protesting at being stretched again.

It is well that I did not stay locked in them for another day. I hope I am allowed enough time to recover, else I might become a slave to the shoes just as I am to the fire drink.

Alasha checked behind several doors before she found Ensis's bathroom, where she drew a pitcher of warm water and bathed herself, letting her abused body relax under the soothing flow. She used one of his towels to dry herself, and found a bottle of scented ointment to rub into her aching feet.

She heard no sound in the study, but when she returned there was a second note on the desk, just as the first one had promised.

In the second drawer, you will find a drawstring bag and a pair of manacles. Place the bag over your head, draw the string snugly closed, and tie it to your collar.

When you are satisfied that the bag is secure, use the manacles to fasten your wrists behind your back. Take care not to over tighten the locking mechanism – I do not want you bruising yourself. That is a job for others.

Once you are prepared, recline on the floor next to my desk, balancing on your elbows and with your legs spread so that you are open and available to whomever might arrive.

Ensis

Alasha set the note down and sat in the chair again. As promised, the manacles were in the second drawer, gleaming against the dark velvet of the bag. She lifted both items out and laid them on the desk.

The bag was heavier than it looked, and she wondered for a moment if she'd be able to breathe once it was tied over her head. She slipped it on and held it to her face, and found that she could draw sufficient air through the material. With the bag loose, she hoped it would be easier.

Alasha groped for the manacles to make sure she could find them on the desk, and then she tightened the drawstring and tied it securely to her collar.

She found the manacles again, and slipped one wrist into their cruel embrace. Her free hand found the jaws and closed them gently, feeling the click that the Marlish mechanism made as it took hold. Then she reached behind her back, holding the remaining bracelet in her shackled hand, and carefully locked it around her free wrist.

Now, where was I supposed to recline? By the side of the desk, or in front of it?

A light sweat broke over her body: she couldn't remember the rest of the instructions.

Perhaps I could slip the manacles down to my feet and step through them. Then I could remove the bag, and read the note, and put my wrists behind me again … but that was not part of my instructions, either.

She decided to remain as she was, and to take a chance on being wrong about the position she was to adopt. She wondered if she was being watched, and started to tremble: she knew that any deviation from her orders would earn Ensis's displeasure.

Alasha stood up and shuffled forward until she felt the cold edge of the desk against her thighs, and then she moved sideways until she found its corner.

I'm almost sure it was to be the side of the desk, she thought, hoping that she wasn't fooling herself. She took one step forward, and then lowered herself to the floor and reclined on her elbows, with her legs extended and spread wide.

Alasha had no way to judge how long she spent waiting in the room. She fumbled for her pulse behind her back, and managed to count several hundred heartbeats, but then the awkwardness of her position distracted her: the carpet that had seemed so soft and luxurious under her feet became harsh and unforgiving, and her arms began to cramp.

She wished she could sit up rather than reclining in this position, but Ensis's instructions had been clear.

Trapped in the timeless dark of the bag, Alasha's world was both confined and expanded. She heard many sounds that she had not noticed before: the creaking of the window shutters when the breeze caught them, the whinnying of horses and the clatter of wagons coming and going in the courtyard below, and distant bustle of the streets of Issing Ford.

As time went on and no one came to disturb her, her position became increasingly uncomfortable. She tried shifting from elbow to elbow in order to relieve the pins and needles that afflicted her arms, but it was of little help. The manacles started to cut into her wrists, too, where her weight pressed them against the floor.

There came a moment when the tedium became even worse than the pain in her shoulders and arms, and that was when, for the first time in her life, Alasha departed from her body.

She found herself hovering near the ceiling, looking down at herself and listening to her own muffled breathing. She could see how her arms were trembling from the effort of supporting her weight, but the discomfort was gone.

Alasha swooped down effortlessly to examine herself more closely.

The bag covered her head completely: all that could be seen was a few dark blonde curls that had tumbled between its neck and her own. Apart from that, there was no hint of who she was.

The fragility and thinness of her body took her breath away for a moment: she was seeing herself from a new perspective, and it had been months since she'd taken the time to consider her naked reflection in a well-crafted mirror. Nevertheless, her recent life seemed to have suited her: she looked as healthy as ever, and to her critical eye, she appeared to have lost weight in all the right places. Alasha had always been a slender girl, but now her waist was tinier and her belly tauter than she ever remembered them. Her skin was flawless, and her body was toned and lightly tanned.

At least my breasts haven't shrunk like everything else, she thought. *Anyway, since this is plainly no more than an illusion of some kind, there is no reason to believe what I see.*

With that, the spell was broken and she snapped back into her body, returning to the discomfort of her arms and the musty smell of the bag. She heard the click of the door latch, and sensed that someone was in the room with her.

If only I'd hung on for a few more moments, I might have seen who it is, and what he does. That would have told me whether the vision was real.

Whoever it was, he approached with a soft tread and stood close to her for a while, as if observing her. Then she sensed him sitting down behind her, and herself being drawn back between his legs to rest her body against his.

Firm hands caressed her shoulders and then her breasts. Strong fingers pinched her nipples and tweaked the rings that pierced her there, and she felt herself stiffening under his touch.

"Who are you?" she whispered.

"Hush," was the only reply he made, and there was no hint of anything she recognized in his voice.

Her manacled hands were pressed against his groin, and there could be no doubt of his desire, yet he maintained perfect control over himself. His fingers quested down over her stomach and found their slow way between her legs, and he started to caress her, collecting the juices of her arousal and trailing them up onto her belly and out to her thighs, painting her flesh with the medium of her own lust.

He held her and caressed her until she came, and he continued to hold her tightly until the final instant when her orgasm was done, as if he were the bowstring that pulled her back and aimed her arrow towards its target, and then released her.

With that, he was gone, and she heard the door closing behind him. Somehow, he had released her hands without her even noticing.

Alasha raised herself from her prone position and knelt on the floor. Her fingers found the knot that fastened the drawstring to her collar, and she fumbled the bag open. Everything was just as she'd left it: the pieces of parchment, the key to her manacles, her shoes and her shift. If it wasn't for the fact that her hands were free and her loins were soaking, she'd have wondered if the entire thing hadn't been a dream.

She pulled herself together, collected her shift and shoes, and left Ensis's apartment. It was dark outside the windows, and she was sleepy. As she made her way back to her chamber in the servants' quarters, she wondered if Mussuf would be waiting for her.

Mussuf was indeed in her room, and he seemed to be in an exceptionally foul mood. He made no move to strike her, though.

Instead, he ordered her to her knees while he made use of her mouth. Before the taste of his cock and the heat of his seed had faded, he threw her onto the bed, forced her legs apart, and fucked her hard. Finally he made her kneel in the middle of the mattress and bent her over a pile of pillows, and made a third use of her.

He remained silent the entire time. His hands on her were forceful and rough, and the attentions of his cock were even more brutally urgent than usual, but at least he didn't hit her again.

12 the firewater trade

"I wish you to put on some sensible clothes and shoes, and to carry a sample of the fire drink to the house where it is to be sold," said Ensis.

"Very well, my Lord. Where must I go?"

"The enterprise is a new one, recently established by a consortium of Arbian women." He handed her a scrap of parchment bearing a scrawled address. "Male Arbians don't approve of females engaging in trade, which is why I'm sending you rather than Mussuf."

"I understand, my Lord."

"These women have also asked me to increase my investment in their business. I'd like you to cast your eye over the place, and bring me your report. Negotiate a price for the firewater, if you think it wise."

"You would trust me in this matter, my Lord?"

Ensis looked at her quizzically. "Don't imagine that I underestimate you, girl. The fact that I consider you my body slave doesn't mean I'm unaware of your other abilities."

His words filled Alasha with confusion, and she made no reply, but simply lowered her gaze submissively.

"Well, what are you waiting for?"

"I'm sorry, my Lord. I shall go immediately."

When she got to the kitchen to collect a case of the fire drink, she noticed that one of the boxes stood on the table. Its lid had been prized off and one of the bottles was missing.

Perhaps Ensis has been sampling it, she thought. *Perhaps it was him in the study last night after all … though surely he would have not have been able to resist taking me, if he had consumed one of the flasks?*

She shook her head and decided to think about it later. For now, she must simply deliver one of the full crates to the address written on Ensis's parchment.

The house was near the center of Issing Ford, and Alasha was glad of the opportunity to have a better look at the town.

She noticed several new buildings shoehorned into too-small plots, as if the settlement was outgrowing the space available. The main thoroughfares resounded with the racket of saws and hammers as carpenters raised wooden walkways alongside the wheel-rutted roads.

They'll have paved avenues and covered sewers here within the year, she thought, as she picked her way across a particularly filthy patch.

Traders jostled through the streets, along with the carts and mules loaded with their wares. Alasha looked down at the crate she carried and imagined for a moment that she was a merchant herself, taking goods to one of her customers and playing a part in the growth of this community.

In a way, I am, she thought. *I was the one who got the recipe from Mussuf, and who made the stuff, and now I'm the one delivering it.*

That thought pleased her, and she started to walk with more of a spring in her step. Several male heads turned as she passed by, but Alasha pretended not to notice.

She found the address she sought easily enough. It was a tall structure, built of timber that still had remnants of bark here and there, and huddled between two larger buildings in a space that might once have been a coach yard. The shutters were painted red, and a red lamp swung over the doorway.

Ensis had told her that the women who ran the place were Arbian, but it was still a surprise when Zanya opened the door.

"Alasha," she said, and held out her hand. "You are welcome here."

Alasha paused before accepting the proffered hand. Zanya – and her friend Xero – had hardly treated her kindly when she was Mussuf's captive. Still, they themselves had not been free at the time, and their discomfort at Mussuf's cruelest actions had been plain. She couldn't find it in her heart to truly condemn them, and anyway, perhaps things would be different now.

She set her burden down for the moment, then reached out and took the girl's hand. "Thank you for your welcome, Zanya. I trust Xero is well?"

"She is well."

Zanya formed her Xendrian phrases as if they had been rehearsed, committed to memory as set-piece responses. Still, her accent had improved in the days since they had last spoken. Alasha couldn't imagine that the women would have had much opportunity to talk to anyone outside Mussuf's caravan, and her heart went out to them: here they were, alone in a foreign land, learning a new language and trying to start a business.

At least Ensis seems to be helping them, she thought, and a pang of envy stabbed her heart. *I wish he would pay as much attention to me; I wonder if he calls them by their names?*

She pushed her feelings of jealousy aside. Her soul belonged to Aric, not to Ensis or his brother, and if her first love truly lived, she knew that he would come to find her. *Ensis will be sorry then, but it will be too late,* she thought, and allowed herself a secret smile.

She entered the house and embraced Zanya, deciding in her heart to forgive the things that had happened between them, and to seek a fresh beginning.

They found Xero sitting on a bench in one of the inner rooms. There was fire pit built below an iron chimney hood, and the room was filled with a delicious warmth. Alasha felt at home straight away. She set the crate of firewater on a wooden shelf.

"It makes happiness that you come," said Xero.

"Thank you," said Alasha.

"Sorry for bad Xendrian. You wish for teach?"

"You'd like me to give you lessons?"

"Yes, lessons."

"Perhaps, if Ensis agrees to it."

"Ensis?"

"My master."

Xero frowned for a moment, as if she hadn't quite understood, and then her expression cleared. "Ah, yes. Ensis. You ask Ensis?"

"I'll ask him."

"Good. Thank you." She gestured at Alasha's mud-spattered shoes. "Roads is bad, no? You wish for bath, before business?"

"That would be good."

Xero rang a small silver bell and another Arbian girl entered, and led Alasha to a cistern room. There was a tub of steaming water waiting.

The girl waited while Alasha undressed. "I take, make clean," she said, picking up the muddy clothes and shoes.

"Thank you."

The Arbian disappeared, leaving Alasha to wash and dry herself, and then to wonder how long the cleaning of her garments would take.

Oh, well, she thought. *I'll just go back to the fire room and ask about my clothes. It isn't as if they haven't seen me naked before.*

When she arrived, the room was clouded with steam. Xero and Zanya were sitting side by side, wrapped in towels and wreathed in the vapors that issued from the fire pit. As Alasha entered the room, Xero ladled more water onto the hot stones, while Zanya handed her a fresh towel and made space for her between them.

"Thank you," she said. "I have never seen anything like this."

"Arbish," said Zanya. "New for Xendrians. *Zhauna,* we call it. Hot-water-smoke bath."

"Steam bath?" queried Alasha.

"Yes." The girl smiled. "Steam. Teaching has started, yes?"

"Yes, the lesson has started."

"Now we try firewater?"

Alasha reached for the crate and handed a bottle to Zanya and another to Xero. "Do you have many visitors, yet?"

"Oh, yes," said Xero. "They like steam bath, and they like Arbian girls. We make Arbish food, too. Now we have firewater, many more will come." She unstopped her bottle and sniffed it, then sampled a small amount of the liquid on her tongue. "Very good. Just like Mussuf make, here in Xendria."

She offered the bottle back to Alasha, who took a polite swallow and returned the flask saying, "Mussuf taught me everything I know."

Both girls laughed at that, and Alasha wondered how much they knew about how she had obtained the recipe. "What will you charge for it?" she asked.

"Charge?"

"Pay. How much will your visitors pay?"

"Oh! Here it is ten silver coins to buy one girl, fifty to stay one night."

"And how much for a flask?" Alasha held one of the bottles up, to make it clear what she meant.

"We try one hundred silver coins. Only for rich, yes?"

"Yes." Alasha thought for a while. Having the fire drink available would certainly help the Arbians' business, and it would be far less onerous to sell a bottle than to take a customer upstairs. Still, she wanted to treat them fairly. "We will charge you eighty silver coins for one bottle."

A look of dismay passed across Xero's face. "We cannot pay for box, then. Only for these two." She indicated the bottles that she and Zanya held.

They haven't been open for long, thought Alasha. *They have no silver yet. Still, it will come.*

"There is no need for you to pay until the box is sold. Then you pay me eighty for each bottle. That's, um, nine hundred and sixty, but those two bottles are a gift, so eight hundred." The amount of silver involved staggered her, even as she said it.

Neither girl seemed to follow her words. They conferred rapidly in Arbian, and then Xero turned back to her. "We sell first, pay when next box come?"

"That's right. And the two flasks we've opened already are yours to keep, as a gift."

"Thank you."

"You will be careful with this? Not too much for any one customer?"

"We know firewater," said Zanya. "What Mussuf did, very bad. For you. Mussuf very bad man."

"Not all bad," said her friend. "You make own drink now, as much as you wish. Can be good, yes?" She put her hand between her legs and pretended to rub herself through the towel, and all three girls collapsed into a fit of shared giggles.

While Alasha was recovering, Xero reached out and touched a lock of her hair.

"Gold," she said. "Not black, not like our hair."

Alasha looked down at the girl's slender fingers twined in her hair, and then her gazed moved up Xero's forearm and to her bare shoulder. For the first time, she noticed the delightfully smooth texture of the Arbian's dark skin, and smelled her exotic fragrance. Alasha felt suddenly shy, and looked down at the stone floor between her feet.

"Not gold," she said. "Gold is brighter."

"Gold not so lovely," said Zanya, moving closer to her other side and letting her towel fall open. The Arbian's hand found Alasha's chin and tilted it back up, and then she leaned in close and planted a deep kiss on Alasha's lips.

Alasha went very still for a moment, and then she returned the kiss with a passion that surprised her. Xero's elegant fingernails were trailing down her shoulder and along her arm, calling shivery crystals of ice into existence on the steam-beaded flesh. The humid heat of the room seemed to penetrate Alasha's loins, and she felt herself opening up like a flower blossoming under a new sun.

"Ten silver coins is not enough," she murmured.

Xero giggled again. "With men we do different," she said. "Very quick. Make them very happy, so they go away. For you, slower." Then she put her mouth on Alasha's nipple.

"Good. I don't want to go away," murmured Alasha, as Zanya lowered her gently down among the discarded towels.

Alasha's legs were opened wide, her thighs pressed against Zanya's shoulders. The girl had spent what seemed like hours there, first planting an uncountable number of delightfully intimate kisses, then flicking her tongue maddeningly over Alasha's pleasure bud, repeatedly bringing her to the very cusp of delight and then backing away again.

Xero knelt at Alasha's head, massaging her temples and occasionally leaning so that they could taste one another's mouths and play lingering, writhing tongue-games.

Captivating rivulets of moisture formed on Xero's breasts and ran down her belly. Some of them fell onto Alasha's lips, and she was consumed by the desire to taste more, to sample everything that the girl had to offer. She couldn't bear it any more. She had to do something, to experience an orgasm, and Zanya didn't seem ready to give her one of her own any time soon.

She reached up and seized Xero's hips, urging the dancer to move forward. Xero complied, and soon she was presenting two pert but-tocks to Alasha's eyes, and a holding a warm, wet pussy over her mouth.

Alasha kept her grip on the other girl's hips, and pulled down. Xero lowered herself eagerly, clamping her sex against Alasha's welcoming mouth and wriggling as if she wanted to cover Alasha's face with her most private, feminine scent.

Alasha paused for a moment, taking stock. Then she extended her tongue and ran it along Xero's vulva, just outside the lips of her sex. She felt the girl's taut legs grip her more tightly, and then spread apart as if to offer easier access to the depths they both sought. Alasha pushed her tongue into the opening that presented itself, and swirled it up and down. Xero rewarded her with a sweet sigh that told of nothing but yearning and desire.

The new sounds and movements seemed to excite Zanya as well, and the quicksilver pace of her suckling increased. Alasha's whole body began to tingle and spark, as if a lightning bolt was gathering itself in her loins. She made her tongue into a hard point and thrust it forward, seeking among the moist folds for Xero's secret pearl, hoping she'd be able to find the right spot.

As she touched it, the dancer's sighs became more vocal.

Zanya was pushing hard against Alasha's own hidden bud, rock-ing her whole body back and forth, and Alasha knew she was about to come. She sent her own tongue flicking ever more urgently over Xero's dripping jewel, and soon the dancer's cries of pleasure were mingling with her own muffled moans.

As they came back down to earth, Alasha saw Zanya looking at them with a satisfied smile on her face. Xero went down on all fours and squirmed her way between Zanya's legs, diving for her friend's pearl. Zanya parted her thighs and held out her arms to Alasha, who folded herself into the Arbian's embrace.

They kissed, so that Alasha's mouth filled with the taste of her own juices that still lingered in Zanya's, and then with the subtle flavor of Zanya herself.

They gave themselves to one another, their breath mingling and their ears filled with Xero's eager mewling as she explored the secrets of Zanya's sex. They kept their tongues touching one another for the entire time, until Alasha felt Zanya trembling in her arms and then becoming still. A wave of tender passion flooded through her, and it almost seemed as if she was climaxing herself for a second time.

As Alasha was leaving, she met Vermillio in the passageway.

She hooked her fingers into his shirt and pulled him into a small parlor. "What in the Gods' names are you doing here?" she hissed.

His mouth became a big O, before he covered it with his hand, and she remembered that he was younger than his manner suggested. Vermillio recovered himself quickly, though, and sat down in one of the over-stuffed chairs. "Ala. This is a most pleasant surprise. I never expected to see you again."

"My name is Alasha, not Ala," she said.

"My apologies, Alasha. I didn't know."

"Of course not. Emon re-named me when I came to be your teacher. Now answer my question: what are you doing here?"

"Lord Fiasco has come to Issing Ford. It seems he's heard of the growing number of pleasure houses here, so I've been sent to inspect this place, to see if the Arbians have anything new to offer him."

"They keep no boys here," she said shortly, "and the girls don't offer themselves to be whipped."

"I know. The mystery draws him, I think, not the girls. He's heard rumors of exotic steam rooms, and delicate sweetmeats, and Arbish love philters."

"My advice is to keep him away from this place, Vermillio. Fiasco's bad enough as he is: you don't want to be near him once he's swilled a flask or two of the fire drink."

"Then the stuff exists? I thank you for the warning. Now tell me, how did you escape? Fiasco said nothing, but his mood was foul when he returned."

"He lost me at cards," she said shortly.

"I see. Quinn and I miss you, Alasha, though I have no doubt you were glad to be rid of such troublesome students. Still, there are words I would speak to you."

"Go on."

"I know that I took advantage of you. Perhaps it's true that I forced you, and I cannot deny that I led Quinn to do the same, but we never meant you any of the harm that Fiasco commanded. I hope you know that."

Alasha thought back to the times she had spent lying on the desk in their classroom, displaying herself for them, obeying them, serving them. She felt herself blushing at the memory of it: how they had humiliated her, and how fulfilling it had been.

"I have no bitter feelings over that," she said, at last. "It wasn't unwelcome to me."

"Then you forgive me? And Quinn?"

"There's nothing to forgive. We all took pleasure from what happened, according to our natures. It's Fiasco who should ask for forgiveness, from all three of us."

"He will never do that."

"I know. He mustn't know I am here, Vermillio."

"I swear I won't betray you. He's sleeping in the house we've taken, in Silversmith Alley. If you leave now, you can make it home before he orders his palanquin and takes to the streets, seeking companions for the evening … he's already growing weary of Quinn and me. Would you tell me where you're staying? Perhaps we could call one afternoon, when Fiasco is asleep."

Alasha hesitated, and then decided to trust him. "At the estate of Merik and Ensis, though I'm afraid my position there doesn't permit me to entertain. In a few weeks it may be different, perhaps."

"Still, we should like to call if we get the chance, to see if you're free."

Alasha smiled at that. "I don't think I shall ever be free," she said.

When she got back to the house, Ensis was waiting for her. "How did the business go?"

Alasha realized that she'd been away for most of the day, and wondered if he'd be angry. "I believe that it went well, my Lord. They accepted the crate, and will pay for it after they have sold the flasks. I took the liberty of providing them with two sample bottles."

"Did you, indeed? And how much are they to pay for each of the others?"

"Eighty silver pieces, my Lord. Their visitors will pay one hundred."

"Then you've allowed them a fair profit. I'm pleased with you, girl. Did the place meet with your approval in other ways?"

"It did, my Lord."

He looked at her sharply. "I thought as much; you spent long enough there. Is there anything else I should know?"

"Only that I met one of Lord Fiasco's people there. Fiasco owned me once, and lost me in a game of cards."

"Then does he have any business with you now?"

"It's possible that he feels he was cheated … I may have inadvertently offered some assistance to the man who won me."

"Really. And what was his name?"

Alasha almost believed that she saw a twinkle in his eye. *He seems pleased with me,* she thought, and had to stop herself from smiling.

"Aric, my Lord," was all she said.

"Where is Aric now?"

"I don't know. I lost him."

"How careless of you. I suppose you regret it deeply."

"Indeed, my Lord. I do."

"What if he should come looking for you?"

"Legally I am still his. He holds my deeds of indenture."

"I see. Now, remember that I wish you to speak candidly: you won't suffer for telling the truth. Does this Aric hold your heart as well as your deeds, girl?"

"He does, my Lord."

"Alas for my brother, then. He seemed to think you have a certain fondness for him."

Alasha thought carefully about her feelings for Merik before replying. "Your brother wasn't mistaken, my Lord. I am indeed fond of him. I would even say I love him … but he doesn't have the strength to hold my heart."

"And do I have such strength?"

"I believe you have the strength, my Lord, but not the desire."

"So that's what you believe, is it? I see. Now, to other matters. There was a flask missing from the kitchen this morning."

"I know it, my Lord. I saw it when I collected the potion to take to the Arbians' house."

"And that was the first you knew of it?"

"Yes, my Lord."

"Then tell me why I found this empty bottle in your chamber, when Mussuf and I searched the house today?"

Alasha's heart filled with ice, and she began to tremble. *Mussuf.* She hadn't realized the depth of the Arbian's hatred. "I don't know, my Lord," she said finally. "I didn't take the flask."

"How strange that it should have ended up hidden under your bed, then. How do you suppose it got there?"

I dare not tell him, she thought. *Then the liberties I've allowed Mussuf to take with me would come to light, and I couldn't bear that.*

"I cannot say, my Lord."

"You cannot, or will not. Very well. I'll think on a suitable punishment for this theft. While I consider, you are to wait in my apartments, unclothed."

Alasha made to leave, but he stopped her with a word. "Wait. Unclothed, I said. You're to strip here, in my presence. Then you may go to my rooms."

He watched with critical eyes as she undressed. As she slipped out of the room, Alasha thought of the mortification she would feel if Marla, or one of the other servants, should see her like this – and of the possibility of meeting Mussuf, which would be even worse, after what he had just done to her.

Ensis's study was just as she remembered it, except that the manacles and the other evidence of yesterday's experience had been cleared away. Alasha stood near the door and waited for whatever might come.

She had no doubt that she was to be punished severely: Ensis must believe that she had stolen a flask of firewater worth a hundred silver pieces or more. *If only I could tell him the truth. Perhaps I will, if the punishment is severe enough. Perhaps I won't be able to help myself.* Alasha cringed at the thought of Ensis discovering her shameful liaisons with

Mussuf.

He seemed perfectly calm when he came into the room. "Now, girl. I've told you of the evidence against you, which is overwhelming. There can be no question of your guilt, or of the punishment that you deserve."

She simply shook her head, railing silently against the injustice, already feeling the tears starting behind her eyes.

"There's no point crying about it now. You should have thought of this before you stole the flask. Did you think that just because you made it, you had the right to take it?"

"I didn't take it, my Lord."

"Saying that won't save you, but I might. I'm going to give you a chance. I'm a fair and honorable man; you saw the offer I made to Mussuf, eh? Now, if you admit what you did, and swear never to steal from me again, I'll forget about this little mistake. It will be as if it never happened. So tell me, did you take the flask?"

She shook her head violently. *I won't dishonor myself by lying,* she thought. *And I've borne beatings before. At least he will have to touch me now, even if it is only with his whip.*

"Very well," said Ensis. He grasped the back of Alasha's collar and marched her to his writing table, where he bent her over the unforgiving surface. He found some lengths of rope in one of the drawers and tethered her wrists to two of the mahogany legs. He secured her ankles in a similar fashion, so that she was spread-eagled between the four corners of the desk.

"Marla?"

Alasha heard the housekeeper's footsteps approaching along the passage outside, and her heart sank.

"Aye, my Lord?"

"Discipline this one, would you? A dozen strokes, I think, unless you decide that more are needed. When you're done, wash her and lock her in her room, if you please."

"Aye, my Lord."

As he reached the door, Ensis turned to look at Alasha. "Consider the cost of your pride, girl. As each stroke falls, consider the cost of your pride."

Then he left, closing the door behind him.

"You should never have come to this house, young lady."

Alasha twisted her head to look at the housekeeper. Perhaps she didn't mean to administer the beating, after all. Perhaps there was a chance to reason with her. "What do you mean?"

"You've turned everything upside down. Things used to be so simple here, and now there's so much coming and going and I don't know who's where or what's what, and that's the truth. Not that truth seems to mean much to some people, lately."

This was all a complete mystery to Alasha. "I don't understand."

"Aye, and no more do I. I know I was harsh with you when you arrived, but that was just me being put out with all the disturbance. It's pity I'm feeling for you now, with the way he's treating you."

"Ensis, you mean?"

"Who else?"

"Will Merik come back soon, do you think?"

"I'm not the one to be asking about that, lass."

"I hope he comes back."

"Aye. You love him, I suppose?"

"Yes, I do. I think I love Ensis too, but in a different way."

"Well, that's hardly to be wondered at. What with them being so close and all, you know, and so alike, in many ways."

"Alike?" asked Alasha. "They seem very different to me."

"That's as may be. Now we'd better to get started on this beating, if we're ever to get it over, hadn't we?"

"I was hoping you might be able to forget about that part."

"Now I'd never go against the young master's orders like that, lass, and neither will you, if you're true to yourself. So tell me, would you like it fast, so it's over quicker, or slow, so there's more of a rest between strokes?"

Alasha thought for a moment. *Get it over with.* "Fast, please."

Marla took a long, flexible cane from where it hung on the wall, and then she swished it through the air and cracked it down across Alasha's naked buttocks.

Even before Alasha could flinch, or finish gasping from the pain, the second blow came. Her yelp was cut short by the third stroke, and then the fourth fell before she could respond.

She gave up trying to anticipate or react. She simply filled her lungs and started to bawl. Marla took no notice: the shower of blows continued to rain down until it seemed they were outpacing her heartbeats.

Mercifully, it was over quickly. Alasha lay on the desk, too cowed even to struggle any more, aware of nothing except for the burning pain and the tears that were streaming down her cheeks.

"There, now. I know it's not the same as when a lover does it, is it? There's no warmth to take the sting away."

"You know about this?" asked Alasha, between sobs.

"Aye, lass."

"Then has he treated other girls in the same way?"

"Ach, no. All that I know of it has been learned on my own account, starting when I was young like you. The master's new interests are all part of the strangeness that began when you arrived."

As she spoke, Marla was untying Alasha's wrists, and helping her up from the table.

"Then perhaps he really likes me after all?" Alasha asked in a small voice.

"Aye, he likes you fine, lass."

Marla took Alasha to the servants' bathroom, and stood her in a tub while she bathed her, dipping a sponge into the cool water and squeezing it gently over Alasha's burning rump.

"You're a bonny lass with a fine body, and you'll keep it too, for a while anyway, unless you make some poor man ruin it for you."

"Make him ruin it?" asked Alasha. "They don't need to be made. Once a man sees my body, all he wants to do is to hurt it. Except for Merik."

"Aye, there's always a different one. But mark my words, it's your own heart as much as their lust that says what's to be done."

Alasha pondered what the old woman had said as the water continued to soothe the hot welts on her behind. *Perhaps she's right. I cannot deny that it's in my own heart, too.*

When she twisted around to look at herself in the chipped mirror, the candlelight proved too dim for her to make out any marks.

"I'll be locking the door when I leave, so you'll not be bothered tonight," said Marla, as she tucked Alasha into her bed.

"Bothered? Then you know about..."

"Aye, I know about him. Not much that happens in this house escapes my notice."

"Then–"

"Don't worry about it, lass. All's as it should be, or as close as it can be, given who you are."

"I don't understand," she said drowsily. "Who do you think I am?"

"You're the Lady Alasha, lass. No more questions now; it's past time for you to be getting some rest."

Obedient as always, Alasha was asleep within a few heartbeats of the housekeeper turning her key in the lock of the bedroom door.

13 ensis

The housekeeper returned shortly after daybreak, bearing hot ti-sane. Alasha woke to the clicking of her bedroom lock, and was curled up facing the door by the time Marla entered the chamber.

"There you are, lass," said the housekeeper as she set the steaming bowl next to the bed.

"Thank you, Marla." Alasha pushed herself back against the pillow and sat up in bed, wincing as she remembered how tender her bottom was.

The other woman pursed her lips when she saw how Alasha flinched. "You'll be sore for a day or two yet," she said, "but I've no doubt a girl like you knows that without being told."

Alasha gave a rueful smile, thinking of the beatings she had suf-fered in Fiasco's house. Compared to them, the housekeeper's cane had been little more than a loving caress.

"Yes. It stings, but it's not too bad. Thank you, Marla, I know you could have done far worse."

"A lifetime's work will teach you to do what's needed, and no more," said the woman shortly.

"Then I'm even more grateful for the tisane," said Alasha with a smile.

"Ach. Well, I've a message for you, and seeing as I had to bring it, and unlock your door, a hot drink was really no extra effort."

"Of course not. What was the message?"

"It's from master Ensis. He asks that you work in the kitchen today, making more of those nasty potions. After that, you're to join him in his apartment for the evening."

"Very well."

"I see you have your doubts, lass. Well, it's not for me to judge. I was to tell you that you may use his brother's room to change, before you call on Ensis. It seems he'd like you to dress for dinner."

"Ensis wants to have dinner with me?" Alasha couldn't keep the surprise out of her voice, and wondered what Marla would make of it: the man had never shown any real interest in her – unless you counted the time in his study, when she hadn't even been sure it was really him.

"Of course he wants to have dinner with you. What man wouldn't, with a bonny young thing like you?"

"Thank you, Marla. You're very kind. But I know Ensis, and I don't think he likes me at all."

"Think what you like, lass, but remember this: I've known young master Ensis for a sight longer than you have."

Mussuf met her on the way down to the kitchen. He gripped her by the elbow and pulled her into a window alcove, where he lifted her shift to inspect her bottom.

"It seems you had an interesting time last night," he said with a self-satisfied smirk. "That will teach you to go running to Ensis every time I give you a playful cuff."

"I don't know what you're talking about."

"You know very well. You forced me to demonstrate that I can have you marked whenever I wish, even if I am not permitted do it myself. And rest assured I can find other ways to torment you, girl. Ways that do not show."

He let her shift drop, but kept his grip on to her elbow. "Well, you had better be about your business, slave girl, or your beloved Master might come to hear that you are lazy and worthless, as well as a thief." He leaned closer to her. "Think on the unimagined ways in which I can bring anguish into your life, and consider whether it would profit you to be more pleasant to me."

He released her, and sent her on her way with a slap that started her rump smarting all over again.

Alasha was familiar with the recipe now; by the end of the day, she had enough flasks to fill ten crates. She considered asking for a padlock so that she could lock them up, but she knew it would be useless.

Mussuf would obtain a copy of any key she was given, and even if he couldn't plant more empty flasks in her room, he would surely find other ways to torment her.

Of the previous batch, only the accusing crate with its single empty slot remained. Perhaps the rest had been taken away, to be delivered by hand barrow or cart. Alasha thought of the various kinds of satisfaction she'd found during her trip to the pleasure house, and sighed. She'd done all the groundwork, but now she seemed to be relegated to working in the kitchen, on simple tasks that could have been done by any scullery maid.

But then I am lower even than a scullery maid, she thought. *At least such girls are free to leave their master's house if they will.*

When she'd finished clearing up the aftermath of her brewing, she took a final look around the kitchen. The crates were stacked in a corner, hopelessly vulnerable to pilfering. Alasha shook her head and decided to ignore the problem: with luck, Mussuf had simply displayed the spite he felt after being told not to strike her again.

Which meant that Ensis had noticed the mark on her cheek, and knew what had happened. She pondered the meaning of that. *Ensis doesn't wish Mussuf to strike me, and last night he had my door locked. Can he be shielding me from the man? Perhaps he has some regard for me, after all.*

Hoping that the time was coming when she would find out the answers to such questions, Alasha left the kitchen and made her way to Merik's bedroom.

Her attire was to be a long sleeveless gown of green silk, with full skirts and a fitted, low-cut top. Marla attended her and helped her to dress. Alasha emptied her lungs and made her waist as small as she could, while the housekeeper pulled on the laces, tightening them until Alasha gasped with surprise.

It seemed a long time since she had worn such a gown, and the maids in Malkenstorm castle had never laced her in so cruelly. Even so, her reflection in the mirror almost took her breath away: she was transformed into a fragile plaything, an ornament so delicate that it seemed she might break in two at an over-eager touch.

The neckline of the bodice was barely sufficient for modesty, and she was uncomfortably aware that a careless move might uncover her, putting her nipples on display, together with the steel rings that pierced them.

Though careless movement is hardly a problem when I can scarcely move at all, she thought. It was true: she could bend only enough to sit down, and when it came time to complete her preparations, Marla had to help Alasha into her shoes, which were precariously high, but at least they had no ankle chains.

"Welcome, Alasha," said Ensis.

He said my name, thought Alasha. *At last, he has called me by my name.*

"Thank you, my Lord."

"We seem to have guests tonight. Friends of yours, I believe?"

She looked past him into the dining room, which was arrayed for a small banquet. Vermillio and Quinn were sitting at the table. Quinn was craning his neck, making no attempt to disguise the fascination he found in Alasha's tight-laced cleavage. Vermillio nodded at her and then turned back to his friend, looking faintly embarrassed.

"Yes, my Lord," she answered, wondering if they had come to call on her, and hoping it wouldn't cause trouble.

"I found them loitering in the courtyard. Hoping to catch a glimpse of her, eh lads? So, I took the liberty of inviting them to join us. I hope their presence will please you, Alasha?"

"Of course," she said nervously. "Vermillio, Quinn, you are most welcome here."

"Thanks, Ala."

"Alasha," corrected Vermillio. "I told you not to say Ala."

"Sorry. Alasha."

"How charming," said Ensis with a smile. "We all seem to know each others' names." Then he rang for the first course to be brought in.

Quinn was using one of the serving spoons to eat his soup, and Vermillio had filled the water glasses with wine. Ensis looked from one to the other with a mischievous grin, and then smirked at Alasha. "I've heard that you taught these two lads all they know of etiquette and deportment."

"Indeed, I gave them some lessons, but I can't take all the credit. I was there for a short time only, and there was another teacher before me."

"I understand they found your lessons very stimulating, and studied hard."

Alasha glared at the two boys. She had confided that part of her life to Aric, during the night they shared in Hazard Inn, but no one else knew the details – apart from the lads themselves. They must have been boasting, trying to impress their host with their worldly experience.

Neither of the lads seemed to notice her discomfiture. Quinn was too busy staring at her breasts, and even Vermillio seemed unable to resist the occasional sideways glance at her low neckline, or to keep the admiration out of his eyes.

The nightmare continued through the main courses. The youths seemed in awe of their company and surroundings, and had little to say, while Ensis did nothing but make one sally after another, teasing both Alasha and her guests. After a glass or two of wine, she found herself becoming quite befuddled, and struggling to hold her own.

As the dessert was being cleared away, Alasha dared to hope that the evening would soon be at an end.

"I understand you two lads have to be back at Lord Fiasco's house by a certain time?" asked Ensis.

Vermillio wiped his mouth on Alasha's napkin. "Yes. But he's attending the new Arbish Pleasure House tonight, so we're free until midnight, at least."

"Then we have a pleasant hour to pass together," said Ensis. "Now, I couldn't help noticing how you two couldn't keep your eyes off my slave."

Both Vermillio and Quinn blushed red as beetroots.

"Um, we're sorry if we've given offence," said Vermillio. "But Alasha is by far the loveliest girl we have ever seen. We never realized how lucky we were when she came to teach us, until she'd gone away again."

"Gallantly said, young man. I suppose you'd like to have her again, eh?"

Vermillio was speechless for a moment, but Alasha saw the twin sparks of lust and of hope that sprang into his eyes. "Oh, yes."

"Yes," echoed Quinn.

"Well, we'll have to see what can be done. Alasha?"

"Yes, my Lord?"

"You know both of these lads intimately, and you know what they have to offer. What do you say?"

"I'm not sure that I understand, my Lord."

"They want to fuck you. As hostess, isn't it your duty to provide for the needs of your guests?"

"Just as you say, my Lord," said Alasha carefully.

"No, not just as I say. I won't command you against your will, though I admit I might enjoy seeing you rutting with them among the crockery. But it's for you to choose."

Then I choose Vermillio and Quinn, she thought. *Since you refuse to touch me, and since the only other choice is Mussuf. Since you have as good as admitted that it would please you to watch.*

"I would be happy to accommodate our guests, my Lord, if it pleases you."

"I said it was for you to choose, Alasha."

She looked into his eyes for a moment, and found no doubt there about what she was to decide. "Am I to lie on the table?"

"Well, lads? You've done this before, haven't you?"

Quinn was already clearing a space. When he was done, Vermillio swung her up between stacked dishes and discarded cutlery. Alasha was grateful for that; strait-laced as she was in her bodice, it wouldn't have been easy to climb onto the table without help.

She twisted her head around and gave a beseeching look to Ensis, begging him silently to dismiss these youths and to lift her skirts himself, but he simply smiled at her and remained in his place at the head of the table.

Vermillio climbed up and straddled her, and then grasped her by the hips, urging her to raise her loins. Alasha complied, wondering if the spike heels would rip the tablecloth, while the youth pulled her skirt up around her waist.

Alasha kept her gazed locked on Ensis's eyes, trying to find a hint of sympathy, or simply the smallest indication that he loved or desired her. She was vaguely aware that Vermillio was fiddling with his breech lacings, and acutely conscious of her own wetness.

It must be the potion, she thought. *Except for that, the idea of being fucked by a boy for the entertainment of my Master would never excite me so.*

Yet excite her it did, and Alasha had no doubt that the evidence of her arousal was glistening between her thighs for each of the men to see. When Vermillio hooked his fingers inside her décolletage and eased it down below her breasts, it was plain that her nipples were betraying her, too.

Next, he put his hand on her sex, and slipped his fingers between her secret lips. He seemed surer of himself than before. *Perhaps he's been practicing,* she thought. *With Liri, maybe, or whoever the latest teacher is.*

She stopped considering such things when he discovered her pleasure bud. All she thought about then was how good it felt, and how much she'd have liked him to tease it with his tongue as well as his fingers.

That wasn't Vermillio's style, though, so when he stopped fingering her, she spread her legs even wider and then wrapped them around his hips as he plunged his cock into her.

She held Ensis's gaze for the entire time that Vermillio rode her, as her own climax came, and then his. She only looked away when the youth had finished with her, and was wiping himself off on one of the napkins.

Quinn's requirements turned out to be as simple as ever. He pulled and twisted her bodice until it came down to her waist, and then he paused and spent several heartbeats simply staring down at the twin objects of his desire.

"Push your tits together." His voice was no more than a whisper.

Alasha complied, and watched while he laved himself with oil from the cruet set and proceeded to rub up and down in the tight cleavage she formed, until at last he gave a deep groan and spurted his seed between her breasts.

She gazed steadily at Ensis for the whole time that Quinn was panting his way to climax, too.

Once Vermillio and Quinn had departed, Ensis allowed her to go into his bathroom and clean herself. She took the gown off and loosened the lacings in the hope that she'd be able to fit it about herself neatly again, but there was no one to help tighten it.

She left the fastenings undone and returned to the dining room, clutching the unlaced bodice against herself to prevent it from falling away. Ensis had retired to a couch close to the fire.

"Come and sit beside me, Alasha," he said.

She went to the couch and sat down, turning her back to show him the loose ties. "Would you like to lace me up, my Lord?"

"No. You were utterly ravishing with your body poured into that thing, but for now I think you look fine as you are."

Alasha felt herself blushing. *He offered me a compliment,* she thought.

"Lean back," Ensis commanded.

He had his arm extended along the back of the couch, and she relaxed carefully into the crook of his elbow. He put his hand on her shoulder and pulled her closer, making sparks jump between his fingers and her skin.

Why is it that these three men should have such power over me?

"Which three men?" he asked.

Alasha started with embarrassment: she hadn't realized she'd been whispering her thoughts aloud. "You and your brother, and Aric."

"I'm privileged to be counted in their company. After the way I've treated you, I'm surprised you have any time for me at all."

"Perhaps it's my nature," said Alasha.

"I think it must be."

She paused, wondering whether to continue, and decided she had nothing to lose. "You show more mastery of me than the others, even though you have scarcely touched me. Even in the act of giving me away, you showed your mastery of me."

"Then you prefer me to my brother, and to Aric?"

"At times," she said with a smile. "Everything has its season."

"And now it is the season for the gown to come off. I hope you liked it, by the way."

Alasha let the bodice fall away, then rose to her feet in order to step out of the skirts. "I liked it very much," she said as she relaxed back into his arms. "Thank you for buying it for me."

"It pleased me to do so. Now, it would please me to chastise you."

She stiffened against him. "Have I displeased you in some way, my Lord?"

"No. Quite the opposite: it would simply please me."

He made no move to bind her, or to compel her in any way. He just seemed to be waiting.

"Very well," she said at last. "How would you like me?"

"Over my knee."

Alasha crawled onto his lap and rested her hands and feet on the floor. She felt the flat of his palm resting gently on her naked bottom cheeks.

"How do you feel about Mussuf?" he asked, suddenly.

Alasha tried to think. Ensis knew about the blow. Perhaps he knew everything. *He has probably given Mussuf permission to have his way with me; what answer does he require from me?*

She decided that the simplest thing would be to answer honestly. "I don't like him."

"I thought not. Everything he has done in this house has been with my knowledge and permission, you know. Everything except striking you. What do you think of that?"

"I wondered if that was the case. Why did you shield me from his violence, my Lord?"

"Because you are precious to me, my slave."

Alasha felt her heart beating faster at that. "Thank you, Master."

There. The words have been said. He has called me slave, and I have called him Master.

Ensis continued, paying no heed to the emotion that coursed through Alasha's brain. "Punishment should be controlled, and Mussuf is too much of a brute for that. Also, one girl can only take so much abuse, and in your case I will not share that entitlement with a man such as Mussuf."

"But he is to continue to have rights over my body?"

"Yes. But remember this: he has only the rights that you choose to surrender, slave. That is the same for every man, including our lately departed guests. Including me."

My Master speaks the truth, she thought. *I have surrendered myself to Mussuf's strength willingly, and will again, even though I hate the man, and even though I know he will leave me in tears.*

Ensis started to stroke her bottom, very gently. "And the girls in the pleasure house? How did you find them?"

"I enjoyed my time with them very much, Master."

"I see." His voice held the hint of a question, but he didn't pursue it.

"They asked a favor of you, Master."

"Oh? And what was that?"

"That I go there from time to time to help them learn Xendrian."

"I see no reason why not. I'll be wanting you to spend some time over there anyway, keeping an eye on my investment."

"Mmmm."

Ensis's hand was spreading a luscious warmth over her buttocks, and out to the rest of her body. He pushed the fingers of his other hand under her belly and into her pussy, and then slid them out before wetly circling her hidden rose bud a few times.

Alasha heard herself sighing with pleasure.

His other hand lifted away from her buttocks and returned with a loud *thwack!*

Alasha gasped, flinched, and then mastered herself. His finger was still running along her pussy lips, and he continued to play with her for several heartbeats.

Thwack!

It wouldn't have been so bad if she wasn't still sore from the previous day's caning.

Thwack!

"Please, Master." She twisted her head back to look into his eyes, hoping that he'd take pity on her. He did, in a way. He bent down, pushing his face close to hers, and he kissed her on the mouth.

At the same time, his finger started to flutter around her pleasure pearl again, and *thwack!* his other hand smacked down onto her buttocks for the fourth time.

Alasha was aware was that she was moaning even as she returned his kisses with mounting passion, and she could feel the pressure of a climax starting to bubble up inside her – not too close yet, but unmistakably there and building under the *thwack!* she tasted salt tears mingling with their kiss, and wondered if he could taste them too.

Thwack!

His finger was deep inside her, and his palm was pressing against her secret jewel, and his tongue was flickering inside her mouth.

Thwack!

Alasha started to come, craning her neck desperately in case she lost contact with his lips, wanting to taste him and taste him for as long as these waves of pleasure continued.

Thwack!

It was softer this time, following her ebbing arousal back down to earth.

Her climax came to a shuddering end, and he was stroking the part of her that he had just punished so severely. Exhausted, Alasha broke the kiss and let her head fall towards the ground, and soon she felt his lips brushing her burning skin, as if he would kiss the pain away.

She had never been happier than this, not even during the night with Aric at Hazard Inn.

At last, she pulled herself from his lap and sat gingerly on the couch again, shifting her weight onto one side in order to spare her smarting bottom.

His breeches were plastered against his thighs, soaked with her juices.

"I'm sorry," she gasped at length. "I seem to have wet you."

Ensis glanced down and smiled. "No matter," he said. "It will give me another reason to punish you, next time."

The next day, Ensis instructed her to accompany the new shipment of firewater over to the pleasure house.

"I took the liberty of sending the previous batch over without you," he said.

"It was no liberty, my Lord."

"Still, I'd like you to take responsibility for the running of the business from now on, if you think you can manage it."

Alasha felt a glow of pride and happy anticipation at that. He was acknowledging her value, and giving her important work to do. "Thank you."

She waited until the crates had all been loaded onto the cart, and then she climbed up alongside the driver and they set off through the streets of Issing Ford.

The journey seemed shorter than the last time she'd come: then, Alasha had taken several detours to gawk at the sights. When they arrived, the crates were unloaded and taken to the storeroom in the twinkling of an eye.

"Shall I wait, Miss?" asked the driver.

"No, thank you. I'll be a while. You go back; I'll make my own way home later."

"Very good, Miss."

Xero and Zanya welcomed her with sweet kisses that held a hint of something more than sisterly affection, and they set to work going over the early firewater sales.

The business seemed to be doing well.

"The large one. Fiasco. He take plenty," said Xero.

"So big, one bottle no good," added Zanya.

"He buy three bottle one night!"

"Is that safe?" asked Alasha – not that she cared much if Fiasco snared himself in the trap, but she would have felt sorry for Vermillio and Quinn, or whomever the Lord's latest companions might be, if he were constantly energized by the potion.

"Oh yes. Big man need more," said Zanya.

Xero handed Alasha a bag of coins: the takings from the first few days. When she peeped inside, it was yellow rather than silver that glinted back at her.

"Gold!" she said.

"Silver too much, too heavy."

"It's still heavy."

"You leave here? Bring cart next time?"

Alasha hefted the bag and considered the matter. The streets of Issing Ford were safe enough, and she planned to leave well before dark. "No, I'll take it with me. I think that Ensis will want it as soon as possible."

The two girls looked at each other, and it seemed to Alasha that a question flickered from one to the other, and that Zanya shook her head very slightly.

"Ensis, your master," said Xero. "You ask him for teach Xendrian?"

"I asked him. We can start now, if you like."

She would have liked to ask what had just passed between them, but she doubted they'd understand what she meant, or be able to explain.

The gold seemed manageable as Alasha left the pleasure house, but the sack grew heavier with every step she took, and it wasn't long before her arms began to hurt.

She set her burden down on the wooden walkway and stopped to catch her breath. Fortunately, it was still the middle of the afternoon: the street was crowded, and she had no fear of being robbed.

When the palanquin paused next to her, she didn't even think to back away.

"My darling niece!" boomed the voice from within. It was very deep, and very loud. "What are you doing out alone, walking among this disreputable rabble? This is not to be borne…"

Alasha heard the muttering that arose from the passers by. It was plain that they would not be disposed to help a niece whose uncle had just spoken such insulting words.

Even as these thoughts were flashing through her mind, a huge arm shot out from behind the curtains of the box and drew her inside with irresistible strength. It was all Alasha could do to snatch her gold up as she was pulled inside and the palanquin started to move away.

"Make yourself comfortable, my dearest Ala."

As her eyes adjusted to the dim interior, she made out the bulk of Lord Fiasco, gesturing at the rugs and cushions that littered the floor in front of him.

Alasha lowered herself delicately into the space he indicated, doing her best to keep her voice steady. "Lord Fiasco. This is an unexpected pleasure."

"Unexpected for you, perhaps, but not for me. I have been following your progress with considerable interest, young lady, ever since you eluded me at Hazard Inn."

"I see." Her voice was shaking, despite her best efforts to remain calm.

"You seem upset."

She tried to pull herself together. "Kidnapping has that effect on me."

"My dear, this is no kidnapping. Your burden seemed too heavy for such a delicate wisp of a girl. I merely wished to offer the use of my transport, and to have a little chat."

"Truly?"

"Truly. I won't deny you made a pleasant toy for a while, but I have moved on to other things. Your maidenhead is what interested me most of all, and I have no doubt that you have squandered it on some worthless scoundrel by now. No matter. I have discovered a most magical pleasure potion in one of the Arbish houses here in Issing Ford..."

"I trust that it meets with your approval?"

"Indeed, it does, and I feel certain my new boys will enjoy it, too."

"New boys?"

"Oh yes. Vermillio and Quinn persisted in being so tediously ignorant whenever I took them to a banquet. When they were so late coming home last night, I simply had no choice but to cast the pair of them out."

"What will become of them?" asked Alasha.

"I care not. Now, to business. I understand that you're quite smitten with the man who won you from me? Aric Albigenses, I believe he's called?"

"Aric meant a lot to me."

"Meant? You speak of the man as if he has already crossed the dark river."

"He was struck down, defending me from Arbian raiders. I don't know if he lived."

Lord Fiasco's rumbling chuckle filled the palanquin. "Oh, he lived, my dear. I can assure you that he lived."

Alasha stared at him, hope blossoming in her heart. "You are certain of this?"

"As certain as you should be, young lady."

"I don't understand."

"Then let me explain. Going by the happy look I noticed as I watched you walking with your sack of coins earlier, I'd wager that you enjoy the love of at least three men. No single paramour could kindle such radiance in a girl's eyes."

Alasha was dumbfounded. "How did you know?"

"By being both persistent and perspicacious, my dear. Tell me, have you ever seen any two of these lovers together at the same time, let alone all three of them?"

"No," said Alasha, her head spinning.

"Well," rumbled Lord Fiasco. "That is something you should consider most carefully, wouldn't you agree? Ah, here we are. Your Master's estate, whomever he might be. I do hope you've enjoyed our little chat, dear Ala, and that it will be useful to you."

As she scrambled out through the door, Lord Fiasco reached forward and ran his jeweled fingers along her bare calf.

"Ah, we could have shared such delightful discoveries in pleasure and pain. Such a shame that you chose the merchant Albigenses over me."

As soon as she was safely outside with her gold, he rapped on the side of the palanquin, and his bearers carried him away.

Alasha paused just inside the front door and did her best to understand what Lord Fiasco had said.

Have you ever seen any two of these lovers together at the same time, let alone all three of them?

Merik had told her that either he or his brother was always on the road, looking after their business interests, and that was why they hadn't been in the house together.

Though it was strange, the way he rushed off so soon before his brother arrived. Surely, whatever ship he was to meet could have waited another hour?

As for Aric and the two brothers, there was no reason why she would have ever seen them together, because they had never met.

Or had they?

A dark clot of suspicion was slowly taking shape at the back of Alasha's mind, and she felt an icy tingling at the nape of her neck.

Aric's dark hair had hung in long curls, and he had worn a Marlish beard; the brothers were short haired and clean-shaven. Merik's hair was beginning to be flecked by middle age; Ensis seemed several years older and grayer.

All of these things could be changed with a sharp blade, and with coloring.

Aric spoke good Xendrian with a pleasant Marlish accent. From their speech, Alasha would have sworn that the brothers had been born and bred within a few miles of Issing Ford.

But Mussuf told me that Aric spoke Arbian like one of his own, and when we were both disguised as Arbians, his Xendrian suddenly sounded Arbish instead of Marlish.

It was clear that Aric outstripped any language tutor she had ever had, much as a hare might outstrip a tortoise. Was it not possible that he could speak perfect Xendrian if he wished, or adopt the accent and dialect of Issing Ford?

Each man wore his own distinct cologne, but to Alasha, there was no distinction to be made between the underlying male scent of either Merik or Ensis. She had put this down to their shared blood, but now that she considered it, surely Aric's own musk, even though she might doubt her memory of the single night they had snatched together – surely there had been a similar quality to that, too?

More than anything, wasn't there the fact that she was powerfully drawn to each of them in exactly the same way, regardless of their manner, or their scent, or their different accents and voices?

One thing alone made her doubt her theory. Merik and Ensis had inherited the same piercing blue eyes, while Aric's were of a greener hue.

And why should she doubt that Merik and Ensis were two brothers instead of a single man? Their requirements of her were certainly very different: one wished to be her slave, the other her Master, while Aric himself seemed to desire neither, but only to be her lover.

Could it be a case of several natures trapped within one body?

Alasha took a deep breath. *I cannot live with these doubts,* she decided. *I must confront Ensis now, and do my best to discover from his reaction whether there is any truth to this.*

Ensis was sitting in his study, working on some ledgers of accounts. He answered Alasha's knock with an invitation to enter, and looked up with an expression of mild impatience.

"I'm rather busy, Alasha, but no matter. I can make time for you this once. I was expecting you to spend longer at the Arbians' house. Did your trip go well?"

"Very well," she said. "Lord Fiasco was kind enough to allow me to ride back in his palanquin."

"Indeed." Ensis seemed suddenly uneasy. He pushed himself away from his desk and leaned back in his chair.

"Yes. I was wondering something…"

"Go on."

"Is there any way for a man to change the color of his eyes from green to blue?"

Ensis's face grew very red, but he seemed unable to reply.

"I am beginning to think that my suspicions are correct," said Alasha. Tears pricked behind her eyes, but she fought them down.

"What suspicions would those be?"

"That you and Merik and Aric are one and the same person, and that you have all been playing a wicked and humiliating game with me."

"Alasha, I'm proud of you. You've unmasked what trained spies and diplomats have failed to–"

"I don't want to hear it, Ensis, or Aric, or whoever you are," she said. The tears were coming freely now. "Take your filthy gold."

She tipped the moneybag on its end, spilling a shower of coins onto the carpet. Through her tears, she saw how his eyes widened, and how he had risen from his chair and was coming towards her.

"Stay away from me, you *traitor!*" she cried, and fled from the room.

Back in her chamber, Alasha thrust the few flasks of firewater she had into the moneybag, crying now because she had no other cases or trunks, and no possessions of her own to pack in any case. She picked up the steel-spiked shoes, debating whether they might come in handy, and that was when Mussuf came in.

"Greetings, my pretty," he said. "I believe we agreed that you owed me a debt this morning–"

"Consider this payment in full," she said as she swung a shoe spike against his temple, as hard as she could. There was a hollow cracking sound and Mussuf's eyes rolled up inside his head. He toppled sideways, crashing into her washstand and smashing the china ewer so that he was doused with water as he fell.

Alasha looked down at the shoes that she still held. "Handier than I imagined," she muttered, and stuffed them into the bag.

Then she left the room and went back down stairs.

"Someone look to Mussuf!" she called as she passed Aric's chambers. "He came into my room and tripped over my shoes, and I believe he has cracked his fat Arbish head open."

She didn't wait to hear if there was any response. She hurried to the front door, let herself out, and set off along the street.

Alasha wished there had been some way for her to keep a little of the gold, but her pride would never have allowed that. She'd only taken the bag because it was of little value, and the shoes because they were the only weapon she had, and were so intimately hers.

As for the rest, she still was dressed in the traveling garb Ensis had provided. There had hardly been time to change, even if she'd had anything of her own to wear. She decided to send the clothes back to the estate, as soon as she obtained some other garments.

In the meantime, she was penniless and destitute. In all the town, she knew only two other places: the Arbish pleasure house, and the tavern where Aric had bought her – *the insufferable man had the impudence to buy me twice over: once with a fortune risked on a card table, and once for a few silver coins.*

There wasn't any choice to be made. Alasha headed for the Arbians' house, hoping that Xero and Zanya would take her in. It bothered her slightly that Aric held an investment in the place, but she knew that the business belonged to the girls, and as she considered the matter, she became certain they would welcome her with open arms once they knew she brought the recipe for firewater.

Xero answered the door and drew Alasha inside before embracing her.

"I not think you come back so soon," she said.

"I have left Ensis," said Alasha. "Aric, I mean. They were all the same man, playing a horrible trick on me. I have nowhere to go … could I stay here for a while?"

"I think so," said Xero. "We talk to Zanya. Come. She in zhauna. Steam Bath. We join, yes?"

They slipped their clothes off outside the steam room, and Xero provided towels. Then they entered the zhauna where they found Zanya waiting for them.

Xero rattled off a long string of Arbian, and Zanya responded with brief questions, clucking sounds, and sympathetic nods.

"So you found out Ensis, Merik and Aric same man?"

"Yes," said Alasha. "You knew?"

"He made us promise for secret keeping. I am sorry."

"It's all right. It's not your fault."

"Now, you stay here, yes? Teach Xendrian every day?"

"Every day," said Alasha. "And I will also make as much fire drink as you can sell."

As she'd expected, the girls' eyes lit up when they heard that. "You teach recipe?"

"Of course," said Alasha. "But remember, you're Arbians. Mussuf was scared that other Arbians might hurt him for giving away the recipe ... might they come after you, too?"

"Not worry. Arbian females not run business, not able. So for us, crime not possible. Must be Mussuf fault!"

Alasha laughed out loud when she heard that, and Xero and Zanya joined her. Then she remembered Mussuf stretched out on the floor of her bedroom, and she felt a guilty chill. There was no doubt that the brute deserved everything he got, but even so...

She hoped he wasn't dead.

The three girls remained in the steam room for an hour, while Alasha held an impromptu Xendrian lesson. Xero and Zanya were eager students, and she was pleased at how quickly they started to grasp the basics of grammar and vocabulary.

They'll be holding normal conversations in a few weeks if they keep this pace up, she thought. *I hope it won't harm the trade among their customers who come here seeking something exotic...*

But she knew that the girls were clever enough to dissemble, and to disguise their growing fluency in Xendrian if necessary.

When the hour was up, Xero made to leave. "No time for playing today," she said with a regretful smile. "Xendrian lesson instead."

Once they were all dressed again, the three friends went through into the kitchen so that Alasha could demonstrate the secret of firewater.

Before they had finished making the first batch of potion, there was a heavy banging at the front door. Zanya disappeared to answer it.

"Visitors for you," she announced, when she returned.

"For me? Did they give their names."

"Names are hard for me to say. Quinn and Ver something"

"Vermillio?"

"Yes. I put in tavern room."

"Thanks. I'll talk to them when we've finished this batch, and then perhaps you could try making some?"

"You watch us, for mistakes?"

"Of course. I'll supervise," said Alasha. She funneled the last of the liquid into its pottery bottle and pushed the stopper in. "There, that's the first twelve done. You won't need to buy from Aric any more, eh? Well, I'd better go and talk to Vermillio and Quinn."

There were already several customers sitting at the tables, drinking and playing cards. Two Arbian dancers moved around the room, serving drinks and sweetmeats and collecting silver. Alasha noticed how the men's eyes followed the girls, and wondered how long it would be before the customers started buying what they had really come for.

Several pairs of eyes turned to Alasha as she entered, and followed her furtively as she made her way to the booth where Vermillio and Quinn were waiting, cradling tankards of small beer.

"Greetings, Alasha," said Vermillio. Quinn said nothing; he simply stared at her décolletage over the rim of his cup.

"Hello, boys."

"We have just come from Lord Ensis's estate. He told us you were gone."

"How did you find me here?"

"It is the only other place I have ever seen you. I hope you didn't leave because of what Lord Ensis permitted us to do last night..."

"No. At least not completely. His name isn't Ensis. He is Aric, the man who won me from Fiasco in a game of cards. He has been playing games with me, as well."

"I am sorry," said Vermillio. "I think this will be of little comfort, but I think his entertainment was intended for your enjoyment, too. I think that he regards you very highly."

"Then why did he give me to you, and watch while you had your way with me?"

"Your pardon, Lady Alasha, but my understanding of the matter was different. I saw how he watched you the whole time. I was terrified that if you gave the slightest hint we did not please you, he would have ended our pleasures and thrown us out."

"Huh?" said Quinn.

"Just leave the thinking and the seeing to me, Quinn."

"Oh. All right." Quinn fell silent.

"You may be right," Alasha said, "but it changes nothing. He deceived me. He let me think he was lying dead in a ditch with an Arbish arrow in his heart."

"He's distraught, Alasha."

"It serves him right. I hope he's suffering terribly. Now, that is enough of him. I don't even want to think about him. Did you hear any news of the man called Mussuf?"

"Alas, it seems he tripped and fell on his head. He is badly hurt and in blinding pain, but is expected to recover."

"That is sad news indeed," said Alasha with a sly smile, although she was relieved she hadn't killed the man. "Now, what of you? What fortune have you been enjoying?"

"Much like you, we have parted ways with our erstwhile Master."

"Yes. I spoke with Lord Fiasco earlier today, and he told me you had both left."

"I'm sure he didn't put it in such delicate terms. He threw us out, Alasha. I could see that we were beginning to bore him."

"Then you are free."

"Free to starve in the streets," he said sourly. "Even Fiasco recognized our worthlessness in the end. He didn't even bother to offer us for sale."

"I believe that his mind may be confused by the Arbish potions he has been consuming," said Alasha comfortingly. "Anyway, it is better to be free than a slave."

"Do you really think so?"

Alasha was silent for a moment. "Perhaps not in every case. But anything is better than having a master like Lord Fiasco. You're young, and not uncomely." She smiled across the table at them. "Perhaps if you had concentrated harder during your lessons, you might be able to find those positions as ladies' companions of which you once spoke."

"That would have been pleasant," said Vermillio with a wistful smile. "As it is, Lord Ensis – Aric, I should say – had offered us some laboring work in his warehouse. Unloading wagons and rolling barrels around, you know the sort of thing. It's better than begging, I suppose."

"Slave work," said Quinn.

"Fortunately for those lacking in skill such as ourselves, Aric doesn't keep slaves," said Vermillio.

Alasha caught his eye, and he flushed and fell silent, taking a sudden interest in the foam at the bottom of his cup.

He recovered quickly enough, though. "Anyway, I have been thinking of what you said, about how we could improve ourselves."

"Yes?"

"You are a fine teacher, Alasha. The best we ever had. Would you take us back as your students again?"

"On similar terms as last time, I suppose?"

"That would be more than acceptable to us, but we understand that things are different now."

"Good. Similar terms then, but different: at the end of each lesson, it shall be you two who place themselves at my disposal, rather than the other way around. And we shall begin with an aptitude test, to ensure you are able to fulfil my needs."

Quinn's face betrayed nothing but bafflement.

Vermillio's, on the other hand, showed a look of considerable intrigue as he rose and offered her his hand.

The room that the Arbians had set aside for Alasha was garish and over-furnished for her taste, but that was understandable given the nature of their trade. At least the four-poster bed was comfortable, and at least Xero assured her that the sheets had been freshly laundered.

Alasha ushered her guests inside, and looked at them critically.

"It was always me displaying myself for your pleasure in the past, wasn't it? Now we shall try something new: a race between you two. The first who presents himself naked to me shall win a prize. One, two, three, go."

Vermillio started immediately, tugging at the buttons of his shirt. Quinn stood dumbfounded, as if he didn't grasp what he was supposed to do, and it was only when he noticed that Vermillio was undressing that the light of understanding dawned in his face and his fingers flew to his jerkin lacings.

Vermillio won the race, but not by much. Alasha made them stand in the center of the room, and spent some time walking around them and admiring their bodies.

"Your physiques are pleasing to me."

"Thank you."

"I expect you to address me properly. Since I am to be your teacher, 'Miss' will be appropriate."

"Thank you, Miss."

"I think the warehouse labor will come easily to you," she said, as she tested Quinn's biceps. "I had no idea that Lord Fiasco worked you so hard."

"He expects his companions to look after themselves, Miss," said Vermillio.

"And I'm grateful to him for it. Now, Vermillio, I promised you a prize."

"Yes, Miss?"

"One of you will have the honor of tasting my very essence." Alasha let her hand drift to her loins, making sure that both youths saw it. She smiled inwardly at the way their eyes widened. "The other will be denied this privilege, but he may be permitted to taste another part of me. Vermillio's prize shall be to choose which of you receives the deepest honor, and which part – if any – the other shall sample."

Vermillio looked from her to Quinn and back again.

"I will allow you some time to decide. You will give me your answer as soon as I have disrobed." Alasha started to unfasten the hooks of her bodice, very slowly.

Their eyes followed her every move as she slipped the garment open and off, revealing the embroidered slip that she wore underneath, and as she loosened her belt and let her skirt slip to the floor. Vermillio's gaze swiveled down as she stepped out of her shoes, while Quinn's stayed fixed firmly on the nipple points that she knew were visible through the flimsy undergarment.

Finally, she gathered the silken thing and eased it over her head before tossing it onto the bed. Now, she was as naked as they were.

"Time's up, Vermillio."

He took a deep breath, as if steadying his nerves. "I would be the one to taste you in truth, Miss. As for Quinn, if it is acceptable to you, I would have him use his mouth to pleasure your breasts."

"Chosen like a good slave and a true friend," she said. "Very well. I shall recline on the bed, and you shall do what you have undertaken to do."

She lay down in the center of the four-poster, parted her legs slightly, and arranged her hands on the pillow above her head.

Vermillio followed her, and knelt between her legs, while Quinn lay beside her.

"Begin," she commanded.

The boys set about their respective tasks with enthusiasm. Quinn soon discovered how she liked to be sucked, licked, and bitten lightly, and after a while she simply allowed him to get on with the job of pleasing her. Vermillio was more hesitant – not that he held back, but he seemed unsure of what to do.

Alasha reached down and guided his mouth to the right spot, and then held him there, pressing harder to encourage him when his tongue approached a rhythm and pressure that pleased her.

All in all, she found it a very satisfying afternoon.

Alasha returned to the kitchen afterwards, and oversaw the production of another twelve bottles of firewater, and then took a hand in the making of another batch herself.

She could scarcely credit the amount of silver that these flasks represented.

Emon the eunuch had paid eleven hundred silver pieces for her, which had seemed a staggering sum at the time, yet a single crate of this potion would fetch more than that.

Was I really worth less than twelve flasks of fire drink?

Alasha knew that the answer was that Xendria contained plenty of slave girls, but no other source of this liquid, and that rich men and women would scramble over one another to secure a supply for their harems and boudoirs.

Perhaps we are selling it too cheaply, she thought, *since we have no inkling of the risks we run. At least we are far from Arbish lands, and Arbish vengeance.*

Xero and Zanya seemed unconcerned about any dangers, and Alasha decided that she should be, too. By the time she had crated up her final batch, it was time for bed.

As she climbed the steps up to her chamber, she could hear the music and carousing that came from the tavern room below, and the deep groans and girlish cries of delight that echoed among the passages upstairs.

Xero came to her room the next morning, dressed in a filmy negligée and bearing a tray of hot khavé and a sealed parchment packet.

She set the tray – which Alasha saw carried two steaming bowls – on the bedside table. Then she climbed into bed next to Alasha and snuggled up against her.

"Letter for you," she said.

Alasha took the packet and studied it. Apart from her name, there was no hint of what it was, or from whom it came. The script was unlike either Merik's or Ensis's.

I never saw Aric's penmanship, though, she thought. *It is probably his, assuming there is truly such a person, and he doesn't turn out to be someone else altogether.*

She broke the sealing wax, unfolded the packet carefully, and spent a few moments trying to ignore the taut smoothness of Xero's legs that were twined between hers, and the deliciously distracting things the girl's lips and fingertips were doing to her bare shoulder and neck.

It was no good. She set the letter down next to the khavé bowls and turned to the dancer, reaching down hesitantly for the warm sex whose secrets she had learned so intimately in the steam room.

The covers rose as Xero opened herself, welcoming Alasha's exploring touch. After that, all Alasha knew was the sweetness of the girl's mouth, and the fresh scent of her hair, and the feel of her lithe body making its unbearably slow way down to Alasha's loins, where the dancer returned in full the favor she had received in the zhauna.

When they were both sated, they lay on the pillows together and Alasha returned to her letter.

Dearest Alasha,

I beg that you grant me a few moments of your time so that I may attempt to explain myself.

The deception that you found so hateful, and that I now find so shameful, was not done through any malice.

Aric Albigenses is a simple fellow who could make love to you for days on end, and take care of you forever (unless shot by some inconsiderate Arbian archer), but he isn't the sort who would revel in taking power over you, or willingly offer you his own submission. Merik and Ensis were alter egos who could step into those roles, and I created them because I felt sure that, alone, I could never be enough for you.

After our night in Hazard Inn, I knew that I loved you and desired you more than any woman I have ever met, and I believed that your feelings echoed my own. But I sensed a depth in you that I could not satisfy. You have traveled a hard road, Alasha, and I was not there to walk with you. The lessons of that road shone like a beacon in your eyes, and in the easy grace of every step you took, and I felt like a sightless fool when I examined myself in that light.

How was I, a blind man, to find my way to the places you wished to go?

When the Arbian shot me, his shaft struck my neck pouch, which being made of velvet would have offered no protection at all. Fortunately for me, your deeds of indenture were also in the purse, and folded so thickly that the force of the arrow was spent. The arrow knocked me from my horse and its point pierced my chest, but my main injury was the blow I took to my head, which knocked me senseless.

Alasha, your deeds of indenture are now soaked with my blood. No one can read them, or tell whose signatures have endorsed them. With no document to match the notarized register entry, you are free. Although you may pay no heed to any other information in this letter, still I would have you know you are truly free.

I followed the caravan into the forest, and dealt with as many guards as I could. When I had reduced them to the handful I knew I could defeat sword-to-sword, I entered the camp and slew those that did not flee. Alas, Mussuf melted away into the woods with you, and I admit that I lost the trail: following wagon ruts along a forest road is a different matter from tracking horses between the trees. I decided it would be best to go to await your arrival in Issing Ford, for I knew that Mussuf must bring you there. I borrowed the house of a grumpy old friend of mine whom you know as my housekeeper, for I have another deception to admit: Marla is no more a housekeeper than I am.

I also escorted the Arbian dancers to Issing Ford and helped them establish themselves, and I sent for the gold we cached in Hazard Inn, and that is the full and truthful account of all that passed between the time we parted and were re-united.

After that, I became like an actor who is trapped inside a play, unable to escape the parts I had invented for myself, and I will confess that my mortification at your discovery was mingled with relief that my deception was finally unmasked.

I can only offer my deepest apologies for the hurt I have caused you, and venture to hope that one day, I will be worthy to be

    Yours
    Aric

Xero did not speak until Alasha had set the letter down. "From Aric, yes?"

"Yes."

"Thought so. Vermillio bring letter."

"So he's using my friends as his messenger boys, now."

"You like letter?"

Alasha thought for a while before answering. "It was interesting," she said.

15 the road home

It was the middle of the morning before Aric arrived.

Alasha had been watching the world go by from her high window, and she saw him coming down the street, accompanied by Vermillio and Quinn.

She drew away from the casement, in case he should glance up – it would be just like him to assume she'd been watching for him – and then crept down the stairs.

Before she reached the first floor, she met Zanya coming the other way.

"Aric here," she said. "With your two friends."

"Thank you," she said. "Would you ask Vermillio and Quinn if they'd like to go to the tavern room?"

"They in tavern already. Aric wait for you in parlor."

"You seem to have this all arranged," said Alasha.

"We try to help," said Zanya. "Xero true romance, want you back together again."

"Xero's a true romantic, eh? I won't say I disagree," said Alasha, thinking of what had passed between them in her bedroom, earlier on. "Very well. I'll see him for a few minutes, but that's all. And he can wait for a while. Tell him I'm having breakfast, and will be with him in half an hour."

Zanya hurried back towards the parlor, and Alasha went to the kitchens to find herself something to eat. She took her time, lingering even longer than usual over her second bowl of khavé.

It would do Aric good to wait.

He was pacing up and down the parlor when she finally joined him. She took the seat close to the window. *If it happens that there are no other chairs close by, and if the light shines straight into his eyes when he tries to look at me – well, such things are no concern of mine,* she thought.

Aric stopped pacing and turned to her, but seemed unable to find any words.

Let him stew for a while.

"Um, you have received my letter?" he asked at last.

"I have."

"And you have read it?"

"I glanced over it."

"Thank you." Aric shuffled his feet for a few more moments, then looked around the room. Alasha saw his eyes alight on an armchair that stood against the opposite wall, but he made no move to sit down. Instead, he turned back to her.

"The letter relates everything I could think of to say, but I wanted to apologize in person."

"I see."

"Alasha, I think that few lives are blessed as ours can be when we are together. Few are fortunate enough to meet the person who is so right for them."

"And which particular person did you think was right for me? Ensis? Merik? You? Or someone completely different, perhaps?"

Aric looked even unhappier, something that Alasha wouldn't have believed possible.

"They were roles I played, but they are all me, inside. Can you honestly not find it in your heart to forgive me, Alasha?"

"Not yet. Perhaps not ever."

"Then tell me what I must do to win you back."

"You don't win me, Aric, no matter how many ogres you may slay, or how many games of cards you win at Hazard Inn. You either have me, or you do not. You had me completely, from the moment you tarried to talk outside my wagon. You lost me on the day I found out you lied to me."

"I see. Well, at least your documents are destroyed. So no man will have you now, unless you choose it."

"You still don't understand me, Aric. It was never a matter of documents, except in the eyes of the law. The man who has me may order my affairs as he wishes because he holds my heart, not some piece of parchment. I'll consent to be shared with his friends and his servants, or be locked in his dungeons, or suffer under his whip. Or not, if he doesn't choose those things. But I'll never consent to being deceived."

"And I'll never deceive you again. You have my oath on that, Alasha, no matter what may pass between us in the future." He hesitated. "It seems there's little else to be said on the matter."

"It's a start, perhaps," she said.

"I should also give you this." He pressed something into her hand. When Alasha looked, she was holding the key to her collar.

"Thank you," she said, fighting the regret that welled up in her chest. She slipped the key into her bodice, resolving to ask Xero to unlock the collar later.

"What will you do now?" he asked.

"I'll remain here for a while, making firewater and saving money. When I have enough, I'll return to claim what is mine."

"What is yours?"

"Yes. My stepfather swindled me out of my birthright. I mean to take it back, and see that he pays the price for what he did."

When the time came, she asked Vermillio and Quinn to accompany her.

"You have excelled in your studies. In all your studies. Do you still have the ambition to serve as companions to a Lady?"

"Indeed, if we could only find one who wished to offer us such a position," replied Vermillio.

"Then while you wait for the right opening, perhaps you could practice with me."

"Ha! Right opening!" said Quinn with a crude guffaw. "I seem to recall finding the right opening last night…" Then he caught himself and his face reddened. "Sorry."

Alasha smiled at him tolerantly. "Don't worry, Quinn. Wit is more than welcome among the fairer sex. But try to make it more refined, all right?"

"All right," said Quinn, and fell silent.

"What would you have us do?" asked Vermillio.

"Last year my stepfather tricked me into signing away my inheritance. I'm going back to deal with him. It would mean a lot to me if you would accompany me on the journey."

"To protect you on the road, you mean?"

"I'd feel safer with two strong men along, certainly. And I feel sure we could find ways to pass the evenings by the campfire."

"I see ... then we shall come, eh, Quinn?"

"Most certainly."

"It might be hard," she cautioned. "We'll need to sleep on the ground whenever there's no inn nearby, and cook our own food. Can either of you handle a weapon?"

"Hard is no problem. I can handle my weapon..." said Quinn, with another snigger.

"Enough, friend," said Vermillio. "Some of Fiasco's associates took the fancy to organize a martial entertainment for their companions." He paused, reddened, and plowed on. "Gladiators, you know? We trained for weeks. I'm no sword master, but I know enough not cut my own head off, and Quinn here is a dab hand with a crossbow."

"Good. Then I shall give you silver to buy whatever weapons and equipment you need. I'll also provide us with horses and supplies, and we shall leave in two days. Are we agreed?"

"Agreed," said the young men, their eyes sparkling with excitement.

Xero and Zanya were both in floods of tears when the time came for Alasha to leave.

"We will miss you so much..." said Xero.

"Hurry back..." sobbed Zanya.

Alasha gave into the tears that were moistening her own eyes, and embraced the two dancers. "I'll miss you, too. I promise to write as soon as everything is settled, and if you're tired of Issing Ford by then, you can come and start a new Arbish House in Malkenstorm."

"Perhaps," said Zanya, laughing through her tears. "We could rescue some more Arbian girls from the market places, and then we could have two houses…"

"Or open an Arbish House in every city in Xendria," said Xero.

"Good idea!" said Alasha, as she climbed onto her horse. "I don't think your plans will founder for lack of ambition … but promise me you'll come to Malkenstorm first?"

"We promise."

"Good. Now, what on earth is he doing here?"

It was Aric, mounted on his big gray and leading a second riding horse behind him.

"Sorry," said Xero. "We could not let you slip away without giving you and him the chance to say goodbye."

Alasha glanced at him again, noting the saddlebags and blanket roll. "I fear he means to do more than bid us farewell."

Aric approached, his beasts' iron-shod hooves striking sparks on the newly cobbled street. "I heard that you were setting out today," he said. "I'm glad that I arrived before you left."

"There was no need to trouble yourself," said Alasha.

"Nothing is ever any trouble for me where you are concerned, my Lady."

Everyone was looking at her, and she felt herself flushing slightly. "Well, I thank you for taking the time to see us off," she said at last.

He looked at her levelly. "I mean to ride with you, Alasha."

"That won't be necessary. I have Vermillio and Quinn as escorts, and as you see we are all three of us armed." She shrugged her shoulder under her quiver, and touched her hand to the hilt of the slender blade that hung at her belt. "We will be perfectly safe."

"I don't doubt it. Still, I would ride with you. I failed to protect you once upon the road, and four is better than three."

Alasha hesitated, thinking of how easily the Arbians had overcome them before. Then she shook her head. *My dress showed me to be one of their slave girls then, and his showed him to be an interloper. Now we are Xendrians, and none dare deny us the use of the King's highway.*

"I thank you for your concern, sir, but my party is complete. Come, Vermillio, Quinn!"

She spurred her horse along the road towards the new bridge.

Behind her, she heard the clattering hooves of her companions' horses as they followed her, mingling with the clinking of the firewater flasks in her saddlebags.

They rode towards the river, passing from the cobbled streets of the center to those that were still little more than cart tracks, and then crossed over the bridge. Alasha glanced down between the railings, remembering the day she had arrived at Issing Ford and waded through the river below.

At the brow of the hill overlooking the river, she reined in her mount and gazed back at the town. In the distance, she saw a horseman preparing to cross the bridge. His steed was gray, and he led another beast behind him.

The woodland on either side of the track seemed utterly different from the dark forest she'd passed through with Mussuf. Partly that was because he had taken her far from any roads in his effort to throw off pursuit, and partly because she was no longer half-naked, barefoot, and bound.

Instead, she was dressed in fine silk and soft leather, mounted on her own horse with a blade at her side, and with two companions that she now counted as friends – and even lovers, occasionally.

The fate towards which she headed was no more certain than before, though, even if she had more control over her course. She had no idea of what she would do once they reached Malkenstorm.

When the sun was overhead, Alasha led them a short way into the woods and chose a picnic spot next to a brook, shaded by an ancient oak tree. They ate some of the bread and cheese they had brought from Issing Ford, and washed it down with cold water from the stream. As she drank, Alasha thought of the other, larger river that she had known so intimately before.

Vermillio fetched a small lute from one of the packhorses, and soon the bittersweet music of his plangent strings and melancholy voice were drifting among the trees.

Alasha opened one of her flasks and took the sip that she knew would still her craving for the firewater for a while. The familiar warmth spread quickly. She reached out to Quinn and he accepted her hand eagerly, allowing himself to be led further along the stream until they found a deep pool.

Alasha undressed first. She stood in a shaft of sunlight that came down between the trees, and stripped lasciviously to the slow rhythm of Vermillio's lute.

When she was naked, she stood with her back to the water and cupped her hands under the breasts that she knew were Quinn's greatest delight, squeezing them together and rubbing her erect nipples between fingers and thumbs.

Quinn simply stared at her, as if hypnotized. Alasha laughed softly, and then stepped back and let herself slip into the cool water. "Strip for me, Quinn," she called.

He did his best, but something told her that he took more pleasure in her performance than she did in his. It didn't really matter: Quinn's strengths lay in other areas.

Like the way his mouth sought her breasts so worshipfully when he finally joined her in the pool, and the way his cock brushed so enticingly against her thighs.

Alasha reached up and grasped a smooth rock that jutted from the bank, and then hoisted herself partly out of the water. She did this partly to save Quinn from drowning himself in his single minded quest to taste her nipples, and partly so that she could balance herself on the tip of his rigid prick, ready to lower herself onto him when the right moment came.

Part of her wondered if Aric was anywhere close by, and if he could hear Vermillio's song.

It was after dark, and Alasha was considering whether it would be best to camp under the stars, when they saw the faint lights of a village further along the road.

"Let us hope there will be an inn, with hot water and soft beds," said Vermillio with feeling. Alasha decided that his day in the saddle had probably affected him more than he cared to admit.

When they rode amongst the huddle of little hovels, they saw that there was indeed an inn: a mean looking building with faint lines of lamplight glimmering through heavy shutters.

"I'm not sure I like the aspect of this place," said Alasha.

"It's just an inn," replied Vermillio. "It may not seem like much, but at least we may hope for clean bedding and for someone to care for our horses."

"Well, there's no harm looking inside. If it seems too flea-ridden, we can always move on after we've taken some meat and wine."

Her words proved optimistic: there was no wine to be had in the place, only leather tankards of beer whose main character was its gassy sourness, and no food except for bread, beef dripping, and watery soup. The barefoot wench who brought their food was thin and smudged with dirt; to Alasha's eyes, the lass seemed only a little younger than herself.

"What is your name?" she asked.

"Lia."

The girl's voice was scarcely more than a whisper, and now she was closer, Alasha could see that one of her eyes was marred by a purple bruise, and that her wrists and ankles bore angry rope marks.

"Who keeps you, Lia?"

"My master's name is Farnham. He is the innkeeper here."

Alasha followed Lia's glance, and saw the man she meant. He was filling cups of beer behind the counter and glaring across the room at his serving girl. "Lia! Stop your idle chatter and get back to work, or I'll have full payment from your hide!"

"Bring me another tankard of this most excellent ale when you have time, girl," said Alasha loudly. "And for my friends, too." She offered her sweetest smile to the innkeeper, and loosened her bodice a little. He reddened and turned away in evident confusion, and she smiled again with satisfaction.

Lia paid no attention to this by-play. She cast a frightened glance at her master and scurried back to the kitchen.

"This is turning out to be an interesting place," said Vermillio. "Something tells me we'll be getting in trouble, later."

"You saw her face and her wrists. You heard what he said."

"You cannot rescue every waif you see, simply because she's troubled. All three of us around this table have known worse plights; and who cares for that? The kingdom is full of such people."

Alasha gripped his forearm and squeezed until he flinched. "The three of us, more or less, chose our paths. Yes, even you, Vermillio. You were free to spend your afternoons in the tavern, and to take advantage of your teacher, and to walk around Issing Ford, yet you did not leave until Fiasco tired of you. As for me, I didn't always have my liberty, but the real chains were in my heart." She indicated the girl with a nod of her head. "She has no such choice to make."

Vermillio nodded slowly, and Alasha released him. He examined the half-moon nail marks she had left on his arm, with a hurt expression on his face. "Very well. What are we to do? Buy the girl and take her with us to Malkenstorm?"

"No. I'll not reward the innkeeper with extra silver; that would only encourage him to brutalize the next waif who comes into his hands. I have a different lesson in mind."

Either through luck or intelligence, Lia waited until Farnham had gone down to the cellars before she returned with the ordered beer. She lingered at the table, as if hoping for another kind word.

"Would you leave this place if you could, Lia?"

"Oh, yes. But it would be hopeless. The other girl ran away, and they hunted her down with dogs. Now I have to do her work, too."

"If we promise to take care of you, would you come with us?"

The girl's whole face lit up. "Oh, yes."

"As a matter of pure interest, how many hunting dogs do they have?" asked Vermillio.

"Six."

"Six." His voice became grave. "Well, Quinn? How many do you think you could stop with that crossbow of yours?"

"It depends. If they all rushed at once, only one. It takes too long to re-load the thing. You never know, though. I might be able to get two."

"Something tells me we're going to find out for sure, tomorrow," said Vermillio.

Alasha turned back to the girl. "Don't worry, Lia. You'll be coming with us when we leave, and everything's going to be all right. I promise. Now, get back to work before Farnham sees you with us."

Their room was cramped and dirty, barely worth the silver piece it cost. If Alasha had been following her own inclinations, she'd have camped in the fresh air under a tree, but now she wished to transact some business with Farnham – the sort of business that could only be done indoors, and under cover of night.

It had been a long time since she had felt such an enervating rush of excitement and fear: not since she'd been a girl, and out after dark on a forbidden hunting expedition with her mother's gamekeeper.

I wonder why he allowed me to come with him? she thought, and then smiled as comprehension dawned. He'd been young and comely, only a few years older than Alasha herself, and he'd never so much as tried to steal a kiss from her.

He's probably gone, now, she thought. *Lord Jarvin has surely dismissed everyone who remembers how things were, back in my mother's time.*

She hugged the memory of those other night time adventures close as she changed into her silken shift and coiled her long tresses artfully about her head, so that the ornamental handle of the poignard that she twined among the curls would seem like no more than a jeweled hair pin.

It wasn't long before she heard the signal for which she'd been waiting. She shot a glance at Vermillio, and saw that he understood. He drifted from the room like a gray ghost.

She set Quinn at the window to watch for the sign that Vermillio's task was complete, and that the horses were ready for them to leave. Alasha herself stood close to the door, listening.

The sounds that had alerted her continued: Lia's soft whimpering, punctuated by an occasional louder yelp of pain, and mingling with coarse oaths and growled threats that could only come from Farnham

"Why is he taking so long?" she whispered.

Quinn just shrugged and looked out of the window again. Then he turned back to Alasha, and nodded.

She slipped silently out into the corridor and padded on bare feet towards the door where the sounds seemed to originate. When she was outside it, she peered through a crack between two timbers to make sure she had the right room.

Alasha couldn't see much, but it was enough: a bare leg, pale and thin and lashed to a bedpost, overshadowed by a bulky figure that was in the midst of undressing.

She tapped on the door, very gently. The voices inside were stilled, and she heard footsteps crossing the room. "Yes? What is it? We're about to go to sleep." Farnham yawned extravagantly, as if trying to convince an unwanted visitor that his words were true.

"Oh, I hope you're not *too* tired," said Alasha, in her most seductive voice. "You see, I couldn't help noticing the girl earlier, and how lucky she is ... I've always *longed* to be tied up by a big, strong man, so that he can do exactly what he pleases with me."

"Er, who are you?"

"You don't know me? I was sure you'd noticed me, downstairs. I certainly noticed you."

"Oh, it's you. Just a moment."

The door opened and she slipped inside. Farnham's eyes widened when he saw her: Alasha doubted if this particular inn had many female night-guests, let alone lithe, silk-clad ones such as herself.

She closed the door gently behind her. "We won't be disturbed, now, will we?"

"No," he said, hoarsely.

"Good. Now, I'd like to hear how you've trained the girl, and what you do to her, so I can imagine how it's going to feel when you do it to me, later."

"Well, I train her with the end of a rope, of course."

"Ooh," said Alasha, wriggling her bottom.

"Yes. She, er, seems to like it, actually, though you might not believe it ... she likes to be gagged, too." He had moved to the head of the bed, and now he stuffed an old rag into Lia's mouth.

"Oh, I believe you, Farnham. I imagine she must like it *very* much."

"Er, yes. Well, when we want to have some fun, I tie her to the bed, just as you see. She likes the ropes as tight as I can make them, so she can struggle against them without worrying about anything coming loose. She seems to find that extra satisfying."

"What a considerate lover you are, Farnham. I can already tell I'm going to be in good hands, when I take her place afterwards."

"Afterwards?"

"Yes. You'll want to … warm yourself up first, won't you? So that you're as ready as you can be when it's my turn? So you won't be tempted not to hurt my ankles and wrists by leaving the ropes the tiniest bit loose, and so your cock is already slick with her when you put it in my mouth? So that you'll *really* lay into my wriggling arse with that long belt of yours?"

Farnham's eyes were nearly popping out of his head. "Oh, yes," he said. "I should definitely warm up first." He tore the rest of his clothes off and then turned back to the girl on the bed.

Silently, Alasha unlatched the door. Then she crossed the room with three long strides, pulling the poignard from her hair with a single fluid motion that ended with its point nestling at the side of Farnham's windpipe. "If you move a muscle or make a sound, you join the others I have killed," she said. "Come in, Quinn."

Farnham stayed very still. The door opened and Quinn came into the room.

"Untie Lia."

Quinn fumbled with the knots for a moment, then cursed quietly and cut them with his dagger. It wasn't long before the girl was sitting in the room's single chair, rubbing her wrists and ankles.

"Now, Farnham. As you might have gathered, I lied to you earlier on. I had no intention of letting you tie me up. Quite the opposite, in fact. Get on the bed."

She kept her blade pressed to his throat as he lowered his bulk onto the mattress. "Tie his hands and his feet, Quinn. Don't be gentle: this one likes it nice and tight, don't you?"

Farnham said nothing. His whole body was quivering.

When he was spread-eagled between the bedposts, Alasha leaned forward and lifted his flaccid cock with the tip of her poignard. "Lia, did you consent to what this man did?"

"No."

"I thought not. It is my custom to castrate rapists," she said.

Farnham started to whimper. "Please, just leave me. Take the girl and go."

"What do you think, Lia?"

"Don't hurt him, please. It will just make things worse."

"Worse? What do you mean?"

"When they catch us."

"If he's going to catch us anyway, then why shouldn't we take our revenge on him while we can?"

"We won't catch you," said Farnham. "I swear we won't even chase you."

"My forbearance is not to be bought with empty promises, innkeeper. The reason you won't catch us is that we don't wish to be caught, and the reason I leave you as a man of sorts is that your victim sees fit to plead for you."

"Thank you." He was close to tears.

"Know that I will be traveling this road again, over the coming months and years. If I cannot come myself, I will send my people. Take better care of the folk under your charge, or I promise that our next meeting will be less friendly."

"I understand," he whimpered. "I swear I'll mend my ways."

"Good. Then you might still be in possession of all your male parts when the time comes for you to cross the dark river, and that time may yet be delayed awhile. Lia, find some clothes, and shoes if you have them. Quinn, it's time to go."

Vermillio shooed the other horses that had been in the stables into the darkness surrounding the village, and the four travelers cantered into the night.

It would take the villagers time to round up their mounts, but Lia seemed certain that the innkeeper would rally his folk to pursue them. All the next day, Alasha rode with an arrow nocked at the rear of the group, looking back anxiously for the first rider or hunting dog to come into view. Quinn rode beside her with his crossbow ready in his hands.

There was no sign of any pursuers, though, and Alasha found herself wondering if someone else had dealt with the problem.

16 malkenstorm castle

Alasha sensed when they were getting close to Malkenstorm. Even before she recognized the shape of the land and the names of the villages, something told her she was coming home. Perhaps it was the soft buzz of Northern Xendrian speech, or perhaps it was just a feeling in the air.

The familiarity brought little comfort, though. She had traveled fast and far, but she seemed no closer to accomplishing the task she had set herself. Sitting with her friends around what she knew would be their final campfire before Malkenstorm Town, she half-wished that this wandering life could continue forever.

She glanced over at Lia. The girl had blossomed in the days they had spent on the road: gentle treatment and nourishing food – not to mention soap and hot water – had shown that there was a comely young woman under the dirt and rags. Alasha had lent Lia some of her own clothes until they arrived in Malkenstorm with its cloth market and its tailors' shops.

Vermillio looked up from where he was roasting the hindquarters of a rabbit on a stick. "Well, Alasha, I'm glad we will arrive in town soon. I hope they serve something other than rabbit; grateful as I am for your skills with the bow, and Quinn's with his contraption, I grow tired of this forage."

"I promise you that tomorrow night we shall have the biggest steak and kidney pie and the finest bottle of wine in Malkenstorm."

"Well, that's something to look forward to, at least. But what then, Lady? How shall we recover your inheritance for you?"

It was the first time anyone had mentioned helping her beyond offering company and protection on the road, and Alasha felt warm inside. "Your offer is most gallant, Vermillio, but I would not have you or Quinn risking your lives for me." She noticed Lia shifting uncomfortably on the other side of the fire. "Nor you, Lia," she added, and was surprised by the grateful glance that the girl shot at her.

"Nonsense," said Vermillio. "We've come all this way with you, and you have taught us much. Well, me, anyway: I doubt that Quinn remembers many of your lessons."

"That's not true," said Quinn. "I may not be as silver-tongued as you, but I can still count myself a gentleman, now. Can I not, Lady Alasha?"

"Indeed. Even so, you cannot risk your lives for me."

"Yes, we can. We're going to stay in your service, like it or not," said Vermillio.

"Yes," echoed Lia, quietly. "I swear I will serve you in any way I can."

Vermillio had taken to drawing plans of the castle in the dust, by the light of the campfire. "Where are the barracks again? And how many soldiers does your stepfather have?"

"The barracks are here, if I read your sketch aright. There are steps leading down, starting here." Alasha used a charred stick to indicate the entry to the barracks. "Here is the mess hall, and there are guard posts here, here, and here. The barracks can accommodate four and twenty soldiers; knowing my stepfather, he'll have at least that many."

"Aye. Given the way the local peasantry moans and groans under his taxes, we must assume he is at full strength, and he may even have extended their quarters since you were last here."

"It doesn't matter," said Alasha. "We could never have taken the place by force, anyway."

Vermillio's eyes gleamed in the firelight. "Then you have some stealthier scheme in mind?"

"No," she admitted. "But once we're there, and have had a chance to look around, I'm sure I'll think of something."

Alasha took two rooms in a modest inn near the edge of the town.

"Won't people recognize a hero like you, when you go outside?" asked Lia.

Alasha turned to Vermillio with a sly grin. "Well, answer the girl. Do you expect to be mobbed when you go out in the streets?"

"Very amusing. There can be little doubt that I *would* be mobbed, if I'd ever spent time here with my lute, but as it is, the only one they're likely to recognize is you."

"I have little fear of that." Alasha glanced in the mantel mirror as she spoke, admiring the way journeying under the sun had tanned her face and lightened her hair. "When I lived here before, I never looked so disreputable."

Her glance strayed to the row of bottles that were arrayed along the mantelpiece. Fewer than a dozen remained; Alasha required a flask every second day if she was not to fall ill.

It has its compensations, though, she thought. *For Vermillio and Quinn, too. I wonder if that's why they're so eager to stay with me?*

She didn't really think so. Their liking and respect seemed genuine enough, not to mention their gratitude for the many things she taught them. "I'm going to need somewhere to make more of the fire drink," she said. A thought struck her. "If we could find the right premises, we could produce it in quantity. After all, we're not getting any richer by sitting here."

"Perhaps Vermillio could go and play in the streets with his instrument," suggested Quinn.

"Thus gaining loot with my lute."

"Indeed, if you count a copper piece or two as loot."

"You're developing into a most famous wit, Quinn. Alasha's teaching is more effective than I ever imagined."

"Of course it's effective," said Alasha. "It's worked wonders on both of you. Now, would you mind getting out of our room and going to see what you can find in the way of premises?"

Lia decided that she wanted a bath after the dusty journey, so they rang for a servant and ordered hot water and perfumed soaps.

Alasha sat in an easy chair and watched her companion undress. Lia made no effort to hide herself, although there was a screen in the corner of the room.

"I like the way you watch me," she said. "Not like Vermillio and Quinn. They watched me, once or twice, when I washed in a stream, but they tried to hide it. You watch me openly."

"I enjoy watching you."

Lia was naked now, but she made no move to get into the bath. Instead, she dipped her fingers into the water. "It's too hot for me. I'd better wait for a while ... would you like to use it first?"

"All right." Alasha made to remove her boots, but Lia hurried over before she could even untie the lacings.

"Let me," she said, and knelt at Alasha's feet. She drew the boots off one by one, and then helped Alasha out of the rest of her clothes before leading her by the hand to the bathtub.

Alasha tested the water again. "It's perfect. Get in before it goes cold."

"You should go first," said Lia.

"Nonsense. The longer we spend arguing, the colder it will get."

Lia climbed in slowly and lowered herself into the tub, careful not slop water onto the rugs. Alasha filled the ewer that the servant had used to fill the bath, and gently poured warm water over Lia's head. Then she lathered some fragrant lotion onto her hands and set about washing the girl's hair.

"I'm really no hero, you know," she said as she worked.

"You are to me. Mmmm, that feels really nice." Lia fell silent for a time, letting Alasha work on her scalp, then she leaned back in the bath to rinse her hair. Her midriff showed for a moment through the bubbles.

On impulse, Alasha put her hand in the water and trailed her fingernails across Lia's stomach, ever so gently.

The girl went tense for an instant and then her body relaxed. She sat up again and smiled. "Do you want me?" she asked.

"Yes."

"Good. Shall I get out, then?"

"No. I want to finish bathing you. Then you can bathe me, and after that..."

"After that, you can have me," said Lia.

When they were finished with the hot water, Alasha felt the need for a sip of potion.

"I've been meaning to ask," said Lia. "What is in the bottles?"

"It intensifies sensual pleasure. I was forced to drink too much once, and now I cannot escape it."

"May I try some?"

"There's no harm in a sip. Never drink more than a bottle at one time, though, or you will end up enslaved as I am."

Alasha offered the bottle, and Lia took a delicate swallow before replacing the stopper and setting it back on the mantel.

"That is marvelously strange," she said, and drew Alasha towards the bed.

When they were sated with one another, they dressed themselves and joined the two men downstairs in the tap room, where Alasha ordered the pie and the wine she had promised Vermillio. As they enjoyed the meal, Vermillio told them of the place he and Quinn had found.

"It used to be a brewer's shop before this Lord Jarvin raised the tax on beer so high, and before his soldiers started to requisition the stock."

Alasha was dismayed: she still felt responsible for what happened in the castle. "The soldiers have been taking peoples' goods?"

"I'm afraid so. People say that Lord Jarvin allows his men to loot as they will, in place of paying them full wages. They do worse than loot too, I fear." He looked at Lia, then at Alasha. "None of us should go out alone, especially after dark."

"Why?" asked Lia.

"I hear they've been dragging girls to the castle and keeping them there, down in the dungeons. Boys, too, sometimes."

"But we passed soldiers on the way here, and they didn't trouble us," said Alasha.

"We were four, well-armed and well-mounted. One or two on foot might be a different matter."

"I see. Then we must all be careful. What of this brewer's shop?"

"It looks to have been a fine business, and the landlord is keen to have it occupied as a precaution against more looting. We could get it for a pittance."

"Good," said Alasha. "Let us all visit it tomorrow, and make the arrangements."

"Will you sell the stuff you make?"

"Why not? We could put it in small vials, so no one will take too much."

"You don't *need* much," said Lia with a self-satisfied smile.

"Huh?" asked Quinn.

Vermillio looked from Alasha to Lia with a knowing look in his eye. "Don't worry about it," he said to his friend. "Small vials will be cheaper, too, which means we can sell more."

"Won't selling it draw attention to us, though?" asked Lia.

Alasha had already considered that. "We won't produce that much, and we won't sell from the shop. I think the local pleasure houses would be the best outlet for our goods, don't you?"

"Just like in Issing Ford," said Vermillio.

"Exactly. We'd probably better brew some beer, too, otherwise we may get Lord Jarvin's men poking their noses in, asking what we're doing."

"Making our own beer? That sounds like an excellent idea," said Quinn.

The next day they left the inn and installed themselves in the rooms above the brewer's shop. Vermillio and Quinn went out straight away to buy ingredients, and Lia set about cleaning the kitchen in readiness for potion making.

"There's a hogshead here," called Alasha, tapping the side of the barrel. It sounded full, so she found a cup and tapped some of the beer. "It seems fine. Lucky we got here before the soldiers took it."

"Shall we find a tavern to offer it to, then?"

"There's little to be gained by selling it, with the taxes as they are, and this is a fine brew. Let's hawk our own efforts around the taverns, and keep this one for ourselves."

The two men returned soon enough, and unloaded their burdens of roots, herbs, and bottles.

"There's a stable yard around the corner," said Vermillio. "Shall we move the horses there? It would be more convenient than having them at the tavern, and the price is better, too."

"Very well," said Alasha, and the men departed again.

"Now, Lia, it's time for you to learn the recipe for firewater."

"You're really going to share this secret with me?"

"Of course. You don't think I want to be the only one who knows how to make the stuff, do you?"

Lia just laughed, and Alasha began to check the ingredients. "Those idiots. They didn't get enough Yohim bark."

"Have we enough?"

"For one batch, perhaps. We can make a start, and if Vermillio and Quinn come back before we're done, we can send them out again.

Alasha showed Lia how to make the potion. The girl didn't seem very sure of herself, and when Alasha suggested writing a detailed list of instructions, she shuffled her feet and looked bashful.

"I'm sorry, but I cannot read," she said.

"Then I'll teach you, as soon as we have the leisure."

Lia seemed a little more confident after that, and Alasha decided that the best thing would be to prepare another batch straight away, so that her pupil could fix the recipe in her mind. "I'll just go to the market and find some more Yohim bark," she said.

"Shouldn't we wait, until we can all go out together? Or send Vermillio and Quinn when they come back?"

Alasha smiled and picked up her sword belt. "I grew up here, remember. No foreign soldier will catch me among the mazy streets of Malkenstorm market, and no local lad would harm me."

Lia shook her head doubtfully. "I still think you should wait."

Alasha put her hand behind the girl's neck and pulled her close. Lia tipped her head up and Alasha kissed her on the mouth, hard. "I'll be fine," she said.

Lia seemed to be too breathless to answer, so Alasha simply smiled at her and left, buckling her blade about her waist as she went.

There was an unfamiliar air to the streets. She'd noticed it before, but now, with time to pause and watch, Alasha perceived its cause.

The people were cowed. Their faces were pinched as if by long hardship, and their clothing was more ragged than she ever remembered. The usual graybeards and matrons were out and about their business, but there were scarcely any young people on the streets. Alasha saw no girls at all, and the few youths who ventured abroad were all armed with knives and staves, hurrying along in pairs and trios as if eager to reach the safety of their destinations.

She began to wonder if she might have been unwise to come out alone.

"Hey! There's one!"

She glanced over her shoulder, and saw two soldiers starting down the street towards her.

Alasha took to her heels.

It didn't take her long to realize that they were faster than she was.

Still, she knew these streets better than anyone. She had played here as a little girl, when she was young enough for the proprieties not to matter. She had even visited several times as a young woman, escaping from a tutor whom she knew would be too shame-faced to report her crime.

She knew all the twisting alleyways and rooftop routes, and most importantly she knew people who would open their doors to her, and let her slip through their shops and into the next street.

Alasha turned into a little alleyway that she remembered from years before, and ran to the shop doorway that she knew would lead her through into Tanner's Court. There was no time to knock, and she had no breath to call out, so she reached out to push the door open.

Even as she grasped the iron handle, she knew something was wrong.

The shop window, which should have showcased an elaborate display of brass and leatherware, held nothing but dusty planks. The door, which should have sprung open at her touch, was securely locked.

More victims of Lord Jarvin's taxes, thought Alasha as she turned to run back down the alley.

It was too late. Her two pursuers stood behind her. They wore the uniform of Xendria and the colors of Malkenstorm, but what Alasha noticed most of all was their stony eyes and lecherous grins.

She whipped out her rapier and dropped to guard position, just as her fencing instructor had taught her.

One of the soldiers sniggered and drew his broadsword. "You're not in some elegant fencing contest now, love." He swatted her slim blade aside and then stepped in close. "Always pays to have a dagger too, in real life. Like this one." She felt the cold prick of steel against her throat, and heard her sword clatter against the cobblestones as she let it fall.

They bound her wrists behind her back, discussing her all the while as if she were a piece of meat.

"What do you think, Krigg? Lord Jarvin's sure to be interested in this, ain't he?"

"What do you mean?"

"Well, it ain't every day we catch a wench like this, dressed for quality and armed for war, eh?"

"So what? I say we just take her back and keep her for a bit. Until we get bored with her, or catch another one, same as always."

"I tell you this one's different. Lord Jarvin will want to see her, for sure. Or Jarvo, maybe."

"I don't know, Danz. It's few enough pretties we're catching lately, now they've all took to skulking indoors. Seems a waste."

"Listen. If they want her, and we take her, we'll pay for it, right?"

"Yes."

"And if they don't want her, and we offer her to them, they'll throw her back."

"Right. So what you saying, Danz?"

"We just got to choose which one to give her to. The father or the son. Who's more likely to give her back?"

"Lord Jarvin. Jarvo might want to her for himself, and that'll be the last anyone sees of her."

"Wrong again, Krigg. Lord Jarvin might not want the wench, but he's bound offer her to his beloved boy before we get a crack at her. That's two chances to lose her."

"I suppose."

"Then we'll take her to Jarvo, and hope for the best. Come on, sweetheart. We've got a lovely surprise waiting for you."

Alasha's stepbrother had been beautiful, once, and he had been unfailingly kind to her, despite being several years her senior. She had always loved him for that.

Now he wore a long, hooded robe, so that only his face was visible. His chiseled features still held a memory of their former grace, but they were giving way to dissipation, like some fleshy hothouse flower that had lived beyond its term. There were loose folds of skin under his eyes, and an unhealthy sheen to his sallow skin.

He smelled of corruption.

"Greetings, brother," she said. "I see you are unwell. Is there some medicine I can fetch for you? A glass of wine, perhaps?"

He ignored her. "Thank you, men. You've done the right thing, bringing this one to me. Take her to my dungeon. If memory serves, my stepsister can be a wild little minx, so you did well to bind her. Strip her and string her up, as usual."

The soldiers manhandled her towards the door, but paused again at Jarvo's command.

"Wait."

"Yes, my Lord?"

"Be as rough as you need to be, but the goods are not to be sampled. You can have her when I'm done."

"Thank you, my Lord."

As they frog-marched her towards the stairs that led to the cells, Alasha began kicking and screaming. One of the soldiers twisted her bound arms up behind her back until she yelped in pain and went still. After that, they bound her ankles too, and carried her down to the dungeons like a sack of flour.

The one called Danz set her feet down and went back out to the corridor, from where he fetched an oil lamp that chased the dungeon shadows into the cobwebbed corners with its pale yellow light.

"Now, Jarvo told us not to sample the goods, but that doesn't mean we won't break a bone or two if you give us cause. You might have just tripped on the steps, know what I mean? So, I'm going to unfasten your ankles now, and if you kick me, we'll both kick you."

"Heh, and we ain't got nice soft boots like yours," said the other.

Danz untied the knots that bound her ankles, and untwisted the rope. Under the circumstances, Alasha decided not to kick him.

"Good girl," he said, as he pulled her boots off and flung them into a corner. Her breeches were next, and both men whistled appreciatively when her legs were revealed.

"What do you reckon, Danz? Cut the top off, or undo her arms?"

"Undo her, I say. I like seeing a tunic coming off over a wench's head. Sort of introduces her tits to the world, nice and slow."

"Right you are." Krigg untied her wrists and then held her arms above her while Danz pulled her tunic off."

Now she was naked. Krigg released her wrists and stepped around to where he could see her properly. Danz simply stood in front of her, letting his gaze roam up and down over her body.

"I can't hardly wait," said Danz. "Let's hope Jarvo finishes with her quick, so there's some left for us. Come on, we'd better string her up."

They shackled her wrists to a chain that hung from the ceiling. Krigg worked a winch, and Alasha was slowly forced back against one of the walls, and then her arms were pulled above her head.

"String her up properly?"

"Reckon so. Jarvo seemed to be specially fond of this one."

Alasha heard the winch working again, and she was forced to stand on tiptoe.

"Good enough," said Danz.

"Don't worry, girl. You'll be seeing us again, if you're lucky," said Krigg, and picked up the lamp.

With that, they left Alasha alone the darkness, slamming the heavy door behind them.

Alasha hung from the chain, swaying slowly. If she stretched her feet down as far as she could, the very tips of her toes encountered the cold flagstones, but it was scarcely enough to ease the pressure on her wrists. She wrapped her fingers around the unyielding links that tethered her, and pulled herself up. That helped, but soon her hands were protesting just as much as her wrists had been.

The dungeon was far below the ground, cut into the rocks deep under Malkenstorm Castle. Alasha knew the layout of the castle very well, although she had never been to the dungeons before. She hadn't expected it to be this cold.

Perhaps it was also fear that made her tremble; it was hard to be sure. She had never been so afraid: Jarvo's promise to his men had surely been hollow. Having seen her sent away as a slave to return as a warrior, he would be a fool to let her out of this dungeon alive.

Whatever else he might be, Alasha knew that her stepbrother was no fool.

Even if he simply holds me prisoner, I will sicken from lack of firewater. That will kill me, in the end, even if Jarvo does not.

Something squeaked in the darkness, and there was a scuttling noise nearby.

Rats and spiders, prayed Alasha. *Please let it be no more than that.*

She would have lost track of time, hanging there in the darkness, and ended up not knowing whether hours had passed, or days. The thing that helped her was the same thing that doomed her: her enslavement to firewater. She knew precisely the effect that denial had on her body, and so when the door finally creaked open, she knew that she'd been held captive for less than a day.

Someone came through the door, and the cold air filled with the stench of Jarvo. "Well, stepsister, it's good to see you looking so well."

"You can't see me at all, since you forgot to bring a lamp."

"Clever, but wrong. I've changed, as you saw, and doubtless smelled, when you paid me that pretty compliment about my appearance. One of the changes is that now I see exceptionally well in the dark."

Suddenly, his voice was a lot closer than it had been. "I'm also much faster, and much stronger, than I used to be."

"What have you been doing to yourself, Jarvo? What dark pact have you made?"

"No dark pact, stepsister. Simple commerce. I have been dealing with the Arbian alchemists."

For a moment, hope flared in Alasha's heart. If Jarvo had access to Arbish potions, perhaps … but the thought died as quickly as it was born. Jarvo would never offer her the drink she needed.

She decided to try something else. "These chains are deuced uncomfortable, Jarvo. Why don't you lower the winch, so we can talk about things sensibly, as we did in the old days?"

"The old days are gone," he said.

"Then why are you here?"

"For the pleasure of your company, sweet stepsister."

Alasha flinched as something cold and hard ran slowly down her body, starting at her lips and ending between her legs. From the way the shadow in front of her moved, it should have been a fingernail, but it felt more like a claw.

"At times like these, I'm glad I have no real siblings. My scruples are somewhat diminished of late, but even I might hesitate to fuck someone who sprang from my own mother's womb."

Something scaly and prehensile was coiling about Alasha's ankles and calves, slowly working its way up.

"Speaking of mothers, what happened to mine?" she asked, hoping to buy time – though for what purpose, she did not know.

It seemed to work, for the moment at least. The thing at her ankles withdrew, and the thing that Jarvo had become stepped away from her.

"It was all part of the same thing. The Arbish alchemy can give unlimited life and strength, or it can take them away. I'm surprised you never suspected that we were poisoning her; such a swift passage from strength to enfeeblement could hardly have been natural."

"I was very innocent."

"I'll say you were." Jarvo's laugh sounded painful, and he cut it short. "Not any more, I'll wager."

Alasha said nothing, and after a while he continued. "It's excellent luck that you should have fallen into my hands, though I use the term loosely these days." He chuckled painfully again. "One of the less fortunate side effects of my transformation is that, whenever I *really* satisfy myself with a girl, she does not, regrettably, survive. That's no bad thing, you might say, as it spares me any inconvenient entanglements. But consider the logistical and supply problems it engenders."

"You're insane," said Alasha.

"Quite possibly. But the delightful thing, stepsister, is that I don't *want* you to survive. So I can fuck you properly with this thing I seem to have nowadays, and it won't matter in the slightest. A happy coincidence, wouldn't you agree?"

Despair filled Alasha's heart. There was no way out of this place. She was going to die here, speared on whatever monstrous object Jarvo had under those robes.

"Don't look so worried, stepsister. I won't broach that particular pleasure, not for a while. That would be too quick, too easy. Many delights await us before the end."

"No."

"Oh, yes. I trust that you glanced around the dungeon, at my collection of whips and braziers and flaying knives? I won't deny that I enjoy your beauty, stepsister, but when the time comes, I'm not planning for there to be much left of it. Anything else would be inappropriate, don't you know?"

The door squeaked again and she sensed that he was gone. A little later, Danz and Krigg returned with the lantern. They lowered her enough to unfasten her wrists, and gave her some bread and a cup of water. Then they hoisted her up again and left her in the darkness.

By the time Jarvo came again, Alasha knew that it had been two days since she had last tasted firewater. She felt light-headed with the beginnings of a fever that made her grateful for the chill air, but she was not yet delirious.

That would come soon, she knew. After that, it wouldn't matter.

This time, her stepbrother bore a lantern in his long-sleeved hand, and he went around the dungeon lighting the torches in their wall brackets. "It's inexpressibly gratifying, sharing darkness with those who can only see in the light," he said. "But today I want you to experience what is to happen to the full."

He unlocked her wrists. Alasha's fingers were numb from clinging to the chains, and he had to prize them open. Her legs gave way when he set her down, and she couldn't stop herself from slumping into his arms.

"So weak," he whispered. "So charmingly vulnerable."

He scooped her up and carried her to a table-like contraption that consisted of a timber cross in the shape of an X, mounted over a glittering array of cogs and cables. He arranged Alasha so that her limbs rested on those of the cross, and then he shackled her ankles and wrists to the beams.

"What is this thing?" Her voice was so cracked and hoarse that she scarcely recognized her own words.

"It's a rack. Let me demonstrate. Don't worry, I won't dislocate anything just yet."

He operated a ratchet and she felt one of the beams shifting under her, pulling her right wrist away from her left ankle. He increased the tension to the point where it was slightly uncomfortable, and then turned his attention a different control. Alasha felt the other beam sliding, just as its mate had, until her body was stretched so taut that it seemed that she was more like a lute string than a girl. The part of her that was slipping into delirium wondered whether she would ring sweetly, if anyone should pluck her.

"Indeed," said Jarvo. "It is very much like tuning an instrument, and a skilful player can coax the most exquisite music from its strings."

Alasha pulled herself back into the present, struggling to keep her fevered ramblings under control.

"It tilts and swivels, too," said Jarvo, and pulled the top of the cross up until they were face-to-face, then spun it so that she rotated down towards his feet.

Something that looked suspiciously like a tail flicked against the inside of his long robe, and Alasha remembered the prehensile thing that had slithered along her leg the day before. A tiny shudder ran through her body, defeated by the tightness of the rack.

"It also holds you ready for beating, or any other torment that I choose." He swung her until she was prone again, and stood between her legs. He'd produced a riding crop from somewhere, and he feinted at the insides of her thighs, her belly, and her breasts. "Conventional whipping posts are poorly designed, presenting nothing but the insensitive skin of the arse and the backs of the legs. The flesh I have to work on here is far more delicate."

As if to underline his words, he cut the crop across the inside of her thigh. Alasha surprised herself with the strength of her yell.

"Just a beginning," said Jarvo. "Finally, it holds you in the perfect position to be fucked. In fact, looking at you spread out and held open like that, I think I'm going to have to relieve myself somewhat. Don't worry, I won't insert myself fully on this first occasion."

He let his robe fall open and Alasha raised her head, trying to see between the dark folds, but the flickering torchlight couldn't pierce the shadows under the cloth. A cloud of foul vapor wafted towards her and she let her head fall back, fighting the urge to vomit.

He leaped lightly onto the machine and straddled the cross, balancing with preternatural ease. Alasha stared at the ceiling, unwilling to watch, unable to face what was happening. She was aware of his hands grasping the timber below her armpits, and of something scaly easing itself under her leg and wrapping itself around her ankle.

Something else, something spiny and metallic and sharp, brushed along her inner thigh.

Alasha started to scream.

The thing, whatever it might be, moved up to the pit of her groin in a horrific, cold caress, and then scraped over her belly and down along her other leg.

She twisted her head aside, gagging at the stench that surrounded Jarvo, and pulling with desperate, panicked strength against her bonds.

The cross didn't so much as creak.

Jarvo went still for a moment and then lowered himself very slowly. It wasn't until she felt the needle-sharp spines kissing the entrance of her sex that the horror became too intense to even vocalize, and her screams were replaced by the sound of desperate whimpering.

The dungeon door flew open and someone entered the room.

"Get your hands off my girl."

"Aric," she sobbed.

Quicker than thought, Jarvo was gone. His leap set the rack spinning, and Alasha ended up hanging upside down, but at least she could see part of the dungeon.

"Have no fear, Alasha. I shall dispatch this thing and be at your side instantly."

Jarvo stalked across the floor, growling deep in his throat. He wielded a branding iron in one hand and a flaying knife in the other. Alasha twisted her head towards Aric.

"He's strong and fast," she said, and then there was no point continuing, or even trying to be heard. Jarvo closed the gap between himself and Aric with a single, inhuman leap, and sword and branding iron were engaged in a bewildering dance, putting the torchlight to shame with showers of blue sparks.

"Damn, he's fast," said Aric.

"You show skill, for a mortal," said Jarvo.

The iron rang off Aric's sword and then returned with incredible speed. Aric ducked, barely in time, then danced aside to avoid the thrusting knife. The branding iron crashed into a torch, cracking the stone that held its bracket and sending it spinning to the floor. The flame died as it fell. Jarvo paused for an instant, and leaped for the next torch.

"He can see in the dark," warned Alasha, in the same instant that Jarvo pulled his new target from its bracket and extinguished it against the flagstones.

The dungeon was almost dark, now. A single torch remained behind Aric, and Jarvo's lantern stood so close to Alasha that she could have reached out and touched it, if her hands had been free.

Jarvo backed away, moving towards Alasha. Aric followed him cautiously. "If you harm her, I shall hold my life cheap when counting the cost of revenge," he said.

Jarvo's low growl could almost have been laughter. "You perish first, you fool, and then I continue to entertain her." He dropped his knife and reached for the lamp. Alasha saw the light die. "Almost dark now," he said.

Aric just laughed. "Have you any idea how long I've been searching for an opponent worthy of me?"

"Have you any idea how long it will take you to die?" countered

Jarvo.

Aric leaped forward, feinting low and then whipping his sword round to cut at his opponent's head. Jarvo stepped inside the blow and caught a handful of Aric's shirt before hurling him with horrific strength towards the final torch.

Aric hit the wall with a sickening thud, and Alasha let her head sink back against the rack, knowing it was over. Jarvo took a few steps backward and smiled at her, and she saw how the light of the remaining torch lit his eyes, as if there was some hellish fire burning within. Then he rushed towards Aric and launched himself across the room.

At the very apex of his leap, he seemed to falter, and then he crashed into the wall underneath the final torch. As Jarvo rolled over, Alasha saw that the hilt of a throwing dagger projecting from his eye.

"Sorry, friend," said Aric, "but you were altogether too fast for a weak mortal like me, and since you insisted on showing me an illuminated target... Maybe in my younger days we could have played some more, but no hard feelings, eh?" He nudged the corpse with his boot, and opened its robe with his sword before flicking it closed again. "I thought not," he said. Then he crossed the room to where Alasha was, and tilted the rack so that she was facing him. "Glad to see me?" he asked, as he started to unbuckle her wrist straps.

Alasha looked at him speechlessly for a long moment, and then she began to cry.

Her clothes were nowhere to be seen, but Aric wrapped his cloak about her and half-carried her out of the dungeon and up the stairs.

"How did you find me? How did you get into the castle?" she managed to ask.

"I found you through Vermillio, who had the sense to remember the name of the inn where I told him I'd be staying. As for getting into the castle, well your friend Lia has been busy making potion, and frantic in case she'd forgotten how."

"You broke into the castle with firewater?"

"Not quite. There was a hogshead of ale at your premises, and we doctored that, as well as several barrels of brandy. Then we simply drove along the castle road until someone requisitioned the lot for military consumption."

"So the guards were too distracted to oppose you."

"Enough were. I think most of them are still pleasuring each other in the courtyard. The rest are dead, or hiding."

"What about my friends?"

"Vermillio and Quinn are with Lia. She insisted on coming; she's brought you some of the drink."

"Let's go to her, then."

"I'm on my way," said Aric, and carried her out into the fresh air.

Alasha drank one of the bottles of firewater that Lia had brought, and then sent Vermillio and Quinn back down to the dungeons to find her clothes. Once she was dressed, she led the group into the castle kitchens where they broke into the store cupboards and made a simple meal.

"There's just Jarvin left, then," said Alasha, when she'd finished eating and drinking. "We'd better deal with him."

"Will you kill him?"

"I don't think so. I don't want his blood on my hands, and there may be a more fitting punishment for him."

She led the way up to the South Tower. There were two frightened-looking guards outside her stepfather's apartments, craning their heads out of the window. By the looks of them, they hadn't drunk any of the doctored beer, but they were watching what was happening in the courtyard below with evident consternation.

Aric stepped forward, sword in hand. "Is Jarvin within?"

"Yes," stammered one of the guards.

"And do you plan to do your duty, and die?"

There was the briefest possible hesitation, and then both soldiers shook their heads.

"Good. Then you'd better go. I'd avoid leaving the castle, if I were you, since that would take you through the courtyard. Instead, make yourselves useful. Bury the thing you will find in Jarvo's dungeon."

"Yes. Thank you," said the taller of the men, and then they both fled.

Alasha pushed the door open, remembering the last time she'd been here: summoned as her stepfather's chattel, to be disposed of according to his whim.

Things were different now.

Lord Jarvin was standing in the sunlight at one of his windows, looking out over the lands of Malkenstorm. He seemed unaware of the lecherous cries and moans that came from the courtyard below his other window.

"Stepfather," said Alasha.

Lord Jarvin turned and smiled at her. "So, you have returned. I trust you had a pleasant holiday?"

"Indeed I did," she said sweetly. "In fact, I enjoyed it so much that I've decided to send you on a similar tour."

A flicker of consternation crossed Lord Jarvin's bland features, but he regained his composure almost immediately. "I thank you for your consideration, child, but at my age, I wouldn't appreciate such a trip."

"Don't worry, Jarvin. I won't place you in the hands of strangers, as you did me. I'm sending you away with your very own troops, so that you can be properly protected."

Now his face showed real fear. "They have been drinking the Arbish firewater, haven't they?"

"You seem to know much of these alchemies, just as your late son did."

Lord Jarvin tottered to a chair and sat down. "Jarvo is departed?"

"Jarvo departed a long time ago. The thing that he became died today."

"Then the Arbish immortality was an empty promise, and the price was for nothing," Lord Jarvin muttered. "To think I might have taken the potions myself…"

They took him up to the battlements, and waited until the frenzy in the courtyard died down and the men were staggering around looking for more of the drink. As they watched, the two guards dragged Jarvo's corpse up the dungeon steps and out to the chapel, where they began to dig a grave.

"Time to go down," said Alasha.

The men formed up in ragged lines at the sight of their Lord, and

Alasha stood on the steps in front of him in order to address them. "You have all drunk deeply of the Arbish firewater," she said. "From this day on, you will know an unquenchable thirst for the stuff. You have already experienced what it can do to you."

The men muttered and shuffled their feet, eyeing one another's stained jerkins and missing armor with evident discomfort. Many of their faces were red, and several pairs of eyes seemed unable to look anywhere except at their owners' boots.

"You will find the cure for your condition in Arbia," she continued. "Or, at least, supplies of the draught that you crave. There's enough of the potion in the wagon to see you safely over the borders, if you take only the smallest sip each day."

"How will we buy what we need from the Arbians?" cried one man.

"You'll have to find something to offer in return."

"But how will we know the way?" called another.

"Lord Jarvin knows the way."

"Of course, he's been dealing with Arbians, hasn't he?" someone muttered.

"Indeed." Alasha paused, and decided to give the knife a final twist. "Where do you think these potions came from? What better way could Lord Jarvin find to ensure his soldiers' loyalty?"

The mutterings increased even more after that, and eager hands plucked Lord Jarvin from the steps and hustled him towards the cart.

Aric was resting in one of Alasha's armchairs when she woke up.

She'd seen her other friends settled in the guest apartments, and then led him back to her chamber, before collapsing into her bed.

She stretched, sat up, and leaned back against the pillows, feeling refreshed and relaxed. Aric offered her a hesitant smile, and she smiled back. "Will you stay here with me?" she asked.

"Are you making me an offer?"

"I don't know. What is it that you want from me?"

"Everything," he said.

"Then I'm making you an offer."

He fished in his pocket and produced the collar she had worn for so many months. "Xanya gave me this. She seemed to think I might need it."

"And was she right?"

"Of course. Xanya is very wise, and a good friend to both of us."

Alasha put her hands behind her head and gathered her hair so that he could fasten the collar about her throat. There was a pleasing finality to the sound of the lock snapping closed; she hoped she wouldn't hear the mechanism again for a long time. "Is this forever?" she asked.

"I think not," he said with a smile.

Alasha frowned. "What do you mean?"

Aric touched his chest. "I mean that Merik is still here, deep inside. He very much hopes to return some day, when his Mistress decides she is ready to receive him."

She thought about that for a while. "Mistress Alasha will summon Merik when she requires his presence, which may well be sooner than he imagines. But today she needs him to be strong. Today she needs him to make the decisions."

"Then his decision is that we should make love. Play games. Hold banquets for our friends."

"Including Lia, and Vermillio and Quinn?"

"Including them, if you'll have them. And you must show me around the castle, of course."

"What would you like to see first?"

"You," he said, and so she rose from her bed and undressed for him. "Anything else?"

"I thought that rack looked very interesting."

"I thought so, too," she replied. "In the right company, of course."

"Of course."

With that, Aric took her by the hand, and she suffered him to lead her out of the room and back down the stairs.

Printed in the United States
83380LV00003B/283-285/A